A MEDITATION ON MURDER

ROBERT THOROGOOD

ISIS
LARGE
PRINT

First published in Great Britain 2015
by
Harlequin MIRA
a division of HarperCollins*Publishers*

First Isis Edition
published 2018
by arrangement with
HarperCollins*Publishers*

A catalogue record for this book is available
from the British Library.

ISBN 978–1–78541–509–8 (hb)
ISBN 978–1–78541–515–9 (pb)

For Katie B

Prologue

Aslan Kennedy had no need of an alarm clock. Instead, he found he woke every morning quite naturally as the sun began to peek over the horizon.

In fact, he'd been waking with the sun ever since he'd decided a few years back that he no longer believed in alarm clocks. Any more than he believed in money, the internet, or any kind of "one cup" tea bag. For Aslan — hotel-owner, yoga instructor and self-styled Spiritual Guru — the wristwatch, with its arbitrary division of seconds, minutes and hours, was a potent symbol of enslavement. A manacle mankind wore while they worshipped at the false idol they called progress.

It made making appointments with him a little trying, of course. But that wasn't Aslan's problem. Not the way he saw it.

On this particular morning, Aslan lay quietly in bed (mahogany, Belle Epoque) until he felt his chakras align. He then swung his legs out onto the teak floorboards (Thai, imported) and padded over to a floor-length mirror (gilt-framed, Regency) where he inspected his reflection. The man who stared back at him looked much older than his fifty-six years — if only because his flowing white hair, beard and white cotton nightshirt gave him a Jesus/Gandalf vibe. But, as Aslan would be the first to admit, the miracle was that he was alive at all. And, as far as he was concerned, the reason why he'd been able to turn his life around was entirely down to his wonderful wife, Rianka.

Aslan turned back to look at Rianka as she slept twisted in the cotton sheets of their bed. She looked so at peace, Aslan thought to himself. Like a beautiful angel. And, as he'd told himself a thousand times over the last decade and a half, he owed everything that was now good in his life to this woman. It was that simple. And debts like that could never be repaid.

Once Aslan had got dressed, he swept down the mahogany staircase of The Retreat, careful his white cotton robes didn't knock over any of the artfully arranged ethnic icons or trinkets that variously stood on pedestals or hung from the wall. At the bottom of the stairs, he turned into the hotel's ultra-modern kitchen and was pleased to see that someone had already laid out a willow pattern teapot and porcelain cups on a tray for him.

Aslan started the kettle boiling and looked out of the window. Manicured lawns stretched down through an avenue of tall palm trees to the hotel's beach, where the Caribbean sea sparkled emerald green as it lapped against the white sand. With a smile, Aslan saw that the guests for the Sunrise Healing were already on the beach, stretching and taking the air following their early-morning swim.

Mind you, his eyesight wasn't what it once was, and, as he looked more closely at the five people in their swim things, he found himself frowning. Was that really who was going to be in the Sunrise Healing session with him? In fact, Aslan realised, if that's who was attending the session, then something had gone seriously wrong.

Aslan's attention was brought back to the room as the kettle came to the boil with a click. He poured the water into the pot and let the familiar smell of green tea calm him. After all, he had much more in his life to worry about than who was or wasn't attending one of his therapy sessions. Perhaps this was no more than karma realigning itself?

He couldn't hide from his past forever, could he?

By the time Aslan took the tray of tea outside, he'd decided that he'd just carry on as normal. He'd lead the guests to the Meditation Space. Just as normal. He'd lock the room down. Just as normal. He'd then share a cup of tea with them all and start the Healing. Just as normal.

"Good morning!" Aslan called out to get the attention of the five guests down on the beach. They all turned and looked up at him. A few of them even waved.

Yes, he decided to himself, it was all going to be just fine.

It was half an hour later when the screaming started.

At the time, most of the hotel guests were finishing their breakfast in the outdoor dining area, or were already wearing white cotton robes and heading off to their first treatment of the day. As for Rianka Kennedy, Aslan's wife, she was sitting out on the hotel's verandah, a wicker basket of sewing at her feet as she darned one of her husband's socks.

The scream seemed to be coming from one of the treatment rooms that sat in the middle of The Retreat's largest lawn: a timber and paper Japanese tea house that Aslan and Rianka had christened the "Meditation Space".

When a second scream joined the first, Rianka found herself running across the grass towards the Meditation Space. It was a good hundred yards away and, when Rianka had covered about half the distance, Dominic DeVere, The Retreat's tanned and taut handyman, appeared as if by magic from around the side of a clump of bougainvillea. As usual he was wearing only cut-off jeans, flip-flops and a utility belt full of various tools.

"What's that racket?" he asked somewhat redundantly as Rianka flashed past him. After a moment, he turned and trotted after her.

Rianka got to the door of the Meditation Space, and, as there was no handle on the outside of it, tried to jam her fingers into the gap between the door and the frame with no success. It wouldn't budge — it was locked from the inside.

"What's going on?" she called out over the sound of screams.

Dominic finally flapped over on his flip-flops and caught up with Rianka, if not the situation.

4

"What's happening?" he asked.

"Dominic, get that door open!"

"I can't. There's no door handle."

"Use your knife! Just cut through the paper!"

"Oh! Of course!"

Dominic grabbed the Stanley knife from the pouch at his belt and clicked the triangular blade out. He was about to slash through the paper of the tea house's wall when they both saw it: a bloody hand pressed up against the inside.

They then heard a man's voice, thick with fear: "Help!"

And then a different female voice: "Oh god! Oh god!"

There was a scrabbling while someone wrestled with the lock on the inside of the door. A few moments later, the door was yanked inwards by Ben Jenkins, who then just stood there in lumpen horror.

Ignoring Ben, Rianka stepped into the Meditation Space and saw that Paul Sellars was lying on his back on a prayer mat, having difficulty waking up. Ann, his wife, was kneeling at his side shaking his shoulders. Rianka could see that both of them had spots of blood on their white cotton robes. As for Saskia Filbee, she was standing off to one side, her hands over her mouth, stifling another scream. There was blood on her sleeve as well.

But it was the woman standing in the centre of the room that drew Rianka's attention. Her name was Julia Higgins. She was in her early twenties, she'd been working at The Retreat for the last six months, and in her left hand she was holding a bloody carving knife.

At Julia's feet a man was lying quite still, his once white robes, beard and hair now drenched in blood, a number of vicious knife wounds in his back.

Aslan Kennedy — hotel-owner, yoga instructor and self-styled Spiritual Guru — had clearly just been viciously stabbed to death.

"I killed him," Julia said.

And now it was Rianka's turn to scream.

CHAPTER
ONE

A few hours before the murder of Aslan Kennedy, Detective Inspector Richard Poole was also awake. This wasn't because he'd trained himself to turn delicately to each day's sunrise like a flower; it was because he was hot, bothered, and he'd been awake since a frog had started croaking outside his window — inexplicably — just before 4am.

But then, Richard thought to himself, this was entirely typical, because if he wasn't being assaulted by frog choruses in the middle of the night, it was torrential downpours like a troupe of Gene Kellys tap-dancing on his tin roof; or it was whole dunes of sand being blown across his floorboards by the hot Caribbean wind. In fact, Richard considered, in all ways and at all times, life on the tropical island of Saint-Marie was a misery.

Admittedly, he'd collected empirical evidence that suggested that Saint-Marie was a popular holiday destination for tens of thousands of other people, but what did other people know? This was an island where it was sunny every second of every single day apart from the ten minutes each morning and night when a tropical storm would appear out of nowhere and rain

7

hard enough to flatten cows. And that wasn't even counting the three months of the year when it was no longer the hot season because it was now the hurricane season — which, in truth, was just as hot as the hot season, but altogether more hurricaney.

And none of this even included the constant and unrelenting humidity, which — Richard often found himself claiming — was well over one hundred per cent. (Of course, Richard knew that this was scientifically impossible, but he also knew that the one time he'd received a precious box of Walker's crisps in the post from his mother, the crisps had gone soggy within minutes of him opening any of the packets. It was like some exquisite punishment that had been specifically designed to torture him. The insides of each packet contained perfect crisps right up to but not including the precise moment he opened the packet and tried to eat one, at which point they immediately went stale in the sultry tropical air.)

This and other wild roller coasters of despair looped through Richard's mind as he lay in bed, wide awake, his bedside alarm clock clicking from 04:18 to 04:19, surely the most miserable minute in the twenty-four hour clock, Richard found himself musing.

A slick of sweat slipped down his neck and into the collar of his Marks and Spencer pyjamas, and before he could stop himself, Richard became a kicking machine, scissoring his legs in a frenzied attack on his sheets until they'd been balled up and dashed to the floor.

He slumped back onto the old mattress and exhaled in exasperation. Why did everything have to be so hard?

There was nothing for it, he might as well get up.

He turned on the lights and padded into the tiny kitchenette and washroom that had somehow been crammed into the inside porch of his shack as if by someone who no doubt felt that the galley kitchens on sailboats were altogether too roomy. Surely there was a way of packing even more cooking and cleaning equipment into even less space?

He went to the metal sink that was squashed in between his fridge and his front door, and discovered that he wasn't the only person looking for a drink. A bright green lizard was already in the sink catching drops of water as they fell from the tap above.

The lizard was called Harry. Or, rather, Richard had named the lizard Harry when he'd discovered that the shack he'd been assigned to live in already came with a reptilian sitting tenant. And, like every flat-share Richard had ever been involved in, it had been a disaster from the start.

As Harry turned his attention back to catching drops of water with his pink-flashing tongue, Richard found himself thinking — not for the first time — that he should just get rid of the bloody creature.

But how to do it, that was the question.

A few hours later, Richard was sitting behind his desk in Honoré Police Station using the internet to research legal and possibly not-so-legal methods of household pest control when Detective Sergeant Camille Bordey swished over to his desk, a gleam in her eye.

"So tell me . . . what do you want for lunch?"

Camille was bright, lithe, and one of the most naturally attractive women on the island, but as Richard looked up from his reverie — irked at the interruption — he frowned like a barn owl who'd just received some bad news.

"Camille, don't interrupt me when I'm working."

"Oh, sorry," Camille said, not sorry at all. "What are you working on?"

"Oh, you know. Work," he said, suspiciously. "What do you want?"

"Me? I just wanted to take your lunch order."

Richard finally looked at his partner. She was young, fresh-faced, and threw herself at life with a wondrous abandon that Richard didn't even remotely understand. In fact, as Richard considered Camille, he found himself once again marvelling at how much his partner was a complete mystery to him. In truth, he knew that he was limited in his understanding of women by the fact that he'd been educated at a single-sex boarding school and hadn't had any kind of meaningful conversation with a woman who wasn't either his mother or his House Matron before the age of eighteen, but Camille seemed even more impossible to comprehend than most women.

To begin with, she was French. To end with, she was French. And in between all that, she was French. This meant — to Richard's mind at least — that she was unreliable, incapable of following orders, and was, all in all, a wild card and loose cannon. In truth, Richard was scared witless of her. Not that he'd ever admitted as much. Even to himself.

"You know what I want for lunch, Camille," he said imperiously, trying to take back control of the conversation. "Because I've had the same lunch every single day I've been on this godforsaken island."

"But *Maman* says she's got some spiced yams and rice she can plate up for us all. Or there's curried goat left over from —"

"Thank you, Camille, but I'd much rather just have my usual."

Camille looked at her boss, her eyes sparkling as she got out her police notebook and made a big show of writing down his lunch order. "One . . . banana . . . sandwich."

"Thank you, Camille," Richard said, somehow aware that he'd been made to look stupid, but not knowing quite how it had happened.

Camille grabbed up her handbag, sashayed out of the room, and Richard waited to see who of Dwayne or Fidel would appear first from behind their computer monitors.

It was Ordinary Police Officer Dwayne Myers. But then, as the elder statesman of the station, this was no real surprise.

Richard tolerated Dwayne — liked him, even — but it was always against his better judgement. Dwayne was in his fifties but looked like he was no older than thirty and, while he wore non-regulation trainers and a bead necklace with his uniform, he was always immaculately turned out. In fact, it was something Richard had always felt he and Dwayne had in common, their sartorial precision. And while Richard knew that

11

Dwayne wasn't really very interested in being thorough, punctual or following any kind of orders, he was a marvel at digging up information through "unofficial" channels. And on a small tropical island like Saint-Marie, there were a lot of unofficial channels.

"Seriously, Chief," Dwayne said. "You can't have the same lunch day after day."

"I went to boarding school for ten years. Watch me."

And now Sergeant Fidel Best's head appeared to the side of his monitor, his young and trusting face puzzled. Fidel was a proper copper, Richard felt. He was meticulous, keen, utterly tireless, and, above all else, he knew correct procedure. The only downside to Fidel was that he was overly keen, so he'd sometimes continue with a line of inquiry long after it was sensible to drop it. Like now, Richard found himself thinking, as Fidel said, "But, sir, don't you get bored eating the same meal every day of your life?"

"Yes. Extremely. But what can I do?"

"Well, sir, order a different lunch?"

"No, I think I'll stick to my banana sandwich, if you don't mind. You know where you are with a banana sandwich."

"I know," Dwayne said, almost awestruck by his boss's dogged determination never to embrace change. "Eating a banana sandwich."

The office phone rang and Richard huffed. "No, it's alright, you two stay where you are, I'll get it."

Richard went to the sun-bleached counter and plucked up the ancient phone's handset.

12

"Honoré Police Station, this is Detective Inspector Richard Poole speaking. How can I be of assistance?"

Richard listened a moment before cupping the phone and turning back to his team.

"Fidel. Phone Camille. Cancel the banana sandwich. There's been a murder."

Rianka had set up The Retreat eighteen years ago when she'd bought a derelict sugar plantation for a knock-down price. The main house had been abandoned for nearly fifty years by this time, but it wasn't its outside that Rianka found herself responding to, it was the inside. Admittedly, the interior wasn't much less damaged, but what Rianka noticed was how the rooms were still as beautifully proportioned and airy as they'd always been; the rotten ceilings were just as high; the main staircase, while leaf-swept and missing many of its boards, was just as grand. To Rianka, the house was no less than a metaphor for the island itself — shabby on the outside, but full of soul on the inside — and, within the year, she'd restored the main house and grounds to their former glory and opened for business as a luxury hotel called "The Plantation".

When Rianka then got together with Aslan, they'd increasingly started to market the hotel as a high-end health farm, and it wasn't long before they'd relaunched the whole venture as a luxury spa that was now called "The Plantation Spa".

The business went from strength to strength.

Then, as Aslan got more involved in exploring the spiritual side of life, he started offering holistic treatments and therapies to hotel guests — either led by him, or by other instructors he hired especially — and it wasn't long before they'd relaunched the hotel for a third and final time as "The Retreat".

For a good few years now, the hotel had been specifically tailored to the internationally wealthy who wanted to heal their minds just as much as they wanted to heal their bodies. Guests could sign up for sessions in healing, be it Crystal, Reiki or Sunrise; or yoga, be it Bikram or Hatha; or meditation, be it Zazen or Transcendental.

Now, as the police drove up the gravel driveway in convoy, their blue lights flashing dimly in the bright Caribbean sunshine, they could see that the main hotel building was the old plantation owner's house; manicured lawns swept down to a private beach, and there were incongruous quasi-religious buildings dotted here and there around the grounds with hotel guests coming and going from them.

Richard, Camille and Fidel climbed out of the police Land Rover and Dwayne dismounted from the Force's only other vehicle, a 1950s Harley-Davidson motorbike that had an entirely illegal sidecar attached to it. No one quite knew where this bike-with-sidecar had come from, or how it had got tricked up in the livery of the Saint-Marie Police Force, but legend had it — and records seemed to confirm — that it had joined the Saint-Marie Police Force just after Dwayne did. Not that Dwayne was saying.

Dominic came out of the house — still wearing flip-flops and cut-off shorts, but the gravity of the situation was such that he'd deigned to slip on a vest.

"Man, I'm glad to see you," he said, running a hand through his lustrous hair before shaking his head a little so his mane would settle.

"Yes," Richard said. "And who are you?"

"Dominic De Vere. The Retreat's handyman."

Dominic was British and Richard could tell from his drawling accent that he was from a moneyed background. In fact, Richard knew the type well. Posh, dim, wealthy, entitled — and therefore able to waft through life exploring the counter-culture as a hobby. No doubt, if Dominic's money ever ran out, he'd make a phone call to one of his old school chums, land a high-paid job in the City and then, for the rest of his life, complain that "the youth of today" were feckless layabouts.

It was fair to say that Richard disliked Dominic on sight.

"If you could just take us to the body," he said.

"Sure thing."

Richard had no interest in continuing the conversation with someone who wore a shark tooth on a string around his neck, so they all walked on in silence until they reached the corner of the house, which is when Dominic stopped and frowned. Richard looked at him.

"Sorry, is there a problem?" Richard asked.

It was clear that there was, but Dominic didn't know where to start.

"Go on," Camille said altogether more tolerantly.

15

"Okay," Dominic said. "Well, it's just . . ."

As Dominic stopped speaking, he started to waft his hands near Richard's body.

"What on earth are you doing?" Richard asked.

"I've never seen this before."

"I'm a police officer, would you stop stroking my arms?"

"But this isn't possible."

This got Richard's attention. "What's not possible?"

Dominic exhaled as if he was about to deliver some very bad news.

"You don't have an aura."

Richard looked at Dominic a long moment.

"I know I don't. Auras don't exist. Now, if you don't mind, I'd like you to stay exactly where you are while we go and inspect the body."

"But your team all have auras."

"We do?" Camille said eagerly, holding up her hand for her boss to wait. She wanted to hear this out.

"Of course you do," Dominic continued, smiling easily for Camille's benefit. "Yours is yellow, golden . . . it's like sunlight. Warm. Impetuous. Open. Sexually adventurous."

Camille seemed delighted by this analysis as Dominic held her gaze much longer than he needed to, and Richard found himself noticing that Dominic wasn't just tanned, muscly and heroically square-jawed, he was also extremely good-looking. In a slightly obvious way of course, Richard found himself adding as an afterthought in his head.

16

Dominic next turned his attention to Fidel and considered the air that encompassed him.

"As for you, you're blues and greens . . . of kindness . . . valour. Hard work. Hey, you're one of the good guys."

Fidel blushed. He was clearly just as thrilled with his "reading" as Camille had been with hers.

"Oh for heaven's sakes!" Richard said. "Thank you, Mr De Vere, but I can see that people are congregated over there" — Richard pointed at the Meditation Space as it sat some way away on the lawn — "and I want to make this clear: my colleagues and I are going over to the crime scene right now, and you're going to stay right here."

"But what about me?" Dwayne said, eager as a puppy dog. "What's my aura?"

Richard huffed in indignation as Dominic turned to Dwayne and took his time to consider. But then a knowing smile slipped onto Dominic's lips.

"You're like me. A shape-shifter."

Dwayne beamed at what he perceived to be the highest of compliments.

"I knew it."

Dominic turned back to Richard. "But I'm telling you, when I look at you, I don't see . . . anything."

"Whereas I see a murder scene over there, so thank you very much for your help. Team, you're with me, but if you try to move even an inch" — Richard said this to Dominic — "I'm going to arrest you for wasting police time."

Richard strode off across the lawn, his team trying not to catch each other's eyes as they got into their boss's slipstream. After all, it wouldn't do to turn up at a murder scene giggling.

But then, there was no chance of Richard or his team laughing by the time they arrived at the Meditation Space, where they found six shell-shocked Brits sitting or standing on the grass. Five of them were wearing white cotton robes that were variously spattered in drying blood. The sixth of them — Rianka — was sitting on the grass on her own. She was wearing a long Indian-style skirt with little mirrors sewn into the hemline, a light summer blouse, and leather sandals.

"Okay, my name's Detective Inspector Richard Poole," Richard said. "And this is Detective Sergeant Camille Bordey. Can any of you tell me what happened?"

"That's simple," said a well-tanned man in his fifties with a Yorkshire accent, a thick gold chain just visible around his neck. Richard also had time to notice a chunky gold watch on the man's wrist. Clearly he was seriously wealthy.

"The name's Ben Jenkins," the man said. "And you should know, that woman over there, she says her name's Julia Higgins. And she's admitted it all. She killed Aslan Kennedy."

Richard could see that Ben was pointing at a young woman in a bloodied white robe who was standing on her own on the grass. She was in her early twenties, had long blonde hair that was tied up in a ponytail, and she was looking back at Richard with doe eyes, seemingly

18

as dismayed by the accusation as everyone else. But she wasn't denying it, either, Richard noted.

With a quick nod of his head, Richard indicated that Dwayne should ghost over to Julia and make sure she didn't make a run for it. As Dwayne started to move, Richard turned back to Ben.

"And where's the body?"

"In there." Ben pointed at the Meditation Space.

Richard turned to the group. "Then if you'd all just wait here, please. The Detective Sergeant and I will only be a moment. Camille?"

Richard headed over to the Meditation Space, Camille coming over to join him, but Richard found himself stopping at the threshold to the building.

"One moment," Richard said as he held his hand up for Camille to pause, because it was only now as Richard approached that he saw that the walls to the building were made of paper. In fact, as he looked closer, he could see that the paper was waxy, clearly very strong, and was even somewhat translucent. Richard put his hand on the other side of the door and noticed that he could still dimly see his hand's shape through the paper.

"What are you doing?" Camille asked.

Richard ignored Camille as he took a moment to inspect the door to the building. He saw that there was no handle on the outside, but there was a Yale-style latch lock on the inside of the door that was screwed deep into the wooden frame — and that there was a corresponding housing on the door frame that it slotted into when the room was locked.

But without a keyhole on the outside, it appeared as though the door could only be locked and unlocked from the inside. Richard filed this information away for later consideration.

Stepping into the room, Richard immediately understood why the walls and roof were made of translucent paper, because every inch of the walls glowed with brilliant sunshine. And not only was it brighter inside the room than it was outside, it was significantly hotter too, like being at the heart of a supernova. Which was just bloody typical, Richard thought to himself.

Camille joined Richard inside and looked at her boss as he prickled in his suit.

"Hot, isn't it?" she said, helpfully.

Richard decided to ignore his partner and instead, squinting against the light, saw that the body of a man lay sticky with blood in the middle of the floor. His hair, beard and white robes were now thick with blood. And there was a bloody knife on the floor by the body.

Richard gave the room a quick once-over, but there wasn't much to see. The floor was polished hardwood planks; there were six woven prayer mats arranged in a circle around a tray of tea things. Six pairs of fabric eye masks and six wireless headphones were also lying here and there, but other than that the room was empty. No furniture — no cupboards, tables, chairs, statues or other ornaments — to hide behind or conceal murder weapons in.

To all intents and purposes the room was entirely bare.

Richard bent down and picked up one of the wireless headsets. He put it to his ear and frowned.

"What is it?" Camille asked.

"I don't know," Richard said, listening, but unable to work out what the noise was.

It was a strange keening.

He listened a bit longer, but, as far as he could tell, it was just more of the same yawling noise. And then dread filled his heart as he realised what it was.

With a shudder, he said, "It's whales singing."

Richard lowered the headphones, sharpish, and put them back down on the floor, before he joined Camille at the centre of the room to inspect the victim.

Crouching down, Richard could see that the murder weapon to the side of the body was a carving knife of some sort. Utterly vicious. The blade was covered in blood, although the handle seemed to be clean.

"We're going to need to get this bagged and tested for prints," Richard said.

Camille was inspecting the body.

"There are no signs of a struggle . . . no fabric or skin caught under the victim's fingernails . . . and no cuts to the hands, wrists or arms. It doesn't look like he tried to defend himself from the attack."

Richard looked at the tray of tea things on the floor by the pool of blood that had spread from the body. The teapot was willow pattern and there were six bone china cups that had all been turned upside down on the floor, one cup in front of each prayer mat. Richard tried to work out what had happened.

If the mats and cups were to be believed, there'd been six people in here. They'd all been sitting on the prayer mats around the tray of tea things. They'd all then had a cup of tea and turned their cup over and placed it down on the floor in front of them to show that they'd finished their drink.

But how did the eye masks and headphones fit into this? And how exactly had the victim been killed?

Camille inspected the stab wounds in the victim's back.

"There appear to be five separate sharp force injuries in the victim's neck, shoulder and back," she said. "Two wounds on the right side of the neck, and three wounds on the right side of his shoulder and back. I'd say the assailant was standing behind the victim — and was almost certainly right-handed."

Richard came over and could see the sense of what Camille was saying. The pattern of wounds suggested that the victim could only have been killed by someone who was standing behind him and striking into his neck and back holding a knife right-handed.

Richard made himself look at the face of Aslan as it lay in a pool of blood on the floor. Who was this man? What had he done to warrant such a violent death?

Richard exhaled. This was his job. To start with the end of the story: the body; the murder. And then he had to uncover the evidence that would allow him to wind time back until he could prove — categorically prove — who'd been standing above the body when the victim was killed; who it was that had wielded the knife.

Richard always made a silent promise to the victims of murder, and he made it once again now: he'd catch their killer. Whatever it took. He wouldn't rest until the killer was behind bars.

A flash of light caught Richard's eye in the far corner of the room. He turned back to look, but the little flash of light had gone as soon as it appeared. So he moved his head a fraction. No, still nothing. He moved his head back. There it was again.

There was something shiny on the floorboards he hadn't noticed before.

"What are you doing?" Camille asked as Richard went over to the wall at the end of the room and got down on his hands and knees to inspect the floor.

"What's this doing here?" he asked.

"What is it?" Camille asked as she came over to join her boss.

Richard found himself looking at a shiny drawing pin. It was just sitting there loose on the floorboards.

"It's a drawing pin."

"And why's that of interest?"

"Didn't you see all of the witnesses out there?" Richard said.

"Of course. What about them?"

Richard turned to his partner as though he was a magician about to reveal the end of a particularly impressive trick. "Because, I'm sure you noticed, Camille, that most of the witnesses were barefoot."

Camille was utterly unimpressed. "So?"

"So who would leave a drawing pin like this loose in a room where people were going about barefoot?"

Camille waited a moment before answering. "That's it?"

"What do you mean, 'that's it'?" Richard asked, irritated.

"Your big revelation? That there's a drawing pin at the scene of crime?"

"No, Camille, that's not what I said."

"But it is. I just heard you."

"No you didn't. You heard me say that it's *loose* on the floor. That's what's interesting. For example," he said, standing up and indicating the rough-hewn wooden pillars and beams that made up the internal structure of the paper house, "if I found a drawing pin in one of these wooden pillars, that would be less interesting. It would just mean that someone had pinned something to a pillar. But here?" Richard pointed at the drawing pin as it sat blamelessly on the polished hardwood floor. "How did it get there? Who dropped it?"

"You're right," Camille said, deadpan. "We've got a dead body over there that's covered in knife wounds, so let's concentrate on a tiny piece of metal we've found on the floor over here. In fact, I think you're right! What if the carving knife we found by the body is a double bluff and the killer used this tiny drawing pin to stab the victim to death?"

Richard decided to ignore his subordinate entirely. Without another word, he went outside again, pulling his hankie as he went and mopping his brow. Really, he thought to himself, his life on Saint-Marie was blighted by bloody sunshine. His shirt collar chafed at his neck;

the dark wool of his suit trousers stretched hot and tight across his thighs; and his suit jacket pressed heavy and scorching against his shoulders and back. Wearing a suit in the Caribbean was like living inside a bloody Corby trouser press. But what could he do? He had to wear a woollen suit. He was a Detective Inspector. And Detective Inspectors wore dark woollen suits, that's just how it was.

Richard saw that an ambulance had arrived over by the main house and paramedics were getting out a gurney.

"Very well, Camille," he said. "While I talk to our apparent murderer, I want you to take the remaining witnesses off. And I want you to get the paramedics to take samples of the witnesses' blood and urine."

"You think the tea they were all drinking was maybe drugged?"

"I don't know, but that was a pretty frenzied attack, I'd be interested to know if anyone was under the influence of anything."

Richard next turned to the youngest member of the team. "Fidel, I want you working the scene — but be sure to bag the drawing pin that's loose on the floor by the far wall."

Fidel looked at his boss. "You want me to bag a drawing pin, sir?"

"Yes."

"That's on the floor by the far wall?"

"That's right," Richard said again.

Before Fidel could ask why his boss wanted a drawing pin bagged for analysis, Richard turned and started heading for Julia, who was still being guarded by Dwayne.

As he approached, Richard pulled a little notebook and silver retractable pencil from an inside pocket. He clicked the lead out and said, "Hello. My name's Detective Inspector Richard Poole. I'm investigating the murder of the man we've just found in that paper and wood structure just there."

Richard indicated the tea house and Julia nodded slowly. She understood. Richard looked at Dwayne and he shrugged as if to say that Richard was right, the witness was indeed this slow.

Richard was at his most gentle and coaxing as he tried to find out who the woman was and what had happened. In truth, Richard didn't really have a "gentle" or "coaxing" side — his idea of doing either was to leave slightly longer pauses in between each of his questions — but he found his manner softened anyway as Julia was so naturally beautiful. It brought out Richard's paternal side. Or that's what he told himself. As she talked, he was able to notice how sparkling and blue her eyes were; and how her skin was bronzed by a golden tan; and how her blonde hair seemed to capture the Caribbean sunlight and radiate it back out in golden strands of light.

It turned out that the young woman's name was Julia Higgins. She was twenty-three years old and had graduated from Bournemouth University the year before having completed a degree in alternative medicine. Since then, she'd been working and travelling, but at the beginning of the year she'd come

26

out to The Retreat for a holiday. She'd loved the experience so much — and had got on so well with the owners, Rianka and Aslan — that she'd asked if she could stay on.

Julia was surprised when they said yes, but, apparently, her timing couldn't have been better. Rianka and Aslan had been looking for help in the office for some time, so they offered Julia free lodging, a small wage — but, most importantly, free access to all of the treatments and therapies — and in return all Julia had to do was a few hours of secretarial support each day. It was an arrangement that had suited both parties and Julia had been happily working at The Retreat for the last six months.

As Julia told her story, Richard tried to work out what he found so puzzling about her. After a while, he realised what it was. Julia was clearly still numbed from the shock of what she'd done — of course she was — but she was also acting as though she was just as keen as Richard to identify the murderer. Which was odd, considering that she was the apparent murderer.

"Then tell me," Richard finally asked, knowing it couldn't be put off any longer, "did you kill the man we found in there?"

Julia blinked back tears as she looked deep into Richard's eyes and said, "His name's Aslan Kennedy. And I think so."

"You *think* so?"

Julia gulped. She then decided that maybe Richard was right to want this point clarified. "I know so."

"You know so?"

27

Julia nodded slowly, frowning.

"Then can you tell me what happened?"

"That's what I don't get. I don't know."

"You don't know how you killed him?" Richard exchanged a quick glance with Dwayne. What was this?

Julia explained how she'd been looking forward to the Sunrise Healing, it was the only therapy Aslan still had time to lead himself.

"So we all went into the Meditation Space," she continued.

"Meditation Space?" Richard asked.

Julia indicated the Japanese tea house. "It's what Aslan and Rianka call that building there."

"And who went inside with you?"

Julia thought for a moment. "Well, Aslan . . . and four other hotel guests. Their names are Saskia, Paul, Ann and Ben."

"So there were only six people in total in there?"

"That's right," Julia said. "The five of us plus Aslan when he locked us inside."

Richard caught Dwayne's eye, both thinking the same thing.

"I'm sorry," Richard said. "He locked you in?"

"That's right," Julia said, puzzled. "It's a Yale lock. You know, one of those latches that closes itself. And Aslan locked it before we all sat down. He said he didn't want us to be disturbed."

"I see," Richard said making a note in his book. "And then what happened?"

"Well," Julia said, "we then all sat on our prayer mats and shared a cup of tea. It's a way of relaxing before the

28

session starts. And then we put on our eyemasks and headphones and lay down on our prayer mats. Although Aslan tends to stay sitting up, cross-legged. He's far more advanced in reaching an autogenic state than the rest of us."

"I see," Richard said, not really seeing anything at all. "And what's an autogenic state?"

"It's a state of perfect relaxation, and it's what the Sunrise Healing's all about. You lie down, put on some headphones and an eye mask and the idea is to let your mind wander as the sounds of nature and the rays of sunlight overwhelm you. It's like being plugged into a recharging station. You wake up half an hour later full of energy. But this time, the next thing I knew, I was standing over Aslan's body holding a knife . . . I killed him."

As Julia was saying this, she lifted her bloodied hand and looked at it as if she couldn't understand how it was attached to her body.

Richard noticed that Julia was holding up her left hand.

"Tell me," he said, as though it wasn't of much consequence, "are you left-handed?"

"That's right," Julia said, puzzled by the question. "Why?"

Richard smiled blandly. "No reason."

"It was like an out of body experience. I could see myself with the knife . . . but if I'm honest, I don't actually remember the moment. You know . . . I was just standing there, the knife in my hand. And that poor man was at my feet . . . not moving . . ."

Julia was overwhelmed by her memories and started to weep. Richard flashed a panicked look at Dwayne. What was he supposed to do now?

Dwayne stepped in.

"Hey. We don't have to do this now. We can take you in, get you a lawyer. Take your statement later."

Julia turned to Dwayne with a look of gratitude, and she wiped her tears from her cheek.

"No," Julia said, after a moment's thought. "You have to know what happened. I owe that to Aslan."

Richard was frankly baffled. Since when did self-confessed killers feel they owed anything to the corpse they'd just created? Dwayne looked over at his boss and shrugged that maybe they should carry on.

"Okay," Richard said. "But don't worry. Only a couple of questions, then we'll be done."

In short order, Richard got the remaining details. Julia was able to explain how she had no particular grudge against Aslan. In fact she liked him. Which was why she was stunned to discover that she'd just killed him. What's more, she not only hated knives, she had no idea where the knife came from that she'd just used to kill Aslan, or how she'd managed to smuggle it into the Meditation Space.

In fact, Richard had to conclude, Julia seemed no less baffled by the murder than he was.

"So, to sum up," Richard said checking over the notes he'd taken. "You say you have no motive — you have no idea where the knife came from — you don't know how you got it into the Meditation Space with you — you have no clear memory of actually killing the victim — but you'd nonethless like to confess to his murder?"

Julia looked at Richard.

"But I have to. It was me. I killed him."

Richard looked at Dwayne. Dwayne looked at Richard. Oh well, a confession was a confession. Dwayne got out his handcuffs and started to bind them to Julia's wrists. As he did this, he cautioned her.

"Julia Higgins, I'm arresting you on suspicion of murder. You do not have to say anything, but it may harm your defence if you do not mention, when questioned, something which you later rely on in court. Anything you do say may be given in evidence."

"But before you go, can I ask you one last question?" Richard said.

"Of course."

"Do you know why there's a drawing pin on the floor of the Meditation Space?"

Julia didn't really understand the question.

"What drawing pin?"

So that was the end of that.

As Dwayne led Julia off, Richard took a moment to look about himself. The old plantation owner's house that was now the main hotel building sat in a sea of manicured lawns, and wouldn't have looked out of place in the French Quarter of New Orleans. It was all wrought-iron balconies and horizontal planks of white-painted wood. But Richard also noted the other structures that were dotted around the hotel's grounds. There was what looked like a red and gold Shinto shrine off in one clearing; a colonnade of vine-entwined

Corinthian pillars straight out of Ancient Greece in another; and, up on a bluff that overlooked the sparkling sea, there appeared to be a Thai temple, with sharply sloped roofs in copper green.

It was all very strange and incongruous to Richard's mind. As for the hotel's guests, Richard could see that they'd apparently all vanished into thin air, although — now he was looking — he could see a clump of them down on the beach looking back at him.

Camille came over from the house and Richard went to meet her.

"Okay," Camille said. "I've sent Rianka — the wife — to her room and I've said I'll go to her as soon as I can. As for the other witnesses, they're off getting changed into their normal clothes. I've then told them to meet by the ambulance so we can take samples."

"Good work. Thank you."

"But what did Julia say? Is she the murderer?"

"Oh yes. She's made a full confession."

Camille looked at Richard and shifted her weight onto one hip, a suspicious look slipping into her eyes.

"And yet . . . ?"

"I don't know, it's just she didn't really make a very good fist at explaining the murder."

"She didn't?"

"No. For example, she didn't say she had any reason to want to kill the deceased. In fact, she said how much she liked him. And she claimed she not only hadn't seen the knife before that she used to kill him, but she had no idea where it even came from."

"But she's the murderer, of course she'd say that. She's lying."

"I know. But seeing as she's already confessed to killing him, why bother to lie that she doesn't know what her motive was, what her means were or what her opportunity was?"

Camille could see the logic of what Richard was saying.

"And she's also left-handed," Richard said.

"She is?"

"Or so she says."

"Maybe she's trying to trick you."

"Maybe."

Camille knew her boss well. "You don't think she did it, do you?"

"I don't know what I think — but it's definitely not stacking up. Not yet. Not if she can't provide us with a decent means, motive and opportunity. And there's something else as well." Richard paused a moment, and then turned back to face the Japanese tea house. "It's this tea house. Because Julia also said Aslan locked her and the others inside it before they started their meditation."

"So?"

Richard looked at his partner. "Well, it's obvious, isn't it?"

Camille refused to be drawn, so Richard explained for her.

"Because who in their right mind would allow themselves to be locked inside a room with four other potential witnesses before committing murder?"

Camille considered this a moment and then said, "Oh. I see what you mean."

"Precisely. Why not kill him in the dead of night? Or when he's on his own?"

Richard looked over at the Meditation Space again.

"If you ask me, there's something about that tea house that's important. Something we haven't realised yet. Either because of how it's made — or where it's located — but the victim had to be killed inside it in broad daylight in front of a load of other potential witnesses. Why?"

CHAPTER
TWO

While Fidel processed the scene, Camille oversaw the paramedics taking the blood samples from the four remaining witnesses, and Richard watched all the activity from the shade of a nearby palm tree. This, in fact, meant standing nowhere near the palm tree in question that was actually shading him, but Richard had long ago learnt that a palm tree's vertical trunk was too narrow to offer any shade from the blistering tropical sunshine. Instead, his technique was to follow the shade of the thin trunk along the ground until he found the much larger clump of shade that was thrown by the bush of fronds at the top of the tree.

Which is why, at this precise moment, if anyone had been looking, they'd have seen Richard standing in the middle of an entirely sun-bleached lawn apparently in his own personal shaft of darkness. But he wanted to take a moment to watch the four remaining witnesses interact with Camille. After all, they'd just been locked inside a room where a vicious murder had been carried out. How were they bearing up?

To this end, Richard had already got the witnesses' check-in details from The Retreat's receptionist.

He could see that Camille was currently talking to a woman he now knew was called Saskia Filbee. The photocopy of her passport had her down as forty-two years old. And according to the hotel's registration card she lived in Walthamstow and worked as a temporary secretary in London. Like the other witnesses, she'd now changed back into her normal clothes and Richard could see that she'd chosen to put on a sensible A-line dress in dark blue. And he could also see from the way that Saskia listened to Camille with her head cocked slightly to one side that this was someone who was happy being told what to do.

He saw Saskia nod her head and go over to one of the paramedics. Yes, Richard thought to himself, Saskia was a sensible secretary. And she would of course volunteer to give her blood sample to the paramedics first.

Richard shuffled the registration forms in his hand and came up with Paul Sellars and Ann Sellars next. According to their passports, Ann was forty-five years old and had been born in Birmingham. Her registration said she was a housewife and, now that she'd changed into her normal clothes, Richard could see that while she was somewhat plump, she seemed to fizz with the energy of a middle-aged woman who, rather than despair at how she'd "let herself go", had instead decided to embrace this fact.

Gold flashed at the thick necklace around Ann's neck, her wrists were similarly festooned with glitz, and she seemed to be wearing electric-blue trousers and gold slippers straight out of an Arabian nightmare, a violently fuchsia blouse, and the whole ensemble was finished off with a silk shawl that she wore draped over her shoulders and which seemed to have been constructed from every colour in the world that didn't actually occur in nature. On it, neon swirls of blue fought with psychedelic greens; and both lost out to attacks of fluorescent yellow.

Richard could see from the way that Ann was now talking to Camille — with almost windmill gesticulations as she pointed from the house to the Meditation Space and back again at the paramedics — that Ann clearly had a personality as colourful and slapdash as her clothes.

He watched as a man wearing tan chinos, brown deck shoes and a white short-sleeved shirt joined Ann. Richard could see from the papers in his hand that this was Paul Sellars, Ann's fifty-two-year-old husband. He was a pharmacist at an independent chemist's in Nottingham, where he and Ann lived. And as Paul calmed Ann down, Richard could see that everything Ann was, her husband wasn't.

For starters, he was rake thin. And almost entirely bald. But it was more than that. It was his manner that was so different. Richard could see that Paul was smooth, conciliatory. In charge. Just a few words into whatever he was saying, Ann quietened down and looked at her husband as though waiting for instruction. And instruction was clearly what he was giving her because, as he pointed off to the paramedics, Ann seemed finally to understand what was expected of her and she went over to give her samples meekly.

Richard saw Camille thank Paul for his timely intervention and Richard then saw him smile briefly and nod once. Paul was clearly a quietly capable person.

Which left only one witness, Ben Jenkins, who Richard had briefly spoken to when he'd first arrived at the murder scene. He could see from Ben's photocopied passport that he was fifty, had been born in Leeds, but he now listed his home address as Vilamoura, Portugal.

As Richard looked up, it took him a moment to find Ben, but then he saw him standing off to one side in the shade of the ambulance. He wasn't that tall, and now that he'd been allowed to get back into his normal clothes, Richard could see that Ben wore what looked like white leather shoes, stone-washed blue jeans and a long-sleeved shirt in vertical pink and blue stripes that was tucked tightly into a thin belt that cinched him tight at the waist.

Richard thought he recognised the type. Ben had done extremely well in life and was now trying to use expensive clothes and accessories to draw attention away from his increasing girth and decreasing attraction. Looking down at the forms again, Richard saw that Ben had listed his occupation on the hotel form as "Property Developer".

Richard found it interesting how Ben was off to one side. Alone. In fact, as Richard watched him, he found himself noting that Ben seemed to be watching Camille and the others, just as Richard was watching Ben.

Richard made a mental note to keep an eye on Ben Jenkins.

Once the witnesses had finished with the paramedics, Camille moved them to the shade of the verandah and Richard joined them all — but not before he'd sent Camille off to check up on the victim's wife, Rianka.

"Thank you for all agreeing to talk to me," Richard said to the four witnesses. "I know this must have been a very trying time for you all."

"That poor man!" Ann said, throwing her hand to her heaving chest. "What do you think he'd done to that girl to make her do that to him? Is she deranged? That's all I can think. Mentally deficient somehow!"

"For god's sake," Paul drawled in a patrician manner, "be quiet, woman."

"Of course, Paul. Sorry."

Ann pulled her mouth into a contrite mou as if to demonstrate how she wouldn't be saying another word — not another peep! — and Richard took a moment to look at Paul. There was so little to him, really. His face was almost skeletally thin, his skin was sallow, what hair he did have was grey and wispy and combed over his bald pate, and yet he seemed to have complete mastery of his otherwise far more punchy wife.

But there was something else Richard could sense between husband and wife, and that was a look of subservience in Ann's eyes. Why should such a larger-than-life woman like Ann be intimidated by a skeletal squit like Paul? But then, Richard reminded himself, all relationships between men and women were essentially a mystery to him.

He put these thoughts to one side. It was time to get on.

"I'd first like to thank you all for your help so far. But before we take your formal statements, can I just try and establish the order of events? What happened this morning?"

"Be happy to," Paul purred, comfortable to take centre stage. "It was a terrible business, wasn't it? Just terrible. But I've been thinking it over, and I think I've got it."

Paul looked to the other witnesses for their assent. Saskia was looking too quiet and withdrawn to mind who told their story — but Richard could see that Ben was twinkling, clearly amused at how Paul thought he was master of the situation.

"If you would?" Richard said.

So Paul told Richard how they'd all had to get up at sunrise, which was why it was called the Sunrise Healing. But before they got to the Meditation Space, they'd been expected to stretch on the beach and swim in the sea as a way of preparing their bodies for the treatment, which was hardly a chore, because, as Paul put it, when someone tells you to go for a swim in a sea that's warm as a bath and teeming with tropical fish, you don't really need a second invitation.

Richard quietly shuddered at the thought. Didn't Paul know that thousands of people around the world drowned from swimming in the sea every year?

Paul went on to say that Aslan then came out of the house with a tray of tea things, and called them over. That's when they put on their white robes.

This detail got Richard's attention. "How do you mean, your robes?"

"The robes we were wearing when you first met us. We'd been swimming before, so all we had on was our swim things."

"I see," Richard said. "And where did you get your robes from?"

Paul explained that there were little huts all over The Retreat that contained tightly wrapped rolls of fresh cotton robes, and they got their robes that morning from the hut on the beach.

"Then tell me, did anyone see Julia put her robe on?" Richard asked.

Ben chortled. "Are you trying to work out how she got the murder weapon into the room?"

Richard met Ben's eyes properly for the first time, and felt a spike of recognition. Closer up, Richard could see that Ben had a chubby face, dark hair — and, with his plummy northern accent, he gave off the impression of being a jolly farmer. Even if this jolly farmer clearly bought all of his clothes from Harrods. But for all of Ben's apparent bonhomie, Richard knew you could measure a man by his eyes. How watchful they were. And Ben's eyes were very watchful.

"That's right," Richard said. "So did any of you see her carrying a knife at all this morning?"

"There's no way she had a knife on her," Ben said, "because I'm telling you, when that girl got out of the sea this morning, all she was wearing was a bikini — and it was barely three pieces of string. There's no way she had a fifty pence piece hidden about her person, let alone a bloody great carving knife."

"He's right, you know," Paul added. "You see, it was me who handed out the robes to everyone this morning. You know, after our swim. And there certainly wasn't anything like a knife wrapped inside the robe I gave to Julia. And seeing as she put it on then and there — and then stayed with us while we all walked to the Meditation Space together — I don't see where she could have got a knife from."

"Then maybe she'd already hidden a knife in the Meditation Space before you arrived?" Richard asked.

"I don't think that's possible," Paul said.

"Are you sure?" Richard asked.

"You've been in that room. It's just an empty box made of paper and wood. And I can guarantee, the only things it contained when we arrived were six prayer mats, six pairs of headphones and some eye masks."

Richard was puzzled. "So you're all saying that there was no way Julia could have been carrying the knife about her person before she got into the Meditation Space — and there was also nowhere inside the room for her to have hidden the knife before you all arrived?"

The witnesses all agreed that this was indeed exactly what they were saying.

"In which case," Richard asked, "just how do you think Julia got the murder weapon into the Meditation Space?"

The witnesses had no idea, and Richard could see their confusion. After all, if Julia came out of the sea in her swimming costume and put on her cotton robe in front of everyone else, it was hard to see how she could have hidden a knife as large as the murder weapon on her person. And Richard had seen the Meditation Space for himself. It was indeed an empty box. Any carving knife hidden inside it beforehand would almost certainly have been noticed by someone. Wouldn't it?

Richard made a note in his notebook and moved the conversation on. What happened after they'd all got into the Meditation Space?

Paul explained that once they were all inside, Aslan placed the tray of tea in the centre of the floor before inviting everyone to take up a position on their prayer mats in a circle around the tea. Then, once everyone was sitting comfortably, Aslan went and locked the door. Apparently, he had been interrupted a few months before during one of his healing sessions and had asked The Retreat's handyman to fix a Yale lock to the door.

Richard noted this detail and once again considered how odd it was. After all, he'd investigated many murders before, but he'd never heard of a murder where the killer allowed himself to be locked inside a room with possible witnesses before carrying out the murder. It didn't make any sense.

Paul explained how, once he'd locked the door, Aslan rejoined the group, sat on his mat and poured everyone a cup of tea. Aslan then told them they all had to drink their cup of tea at the same time.

"At the same time?" Richard jumped in.

"That's right," Paul said, before explaining that it was apparently an old Japanese ritual that dated back to the days of the shoguns. Everyone had to drink their tea at the same time and then turn their cups over to show that they'd finished.

"Very well," Richard said. "So you all drank your tea and turned your cups over. What happened next?"

"Well, then we all put on our eye masks and wireless headphones," Paul said. "Aslan told us that we then had to lie down, close our eyes, open our minds, and listen to the whale music. This was how we were going to heal ourselves."

"Whale music was going to heal you?"

"It was about losing ourselves in the immensity of the deep. And I was as sceptical as you to start off with. But it's an odd one, because when you're lying there — and you can feel all that sunlight on your skin — and you've got your eyes closed, and you're listening to distant whale song, you do start to drift off."

"It's so true!" Ann said. "You go all dreamy."

"Dreamy?" Richard asked a little too keenly, and he saw understanding slip into Ben's eyes.

"You think we were all drugged, don't you?" Ben said. "That's why you wanted us to give samples to the paramedics."

The witnesses looked at Richard and he realised he had an explanation to give. "It's a possibility I'm not ruling out. After all, it's somewhat unusual that a murderer would have the confidence to strike in a confined space in front of so many witnesses. One explanation might be that you were all drugged and the killer wasn't."

"I definitely felt woozy when I woke up," Ann said. "And so did Paul. He had difficulty waking up in fact. I had to shake him by the shoulders."

Paul looked at his wife with quiet disdain. Clearly, while he was happy to talk on the behalf of others, he wasn't so happy when his wife talked on his.

"So did I," Ben said.

"And me, too," Saskia said, speaking for the first time. "I couldn't wake up to start off with, and my head was throbbing. Although I soon forgot about all that when I saw what had happened while I'd been wearing my eye mask."

"Of course," Richard said, making a note. "And what exactly did you see when you took it off?"

Saskia looked at Richard a moment, clearly reliving her horrifying experience and unable to put what she'd seen into words.

"That woman," Paul said. "Julia. Whoever she is. Standing over the body. That's what we all saw. Screaming her head off and holding a carving knife in her hand. It was covered in blood."

"And is that the same for all of you?"

The witnesses all agreed that the first they'd known that anything was wrong was when they'd heard a woman's scream. Then, at different times, they'd all taken their headphones and eye masks off and seen Julia Higgins standing over Aslan's body, screaming and holding a bloody carving knife.

"I see," Richard said, making a note of this fact. "But did any of you see Julia stab the victim?"

The witnesses hadn't.

"So you all agree," Richard wanted to clarify. "The first you saw of Julia, she was standing over the dead body holding a knife, but none of you saw her stab the victim at any time?" Richard asked.

"That's right," Paul said for them all.

"I see," Richard said. "Then can I ask, are you all sure you were the only people in the room before you put on your eye masks and headphones?"

"Of course," Ben said a touch dismissively. "There's nowhere to hide in that box. I'm telling you, it was just the five of us in there when Aslan locked the door and we all sat down."

"Suggesting that it could only have been one of you five who killed him."

This got all of the witnesses' attention.

Paul was the first to recover.

"Yeah, but that's okay. That other woman. Julia — or whatever her name is. She's already confessed to the murder. Hasn't she?"

Richard decided this was a question that did not need answering.

"Then can you tell me," he continued, "how long were you all lying down and listening to the sounds of the deep before you started coming round?"

"Ten minutes," Ben said. "Fifteen at the most."

"Really? That's quite a precise figure."

"I checked my watch when we went into the room. It was a quarter to eight. I reckon we all drank tea for about ten minutes, so that means we lay down and put the headphones on some time before eight. And when we started coming round, I looked at my watch and it wasn't much past 8.10am."

"So you were all wearing eye masks and listening to music on headphones the whole time you were lying down?"

The witnesses all agreed, and Richard took a moment to look at them all again.

Saskia had only spoken once, but Richard could see that she was meeting his gaze evenly, her hands folded neatly on her lap, her back straight. She looked worried — upset, even — but these were quite natural reactions; she didn't look like she was hiding anything.

As for Ann, she'd followed what she could of the conversation like someone watching a tennis match for the first time — and without any idea of what the rules were. If she was guilty of anything, Richard mused to himself, it wasn't going to be of having a razor-sharp intellect.

And then there was Paul. Richard still couldn't quite work out how someone so drab — so "middle management" — could have such an apparent hold over his wife. After all, the way Richard saw it, Paul was just one toothbrush moustache away from being the spit of Roger Hargreaves's Mr Fussy.

Which left only Ben, and Richard continued to be quietly puzzled by him. Why was his manner so off-hand?

This made Richard remember what he had to ask next.

"Can I ask," he said, "who here is left-handed?"

The witnesses looked at Richard, surprised, but they were all happy to tell him that they were all right-handed.

Richard took a moment to consider the significance of this fact. After all, it already looked as though the wounds in the victim's neck and back had to have been inflicted by someone who'd been wielding the knife right-handed. So how come the only person who'd confessed to the murder was the only person in the room who was left-handed?

"Then one last question, if you don't mind. Can any of you imagine why Julia — or anyone else for that matter — would have wanted to harm Aslan Kennedy?"

The witnesses said that they had no idea. After all, as they put it, none of them had ever been to Saint-Marie before, they barely knew Aslan.

"And I only arrived on the island last night," Saskia said. "The first time I even met Aslan was this morning."

"Really?" Richard said.

"That's right," she said, but Richard noticed that Saskia had something else on her mind. Something was troubling her.

"And?" he asked.

Saskia looked at Richard, unsure, and Richard decided that the dutiful secretary needed to be told what to do.

"If you have any information that may have a bearing on the case, you're obliged to mention it."

"No, of course," she said, suitably chastened. "And it may be nothing, but yesterday, after I arrived, I got a bit lost in the hotel and I found myself outside Aslan's office. Although the door was closed, I could hear voices inside. Raised voices."

"What time was this?"

"About 6pm I think," Saskia said.

"And you're sure it was Aslan's office?"

"Oh yes. But the thing is, the voice I heard belonged to a man, but I don't think it was Aslan. Anyway, I heard this man say 'You're not going to get away with it!'"

"You did?"

"That's right. And he was angry. But I heard it quite distinctly. 'You're not going to get away with it!' he said. And a few moments later, the door opened and I saw Aslan flee. He looked seriously distressed."

"You didn't see who he left behind in the office?"

"No. The whole thing was so strange, I didn't hang about to find out who the man was who'd been shouting at Aslan."

Richard considered what Saskia had said before turning to look at Ben and Paul.

"I don't suppose either of you were in Aslan's office yesterday shouting at him at 6pm, were you?"

Paul looked affronted.

"Certainly not."

"So can you tell me? Where were you at 6pm yesterday?"

Paul had to think for a moment before he answered. "I was down at the beach. Wasn't I, darling?"

Ann looked at her husband, uncomprehending. "You were?"

"Of course I was!" Paul said, exasperated. "I was with you."

It took Ann a moment to register this fact. "Oh, of course!" she eventually said. "That's right. We were both down on the beach, weren't we?"

Richard found himself briefly wondering why it took Ann so long to remember that she and Paul had been on the beach together. Had she really forgotten?

Richard turned to Ben and waited for his answer.

"Alright," Ben said, "I was in my room. On my own."

"So you're saying that no one can alibi you for about 6pm yesterday evening?"

Ben looked at Richard with the first hint of irritation.

"That's right. I went to my room at about five for a bit of a lie down. I'd had too much sun. I then didn't leave my room until seven when I came down for dinner. But I don't need an alibi, I didn't kill Aslan Kennedy."

"I see," Richard said, making a note of this fact.

Richard decided he'd got enough from the witnesses for the moment. At the very least, he needed to corroborate what they'd so far said with Aslan's wife, so he thanked the witnesses for their time, told them that an officer would be asking them to write out their formal statements later on, and then he went off to find Camille.

She was upstairs comforting the grieving widow in her bedroom.

Richard felt himself relax as soon as he entered Rianka and Aslan's bedroom. The shuttered windows let in only the thinnest stripes of sunlight, the dark floorboards were polished and cool, and a ceiling fan ticked lazily overhead. There was even an aspidistra in a pot in the corner of the room, Richard noted with a sigh of quiet approval.

Camille and Rianka looked up as he entered.

"Mrs Kennedy?" Richard asked.

"Please . . . it's Rianka."

Richard took a moment to consider Rianka. She was slender, her hands were elegant and long-fingered, her grey hair was fixed behind her head with two chopsticks, and while her clothes were colourful and ethnic, she herself appeared quiet and demure. Prim, even. Even so, it was easy to see the beautiful young woman who had turned into this beautiful sixty-something-year-old woman.

A woman who was now experiencing the shock of sudden grief, her cheeks tear-stained, her eyes wet with pain.

"I'm sorry to intrude, but I do have a few questions."

"No . . . of course."

"I'll be as brief as I can."

Rianka nodded.

"Starting maybe with last night. You see, we've got a witness who says that she heard a man arguing with your husband in his office yesterday at about 6pm. Do you happen to know anything about that?"

"An argument?"

"Apparently so. At about 6pm."

Rianka had a good think, sorting through her confused thoughts. "I'm sorry. I was in the kitchens then, I don't know anything about that."

"Then perhaps your husband mentioned an argument to you later on?"

"No. Aslan didn't argue with people. He wasn't like that. And he definitely didn't mention any kind of argument to me yesterday."

Now that was interesting, Richard thought to himself. Saskia said she overheard Aslan having an argument. So why hadn't he mentioned this fact to his wife later on?

"Then can I ask," Richard continued, "whether or not there was a man in your husband's study shouting at him yesterday, did anyone have any grievances against him?"

"No, of course not. Aslan was wonderful. Everyone loved him . . ."

Rianka trailed off and Richard could see that something was on her mind.

"Although?" he prompted.

"Well, it's maybe nothing, but he and Dominic haven't been getting on for a while."

"And who's Dominic?"

"The handyman. It was Dominic who brought you to the Meditation Space."

"Oh, *him?*" Richard said, surprised.

"Although Dominic was outside the Meditation Space when it was opened up, so I don't see how he could be involved."

"Don't worry," Richard said. "We'll look into it. But if we come on to the events of this morning. Can I just start by asking, when did your husband get up?"

"At sunrise. That's when he gets up."

"I see. And you?"

"I lay in bed for half an hour or so longer and then I got up as well. I had some breakfast, and then I remembered there was some sewing I could be getting on with. So I went out onto the verandah to do it." Rianka gathered her courage as she forced herself to remember. "I saw Aslan and the others go into the Meditation Space. They closed the door. And that was the last time I saw him . . ."

"And do you know what time this was?"

"I have no idea. Not really. Maybe half past seven? Or just after?"

"Then can I ask, did you stay on the verandah the whole time your husband and the other guests were inside the Meditation Space?"

"Yes."

"Did you perhaps see anyone enter or leave the Meditation Space during that time?"

"No. I didn't."

"Are you sure?"

Rianka seemed to piece together her memories as she spoke. "I could see the whole lawn. The Meditation Space is in the middle of it. The only people I saw go inside it the whole time I was on the verandah were Aslan and the five guests. And once the door was shut, it didn't open again. Not until later on, after I heard a woman scream. And that's when I ran . . ." Rianka trailed off as the pain of her memories overwhelmed her.

"Thank you," Camille said. "We won't be asking anything else."

"Just one more question, though, if that's alright," Richard said.

Camille flashed a look at Richard that might have killed a lesser man, but Richard was impervious. He had a killer to catch. And Camille should have known by now that he wouldn't be wasting Rianka's time unless it was important.

"Do you have any idea how a drawing pin ended up on the floor of the Meditation Space?"

"I'm *sorry?*" Richard was surprised to see that Rianka had apparently said this without moving her mouth. And then he realised it had been his partner who'd spoken.

Ignoring the look of fire in Camille's eyes, Richard turned back to Rianka.

"You see, we found a drawing pin on the floor of the Meditation Space, and it could be important. After all, why would there be something as dangerous as a drawing pin left on a floor where people are walking around barefoot?"

"I don't understand. Are you asking me how a drawing pin got into the Meditation Space?"

"Yes I am."

"Then I'm sorry. I don't know."

"Very well then, thank you very much for your time." Richard turned to his partner. "Camille, if Rianka's up to it, I'd like you to take her formal statement — and

54

then I'd like you to take the statements of the other witnesses who were in the Meditation Space."

"Yes, sir," Camille said.

Richard could tell that Camille was irritated that he'd asked the grieving widow about a drawing pin, but he refused to apologise for what he felt was a valid line of inquiry, and that was that.

Outside again in the glaring sunlight, Richard tried to make sense of what he'd learnt so far, but it was hard to get a handle on everything. After all, they'd already arrested the self-confessed killer. Surely that made it an open and shut case?

But Richard wasn't so sure. There was a long and ignoble history of weak-minded people admitting to murders they hadn't committed. And there was no getting away from it, Julia hadn't behaved like any kind of murderer he'd ever met before. After all, who'd confess to a murder and then be unable to explain to the police why they did it, how they did it or where the murder weapon came from? It also didn't help her case that the wounds to the right side of the victim's neck and back strongly suggested that the killer had been right-handed, and Julia said she was left-handed.

And then there was the mystery of the drawing pin. Richard didn't care that Camille thought it was irrelevant. He'd learnt long ago that the most important object at a crime scene was sometimes something entirely humdrum that wouldn't be of interest except for the fact that it was in the wrong place. And a drawing pin that was loose on the floor in a room where people went around barefoot was definitely a humdrum object in the wrong place.

He also couldn't shake the feeling that the location of the murder itself was important. Aslan was killed inside a locked room that was only made of paper — and in front of a load of potential witnesses — but why was he killed there?

Richard looked through a heat haze at the Meditation Space as it sat shimmering in the middle of the lawn.

What had happened in there while it was locked down?

Richard considered that maybe Julia was their killer. Maybe she wasn't. But if she wasn't, then that meant that one of Saskia Filbee, Paul Sellars, Ann Sellars or Ben Jenkins had in fact done it.

But why on earth would any of them want to get a carving knife and viciously slay the owner of a hotel none of them had ever visited before?

CHAPTER
THREE

"Right then," Richard said when he and Camille had rejoined Dwayne back in the police station. "We have a killer to catch. Let's get this up on the board."

Richard dragged the ancient whiteboard on its juddering legs across to the centre of the room and took a moment to marvel — not for the first time — at how rudimentary the Honoré Police Station was.

There were four wooden desks for each of the station's police officers — each with a computer on — and that was about it. Everything else that was piled around, and there was a *lot* of everything else, was generally broken or defunct somehow. The office noticeboard carried rotas for officers who'd long since left the station; the Wanted poster on the wall was for a man who'd apparently long since died; and there were ancient metal filing cabinets propped up around the walls like drunks at a party, their files spilling out of their drawers. And under all the mess of paperwork that littered everywhere, there were whole sedimentary layers of ancient office equipment that hadn't been discontinued so much as abandoned in place.

Richard had come to the island of Saint-Marie just over a year ago when he'd been sent out to solve the murder of the incumbent Detective Inspector, a man called Charlie Hulme. Richard had hated the tropics from the moment he'd stepped off the plane, but he'd consoled himself at the time with the knowledge that he'd be able to go home just as soon as he'd solved the case.

But Richard hadn't been counting on the political manoeuvrings of the island's Commissioner of Police, Selwyn Hamilton, and by the time that Charlie Hulme's killer had been caught, Richard was astounded to learn that he'd been invited to stay on as the island's Detective Inspector.

Richard had been horrified, not least because it finally confirmed a suspicion he'd held for many years that his Superintendent back in Croydon had been trying to get rid of him. But now that Richard had had this fact confirmed, he decided that he was too proud to ask for his old job back. As far as Richard was concerned, no one should ever be made to beg to go back to Croydon. So, instead, he accepted the job on Saint-Marie as a stop-gap and spent every subsequent spare moment he had applying for jobs that would allow him to go back to a different station in the UK.

But a strange thing happened as the months passed, not that Richard was anything more than dimly aware of it. Because, separated from a Metropolitan Police hierarchy that he'd never quite fitted into — and now surrounded by a talented team who seemed to forgive him his idiosyncrasies while championing his strengths — Richard had finally started to find the sort of success that had proved so elusive in the UK.

He still hated the tropics of course: the climate, the spicy food, the shack he had to live in — the sand that got everywhere — and the fact that even though Saint-Marie was larger even than the Isle of Wight, it wasn't possible to get a decent pint of beer anywhere. But while Richard told himself that he was still hell-bent on getting posted back to the UK, he hadn't noticed — although his team had — that he hadn't actually applied for any jobs back in the UK for the last few months.

This didn't mean that he was happy, of course. Someone like Richard could never be happy — but his levels of unhappiness had perhaps bottomed out.

On this occasion, though, Richard was having a typically frustrating time trying to find even a single whiteboard marker with enough ink in it to work. Once he'd finally found one that would just about do, he turned to face his team.

"Very well," he said. "Five guests at a fancy health-spa-cum-hotel get up at dawn and go for a morning swim. Saskia Filbee, Ann Sellars, Paul Sellars, Ben Jenkins and Julia Higgins." Richard wrote the names on the board, leaving plenty of space between the names so they could later annotate the board with evidence as they collected it.

Richard carried on making notes on the board as he recounted how the witnesses all went swimming that morning, and how one of their number — Paul Sellars — handed out fresh cotton robes to them all, Julia Higgins included, before they all went with Aslan to the Mediation Space, and how all of the witnesses agreed that Julia couldn't have hidden a knife about her person before the room was locked down.

He then went on to explain that once inside, it was Aslan who locked the door from the inside. All five guests and Aslan then drank from the same pot of tea and all turned their cups over. They then all put on their wireless headphones and eye masks and lay down on their prayer mats.

And then there was a ten to fifteen minute window in which Aslan was brutally slain, somehow without any of the witnesses hearing or seeing anything until Julia started screaming, which was when everyone inside the Meditation Space woke up and saw Julia standing over the body holding a carving knife in her left hand.

"Even though the wounds in the victim's neck and back look like they were delivered by a right-handed person," Camille said.

"Precisely."

"And you should know," Camille said, "when I watched Julia write out her witness statement, she used her left hand to do the whole thing."

"So what do we think? Is she really our killer?"

"She's confessed to the murder," Dwayne pointed out.

"I know, but I don't want us to rule anything in or out for the moment. Not until we know more about what we're dealing with. And you should know, all the witnesses said they felt groggy when they woke up. Camille, did we manage to get samples of the tea they were drinking off to the labs in Guadeloupe?"

"Yes, sir."

"And samples of the witnesses' blood and urine?"

"Yes, sir."

Richard looked at the board and realised something.

"Because there's something you should all know," Richard said. "Paul Sellars's registration card for the hotel had his profession down as a pharmacist. If the tea was doctored in any way, he's the person on this list who'd have had the easiest access to any kind of mind-altering drug."

Richard recorded this fact by Paul's name on the whiteboard.

"And two more things," Richard said. "Firstly, why was Aslan killed inside a house made of paper and wood? It's such a strange place to commit murder. Don't you think? And secondly — and just as important — why did we find a drawing pin loose at the scene?"

As Richard finished writing his notes up, it was fortunate that he couldn't see the sceptical looks that passed between Dwayne and Camille behind his back.

"Very good," Richard finally said, looking at the board. "Yes. That's a start. Have you got the witness statements?" he asked Camille.

"Of course, sir," she said.

As Camille hunted for the statements among the slick of other casework on her desk, Richard marvelled once again at how he managed to work so effectively with a partner who was so very disorganised. Her desk alone was enough to send him into conniptions with its mess of paperwork, files, bits of old orange peel and desiccated tubs of make-up that she'd leave the lids off and then lose interest in entirely. Richard's desk, on the other hand, was of course neat and tidy; his in tray empty, his out tray just as empty. There was no pending tray. As far as Richard was concerned, pending trays were for wimps.

"Got them!"

Camille triumphantly held up a manila folder containing the witness statements.

"Yes. Well done, Camille."

"What do you mean by that?" Camille asked, picking up on her boss's tone.

"Only that it shouldn't be such an achievement to find the witness statements to a murder case."

"I knew where they were."

"Self-evidently you didn't."

Camille pointedly opened the buff folder by way of a reply, and, as she gave her verbal report, Richard wrote up his version of what Camille was saying on the whiteboard.

"Okay . . . as for witnesses, first we've got Rianka Kennedy of course. And it's basically what she'd already told us: she sat down on the verandah to do some sewing at about 7.30am, and no one other than Aslan and the five known witnesses went into the Meditation Space before 8am. She then saw no one else enter or leave the building, and the only person who was even remotely nearby was Dominic De Vere, the handyman. But Rianka said that although Dominic had a history of arguments with the deceased, he was definitely outside the Meditation Space when the screaming started."

Dwayne said, "And if he was outside, he can't be our killer."

"Quite so," Richard agreed. "Then what about our actual suspects? The people who were inside the locked room with the victim. What did you make of them all, Camille?"

Camille fanned out the witness statements so she could see them all. "So first we've got Saskia Filbee," she said. "I thought she was the classic innocent bystander. Shocked, but willing to help."

"I'd agree. That's what I thought of her, too."

"And then we've got the husband and wife, Paul and Ann Sellars. And they're an odd couple, aren't they?"

"Go on," Richard said.

"Because she's kind of crazy. I had an aunt like that. You know, larger than life. Talked too much. But it was because she never married and she had to keep noisy or she'd notice there wasn't much going on in her life."

"You think Ann's unhappy?" Dwayne asked.

"I don't know. But she definitely talked too much. You know?"

"Maybe she's feeling guilty?" Dwayne offered.

"Maybe," Camille conceded, though she wasn't too sure.

"Then what about Paul?" Richard asked.

"He's so sure of himself. And in control. Isn't he?" Camille said, and Richard couldn't help but smile as this tallied with his impression of Paul as well. "And patronising. I got the distinct impression he didn't take me seriously because I was a woman."

"Then what of Ben Jenkins?"

"I don't know," Camille said. "He was happy to give his statement, but there was something about him I couldn't quite pin down."

"How do you mean?"

"He was helpful enough, but I felt he was being careful. Like he'd had a brush with the law in the past."

"That's exactly it!" Richard said, delighted. He'd been unable to place Ben's manner himself, but Camille was right. When Richard talked to Ben it was as though Ben knew he had to be guarded around policemen.

Richard turned to Dwayne.

"Dwayne? According to his registration document, Ben Jenkins lives in Portugal. When you do your background checks, see if he's ever had a run-in with the authorities, would you? Not necessarily criminal. He's a property developer there, it could be financial. Or legal. Or maybe he was investigated by the tax office. Or by the government's Planning Department. But Camille's right, the man was too canny for someone giving evidence for the first time."

Dwayne looked puzzled.

"Problem?" Richard asked.

"Sure. I'll do all that, but I don't know if you've noticed, Chief, but we've got the killer in our cells. She's already confessed to the murder."

"I know, Dwayne, but it doesn't mean we should believe her."

Dwayne looked at his boss. "You don't think we should believe criminals when they confess to their crimes?"

Before Richard could answer, there was the thump of footsteps on the verandah and everyone turned to see Fidel enter the station, his hands holding a manila file full of statements.

He was hot and he was very, very bothered.

"Ah, Fidel. How were the other hotel guests?"

Fidel dumped the notes onto his desk before responding.

"Confused. Panicked. Shocked. And all I got from them was a whole heap of nothing."

"Well, let's see about that."

"I'm telling you, sir, I spoke to thirty-seven different guests and they're all saying the same thing. Aslan was kind, quiet — a 'man of peace' a few of them said." Fidel spread out his notes on his desk and read out a few choice quotations. "'He was the person I aspire to be.' 'He's the reason I come to this Retreat year after year.' 'He had a soul of pure gold.' I'm telling you, sir, they all think he was some kind of a saint."

"Then how come he ended up getting knifed to death?"

"Not one of them has the first idea. But a couple of people did say something interesting."

"Oh?"

"They said the only person at The Retreat who didn't seem to like Aslan was Dominic, the handyman. Dominic would apparently make comments. He thought Aslan didn't live in the real world."

"Which would be interesting," Richard said, "except for the fact that he wasn't in the Meditation Space when the murder was carried out, so I don't think we can consider him a suspect. Did you get anything that suggested that anyone inside the locked room with the victim at the time of the murder had a grievance with him at all?"

"I'm sorry, sir. I got nothing like that."

"Then what about the argument? Did any of the guests hear a man shouting at Aslan in his office at 6pm the night before?"

"And nor could I find anyone who heard any kind of argument at 6pm yesterday — either in Aslan's office or anywhere else."

"And is that likely?"

"How do you mean?"

"That the only person in the whole hotel who heard a man shouting 'You're not going to get away with it' to Aslan was Saskia Filbee?"

Fidel thought for a moment. "I don't know. It was pretty hot yesterday, most people would have been outside at that sort of time, I reckon."

Richard considered this a moment before continuing. "Then what did the hotel guests have to say about Julia Higgins?"

Fidel started checking through his notes again as he said, "And that's just as much of a dead end, sir. I couldn't find anyone who had a bad word to say about her. She helps out in the office and she's always polite. Cheerful, that's a word a few people used. As for her relationship with Aslan, everyone said she hero-worshipped him. I couldn't find a single person who believed for a second that she could be our killer."

Not for the first time, Richard felt as though he were looking at the case the wrong way round. After all, why would a woman no one had a bad word to say about, kill someone who, by all accounts, she adored? And why would she do it inside a house made of paper? And in broad daylight? In front of four other potential witnesses? And, having killed a man everyone said she hero-worshipped, why would she then confess to the murder — but then fail to provide the police with any of her means, motive or opportunity?

Well, Richard mused to himself, there was one way to find out. Julia was currently in their police cells. He could ask her.

"Very well," he said. "Dwayne and Fidel, I want you to finish processing the evidence. And Fidel, I want you dusting the murder weapon for fingerprints, of course, but first I want you to lift whatever prints you can find on the drawing pin I asked you to bag at the scene."

Fidel looked at his boss. "You want me to lift whatever prints I can find on the drawing pin I found on the floor of the Meditation Space?"

"That's right," Richard said, a little irked. Hadn't he made himself clear? "Whatever prints you can lift from the drawing pin."

"And you want me to do that *before* I start processing the actual weapon that was used to kill the victim?"

"Yes. I said. As for you and me, Camille, I want to have another chat with our killer. And this time I want her to tell us why she killed Aslan Kennedy and how she smuggled a knife into the murder room without anyone seeing."

Richard led through the bead curtain into the cells at the back of the station. This was his least favourite place on the whole island — which, whenever Richard thought about it, was really saying something. There were just two steel-barred rooms, an iron bed in each, a high strip of window above them both, and ancient paint that was peeling from the wall, exposing the crumbling bricks underneath.

Richard and Camille found Julia with her eyes closed and sitting in a lotus position on the floor of the first cell. Richard could see that she was now far more sensibly dressed — although he found himself musing that he'd personally not choose to go to prison wearing cut-off jeans and a tight T-shirt in bright lime green promoting hashish, but he supposed it was each to his own.

Julia opened her eyes as the police approached.

"What have I done?" she asked, so grief-stricken that neither Richard nor Camille said anything for a moment.

"You know," Julia said, "I've been trying to put myself into a trance and go back in time."

"You have?" Richard asked, already pre-emptively weary. This was what he found so tiresome about the New Age movement: they seemed to use the most cumbersome methods to reveal things that were actually already known. Like trying to go into a trance when a normal person would just use their memory. Or inventing ley lines to explain the mystery of

Glastonbury Tor, when really it was just a hill in a surprising place. As for Stonehenge, Richard had always felt that the guy who'd commissioned it had probably only wanted a nice side table, but had made the mistake of asking a bunch of druids with too much time on their hands to do it.

Correctly interpreting her boss's dismissive look, Camille tried to move the conversation on. She asked Julia, "And have you been able to access your memories?"

Julia looked at the police. "Not consciously."

"Not consciously?" Richard asked, exasperated.

"But I could access them subconsciously, I'm sure of it. If I could just get Dominic's help."

Richard's antennae twitched. For a man who wasn't a suspect, Dominic's name was appearing a little too often in the investigation for his liking.

"You mean The Retreat's handyman?"

"That's right. He's a wonder."

"Well, we can both agree about that, he's certainly a wonder. But this case is peculiar enough as it is without bringing in a handyman to extract a confession."

Julia smiled slowly. "But he's not a handyman. He's a Seer."

"A Seer?"

"That's right."

"Please could you tell me what a Seer is."

"He can see things."

Richard took a deep breath and waited for the surge of irritation to wash away.

It didn't, so Camille stepped in. "And what sorts of things can he see?" she asked.

"The future of course. But he can also see the past."

"And how does he do that?"

"Well, in this case, he'd put me into a trance state. You see, he used to be The Retreat's hypnotherapist."

"Used to be?" Camille asked.

"That's right. He stopped doing that just after I arrived." Richard and Camille shared a glance.

"Is that why Dominic and Aslan have been arguing?" Julia was puzzled. "You know about that?"

"Why don't you tell us?" Richard said, probing.

Julia smiled sadly. "It's hard to talk about without making it sound worse than it is, but they weren't ever going to get on. You see, Dominic's a Capricorn and Aslan's a Libran," Julia said as if that explained everything. "And I think Aslan felt that Dominic was taking advantage of the guests in his hypnotherapy sessions. Not that he was. Dominic's hypnotised me often enough. So I know how gentle and supportive he is. He doesn't take advantage of anyone. But Aslan told Dominic he didn't want him offering any more hypnotherapy sessions. Dominic was furious, but there wasn't much he could do. The hotel belongs to Aslan and Rianka. But here's the thing, Aslan said Dominic could stay on as the hotel's handyman. That's the sort of guy Aslan was. He still offered Dominic a job even though they'd argued so badly."

"And Dominic took it?" Richard said, surprised.

"It allowed him to stay on the island," Julia said.

"I see," Richard said, even though he couldn't.

"But the thing is, you have to believe me, Dominic is amazing at getting people to remember memories they've buried because they find them too upsetting. And if you let him hypnotise me, I bet I'll be able to tell you how I got the knife into the Meditation Space. And why I . . . did what I did," Julia finished with a gulp.

"Unfortunately," Richard said, "that would be totally unethical. So why don't we just leave you here for a bit longer, and when you remember anything that might help us, you just call out. We're only next door."

Sensing that Camille was disappointed with this ruling, Richard returned to the main office, calling out to Fidel as he entered through the bead curtains.

"So have you dusted the drawing pin?"

Fidel looked up from his desk in surprise.

"Yes, sir, I have."

"And what did you find?"

"Well, sir, I was only able to dust the flat bit you press down on with your thumb."

"Of course. But is there a fingerprint there?"

"No, sir. There's no print on it, it's entirely clear."

"Now that is interesting," Richard said, excitedly.

"Yes, sir," Fidel said, baffled by his boss's sudden enthusiasm.

"But doesn't that just mean it's never been used?" Dwayne asked.

"And that's where you'd be wrong," Richard said as he started writing on the board.

"I would?" Dwayne asked, puzzled.

"Yes, because I think that drawing pin was part of the killer's plans — and they then wiped it clean of prints once it was used."

Richard wrote up this latest development on the whiteboard, and then he took a step back to look at his handiwork.

The Murder
Five guests go for a swim
Paul hands out robes
Aslan prepares the tea
5 guests + Aslan go into Meditation Space
Aslan locks it down from inside
Drink tea — all cups turned over
10–15 minute window for murder, (8.00–8.10/ 8.15)
Right handed killer?

Investigation / Leads
How did the knife get into the room?
Was the tea drugged?
WHY KILL IN PAPER HOUSE?
WHY A DRAWING PIN? Who wiped it of prints?
Who was in Aslan's office @6pm the night before shouting "You're not going to get away with it"?

Outside the Meditation Space

Rianka Kennedy
Wife
Has no idea who'd want Aslan dead

Dominic De Vere
Ex-hypnotherapist. Now handyman
Sacked by Aslan
Argued with Aslan

Inside the Meditation Space

Aslan Kennedy
Victim
Everyone says he's nice

Julia Higgins
Worked at The Retreat last 6 months
Confessed to murder
But NO MEANS: where did she get the knife from?
NO OPPORTUNITY: how did she get the knife
  to the room?
NO MOTIVE: why kill Aslan?
PLUS: left handed, but the killer was right-handed?

Ann Sellars
Housewife
Married to Paul

Paul Sellars
Handed out the white robes
Pharmacist

Saskia Filbee
Single, 45 yrs old

Here on her own. Says she arrived night before
Heard argument in office night before — at about
6pm — a man, but couldn't identify him

Ben Jenkins
Property Developer. Portugal. Brush with authorities before?

"Okay, Dwayne," Richard eventually said. "I want background checks on our suspects. One of the five people locked inside the Meditation Space with Aslan Kennedy killed him. Who was it? And why?"

"Yes, sir."

"As for you, Fidel, I want you trying to lift whatever fingerprints you can from the murder weapon. And if you can't get any admissible prints from the handle, at least see if you can tell if it was wielded left-handed or right-handed."

"Yes, sir."

"Which leaves you and me, sir," Camille said, "and I think we should go back to The Retreat."

"You do?" Richard asked, already suspicious of his subordinate's motives. "And why exactly is that?"

"Well, sir," Camille said, her eyes shining with innocence, "you said it yourself. There's something about the Meditation Space that meant Aslan had to be killed in there and nowhere else. I think we need to inspect it again."

Richard took a step towards Camille and drew himself up to his full height.

"And this has got nothing to do with finding Dominic so we can ask him to put Julia into a hypnotic trance, has it?"

Camille was shocked by the suggestion. "Of course not, sir. You've already said that would be unethical. But there's also the matter of the murder weapon to consider. Because if Julia didn't have the carving knife about her person when she went into the room, it must have already been hidden in the Meditation Space beforehand. I think we need to work out how Julia got the carving knife into the murder room."

Richard looked at Camille a very long moment.

"And you promise that this has got nothing to do with asking Dominic to put Julia into a trance?"

"Of course not, sir," Camille said, shocked by the suggestion.

"Very good," he said. "Then I think you're right. We should go back to The Retreat."

Satisfied that he'd clipped Camille's wings for once, Richard went off to get his briefcase. But what he didn't see was the sly grin and slow wink that Camille gave Dwayne and Fidel the moment her boss's back was turned.

Getting Dominic to put Julia into a trance was *precisely* why Camille wanted to go to The Retreat.

CHAPTER
FOUR

Richard didn't know when exactly it had been established that Camille would do all of the driving when they were in the police jeep. It's not that he disliked her driving — Camille drove very well, if a little fast for Richard's liking — but he didn't like ceding control over any aspect of his life, and the jeep was no exception. In particular, he didn't like how Camille would agree to drive him to one destination, and then drive him to a different one entirely.

For example, her mother Catherine's beachside bar — which is where Richard now found himself sitting at a rickety table, being served a cup of tea by Camille's entirely baffling mother, Catherine. But then, if Richard didn't understand Camille, he found her mother off-the-scale impossible to comprehend. As far as Richard could tell, she only ever spoke in riddles. For example, she'd tell Richard he'd only find the answers he was looking for when he stopped looking. Which just irritated Richard; he wasn't looking for answers. Or — on another occasion — that he wouldn't be able to start running until he learnt how to stand still. Generally, Richard just nodded along as politely as he could to whatever she was talking about and then tried to change the subject to the weather. That was a much safer area for discussion. You knew where you were with the weather.

On this occasion, though, Camille had stopped off at her mother's bar because she knew that Catherine had holidayed at The Retreat a number of times and knew Aslan well.

Wearing a floor-length orange dress, big silver hooped earrings and with her hair tied up in a purple silk scarf, Catherine swished over and joined them both at their rickety table on the bar's little verandah that overlooked the bay.

"How's your tea?" Catherine asked silkily as she sat down.

This was an area of conversation where Richard felt entirely on safe ground. Catherine, despite being French, made a cracking cup of tea.

"Perfect, thank you."

Catherine smiled in pleasure. "So. How can I help you both?"

"Well, *Maman*," Camille said, "have you heard about the murder?"

"Of course. Poor Aslan. I liked him very much."

"Camille said you knew him," Richard said.

"Of course. A little."

Catherine had run her bar for years. There weren't many people on the island she didn't know.

"Then can you tell us a bit about him?" her daughter asked.

Catherine was happy to. According to her, Rianka had come to the island a couple of decades before and had set up The Retreat on her own. In fact, as far as Catherine was concerned, Rianka was an inspiration to all single women trying to run their own business. But Catherine then explained that it was only when Rianka met and fell in love with Aslan that the business really took off. It was such a sweet romance as well. Catherine remembered it well.

"They were both in their forties, but found love," she said with an encouraging smile that Richard noted seemed to be for his benefit. Why was Catherine looking at him like that?

Catherine sighed at Richard's lack of comprehension, and carried on with her story. It was Aslan who introduced a spiritual side to what they were doing at The Retreat. Before then, it had just been a normal spa hotel. But Aslan's interest in mysticism transformed the place. What's more, the way Catherine explained it, Rianka and Aslan were a formidable team. Rianka was the brains behind the business; the person who did the books and looked after the money.

"Whereas Aslan was hopeless with money. Had no interest in it. But he was the public face of The Retreat," Catherine said, "and what a face it was! You only had to look into his eyes to know the wisdom he had. He was soulful, you know?"

As Catherine continued to explain Aslan's various virtues, Richard found himself looking over the sparkling sea to the far distant horizon. Somewhere over there was England. Where you could go about your business without sweat clinging to every inch of your body. And where your feet didn't throb from the heat trapped inside your shoes. Richard felt his love for England like a physical yearning.

"Are you even listening to me?"

"Of course, Catherine," Richard lied as he returned his attention back to the conversation. "And it's very interesting what you're saying, but I just want to know, do you think anyone could have killed him?"

Catherine seemed shocked by the suggestion. "No. Aslan liked everyone. Everyone liked him."

"Even his wife?" Richard asked.

"How do you mean?"

"Well, he wafts around in white robes going 'om', it would test any relationship, you'd have thought."

Catherine smiled tolerantly at Richard's description. "But that's where you're wrong. Rianka worshipped Aslan and he worshipped her back even more. I remember him once telling me that he owed his life to his wife." Here, Catherine leant forward conspiratorially. "In fact, I got the sense from Aslan when he was telling me this that something very bad had happened to him in his past, and Rianka had saved him somehow."

This got Richard's attention. "Did he say what the bad thing was?"

"Oh no. This was just me reading between the lines. But I'm telling you. Those two loved each other. Whoever killed him, it wasn't Rianka. And I don't know who else it could be. Everyone liked Aslan."

Richard considered what Catherine had said before downing the last of his tea.

"Well, thanks for your time, Catherine, but I really think we must get on."

As Richard got up from the table and left without so much as a backwards glance, he didn't see the amused look that passed between mother and daughter. Because what Richard never knew — and would certainly have never understood — was that both Camille and Catherine were set on reforming him. They'd get him to loosen up. To relax. Admittedly, it hadn't worked yet, but neither of them were prepared to give up. Not yet.

With a kiss for her mother, Camille followed Richard out.

Half an hour later, Richard and Camille arrived back at the murder scene and Richard found himself pausing before he entered the building.

"Problem?" Camille asked.

Richard turned on the spot — taking in how the Meditation Space sat isolated on the wide lawn, the main house standing bright white against the blue sky — and a few shrubs of colourful tropical flowers in bushes dotted here and there.

"Why here?" he said.

"You mean, why commit murder inside a Japanese tea house?"

Richard nodded. It still didn't make any sense to him. The tea house was extremely exposed, but its translucency and lack of any kind of sound-proofing also seemed to make it the least likely place you'd want to carry out something as private as a murder.

He started walking around the structure. It was a large rectangular box-shape just sitting in the middle of a lawn with thick cream paper for walls and thick cream paper for the roof. What was more, the light that was trapped inside it made the whole thing seem to glow. It was as if a strange spaceship had landed in the middle of the lawn.

As Richard got closer, he could see thick vertical bands of dim shadows through the paper walls. These were the wooden pillars that made up the building's internal structure. There seemed to be about a dozen such vertical pillars along each of the long sides of the room. But how was the paper attached to each of these pillars? Richard looked closer at the walls and saw hundreds — if not thousands — of staples attaching the paper to the pillars. The staples were deeply embedded into the wooden frame, were all quite rusty, and had all clearly been there for some time.

"I wonder how the walls survive hurricane season?" Richard asked.

Camille watched her boss press his hand against the paper wall. Clearly it was thickly waxed; extremely strong. But even so, there'd be no way it could survive the worst of the region's weather.

"The frame would be okay, but you're right, I'm sure they need to replace the paper from time to time."

Richard finished his circumnavigation of the Meditation Space. There were no rips or tears in the paper anywhere, and the rusting staples made it clear that this current batch of paper walls had been *in situ* for many months.

"So what do you think?" Camille asked. "Could the killer have got through the paper walls?"

"No way," Richard said. "Not without damaging the paper. And the staples all around the outside of the building make it clear that no one's tampered with any of the walls any time in the recent past. They're all rusty."

"Then what about the door? Could the killer have got in that way?"

Richard considered the wood and paper door. It was like the rest of the building: a simple wooden frame with thick white paper stretched across it tight like a drum.

Richard looked back at the hotel, a hundred yards away. A considerable distance, perhaps, but he could see that the Meditation Space was slap bang in view not just of the verandah, but of everyone who'd been up at the hotel. If Rianka said no one entered or left through the door to the Meditation Space once her husband had gone inside with his guests, then she was almost certainly right: no one had entered or left through the door.

Richard said, "The door's kind of a moot point, isn't it? As everyone says the room was locked down by Aslan before they even sat down. But let's see anyway."

Richard opened the door and inspected its latch lock. It seemed an entirely normal Yale lock such as could be found on the inside of any front door in the UK. It was screwed firmly into the wooden frame of the door — just as the housing was screwed firmly into the doorframe that it slotted into.

"Camille, could you go inside the room and lock me out please?"

"Of course."

Leaving Richard outside on the grass, Camille entered the Meditation Space and shut the door, the bolt of the Yale lock automatically slotting into the frame as it locked the door fast with a firm metallic clunk.

Richard could see that there was no handle on the outside of the door — or any other way to get purchase on the smooth papered surface. There was no keyhole on this side of the door, either, and the door fitted tight within the doorframe. Richard tried to get his fingers into the gap — tried to imagine how the door could have been opened or jemmied from outside without damaging it — and failed.

"Okay, so I think that answers that question," he said. "Once locked down from the inside, there's no way anyone could have broken in through this door from the outside. Not without damaging the frame or ripping through the paper walls."

Richard heard the bolt clunk back, and Camille pulled the door open.

"So no one got in through the door any more than they got in through the walls," Richard said as he entered the Meditation Space and once again was hit by the pounding heat and searing light. He yanked out his already-sodden hankie and dabbed at his forehead. Really, the heat was unbearable.

"You can take your jacket off," Camille said.

Richard looked at his partner as though she were insane. He then returned to the job in hand.

The room was a perfect rectangle and Richard was pleased to see that he'd been right. There were twelve vertical wooden pillars running down each of the long sides, just as he'd expected. The paper attached to the outside of the pillars was translucent — of course it was, it was cream paper — the floor was highly polished hardwood planks, and there was nothing else in the room to break the perfect geometry of the space apart from half a dozen prayer mats, the wireless headphones and the cotton eye masks.

There was no way the killer could have been hiding in the room before the witnesses arrived. And Richard had just proven to his own satisfaction that it wasn't possible to break into the room after the door had been closed and locked down from the inside.

This meant that there were only five possible people who could have killed Aslan Kennedy: the five people of the Sunrise Healing who were already in the room with him when he closed and locked the door.

Richard's irritation spiked. He could feel in his bones that there was something about the room that was important. Something to do with it being made out of paper. After all, why was it inside *this* building that Aslan was killed? At the very least, it offended Richard's sense of the natural order of things that paper could prove so impregnable. It was only paper for heaven's sakes, but Richard knew that for all that it was possible to break in from the outside, the Meditation Space's wall and ceiling might as well have been constructed from stone, and the door from iron.

"It really is a locked room. Isn't it?" Camille said.

"I'd agree with that. Which means that if Julia's not our killer, then it has to be one of Saskia, Paul, Ann or Ben."

"But why would any of them want to kill Aslan?"

"Precisely," Richard said just as he saw a flash of light across the room where the wooden floor met the paper wall.

"Camille?"

"What?"

"You know what, I think that's another one."

Richard went over to the paper wall and dropped to his knees to inspect the floor.

"Another what?"

Richard got out his silver retractable pencil and used it to flick the tiny metal disc away from the wall.

"I don't believe it."

It was another drawing pin. But whereas the first pin they'd found had been pristine, this one's spike had been bent to the side before it ended up over by the paper wall.

Even Camille had to concede that the presence of a second drawing pin at the scene of the crime was beginning to look less coincidental.

"Okay, Camille, on our hands and knees please, I want every inch of the Meditation Space searched for drawing pins."

It was a few minutes later that Camille found the third drawing pin. It was pressed into one of the vertical wooden pillars only a few inches up from the floor.

"Why's it been pushed into the pillar so near the floor?" Camille asked.

It was only when Richard looked over at the door to the room that he began to realise what it might have been doing there.

"You know what? I think this was how the knife was hidden in here beforehand," Richard said.

Camille looked at her partner. "I find a drawing pin in a wooden beam and you say that's how the knife was hidden?"

"But think about it!" Richard said. "Do you think anyone would have been able to smuggle a carving knife in here without any of the others noticing?"

"Seeing as they were only wearing swim things — and cotton robes that were handed out by Paul Sellars . . .? I don't think so."

"And nor do I. So — logically — the murder weapon must have been in here before the room was locked down."

"Okay. Agreed."

"Even though there's nowhere to hide the knife, is there? Or so it would appear at first."

Richard explained how there were twelve vertical wooden pillars along the longer sides of the room, and the drawing pin they'd just found was stuck into the eleventh pillar along. And on the side of the pillar that wouldn't have been visible as the hotel's guests came in through the door.

"In fact," Richard said with increasing excitement, "how wide would you say the murder weapon was at its very widest?"

"Three inches. Maybe four."

Richard got down on his knees, pulled out a little metal ruler he always kept in his inside jacket pocket for just such occasions, and measured how far the pillar stuck into the room. "And this pillar is a good five inches wide. But you'd have to make sure that any knife hidden here was tight up against the wood, and perfectly vertical, which wouldn't be easy. So if you wanted to hide a knife in the shadows here, how could you stop it from falling over or being seen?"

Camille looked at Richard. "You'd maybe get a few drawing pins and pin the knife blade to the wood so it didn't fall over."

"Exactly! And I think that's exactly what happened. All it would take is a couple of pins under the handle — or around the blade — to make sure it stayed flush against the beam. And, having pinned your knife behind this pillar — just off the floor a bit — it would have been all-but impossible for witnesses to see as they came into the room."

"Unless they came to this end of the room."

"But we know they didn't do that." Richard indicated the door in the opposite wall. "They all came in through that door and went straight to the centre of the room where they then sat down in a circle and started drinking tea." Richard strode to the centre of the room as he continued to explain. "All the killer had to do at some point before then — either the night before, or very early that morning — was come in here and pin the knife to the further side of that pillar. And then he or she was at liberty to enter the Meditation Space later on wearing whatever skimpy clothes they wanted. And they didn't even have to worry about the room being locked down while they were all inside because the murder weapon was already planted in the room."

"And while everyone else was meditating —"

"Wearing eye masks so they couldn't see — and listening to whale music on headphones so they couldn't hear — the killer gets up, comes over here, liberates the murder weapon, and, in the process, two of the drawing pins ping off. And the third drawing pin stays pinned into the pillar. But with the knife now freed from its hiding place, the killer approaches Aslan as he sits cross-legged on the floor."

"And knifes him in the neck and back."

"Knifes him five times."

Richard sighed.

"Which is both good and bad news."

"It is?" Camille said.

"Because what we're increasingly seeing is a premeditated murder, Camille. A *rational* murder."

"So?"

"Well, isn't it obvious?"

"No, or I wouldn't have said 'so'. So?"

Richard looked at his subordinate a moment. "So, why on earth would an otherwise rational killer plan to kill someone inside a locked room which also contained a load of other potential witnesses? And, if Julia is indeed our killer, why would she commit this carefully premeditated murder only to start screaming the moment she'd done it so that the witnesses who had previously had their eyes closed now took their masks off and saw her standing over the body with the murder weapon in her hands? It doesn't make sense."

Richard let this settle for a moment.

"But that's the bad news."

"Okay," Camille said. "Then what's the good news?"

"I was right about that first drawing pin we found, wasn't I? It was important."

Camille considered Richard a moment and realised that, yes, he was indeed the most infuriating person she'd ever met in her life.

"But who's our killer?" Richard continued. "Saskia Filbee, our meek secretary from Walthamstow? Paul Sellars, our self-regarding pharmacist? His flamboyant wife, Ann? Our property developer Ben who we both think has maybe had a brush with the law in the past?"

"Or is it," Camille finished, stealing Richard's climax, "Julia Higgins, the woman who's actually confessed to the murder?"

Richard was about to reply to Camille's interruption when he saw a shadow fall onto the wall of the Meditation Space. He held up his finger for Camille to be silent and together they watched the shadow of a person move furtively along the side of the paper. Clearly, whoever was out there had no idea that they could be seen by Richard and Camille from the inside.

Richard pulled out a little penknife from his pocket. It was ivory-bodied, steel-bladed, and it had been given to him by his Great Uncle Harold to mark the occasion of his first day at boarding school. Richard had been eight years old at the time and Uncle Harold's rambling rhapsody on the wonders of boarding school had left the eight-year-old Richard with the distinct impression that, from now on, he'd have to be hunting for all of his food. Which wasn't far from the truth, of course, and Richard had kept the knife close ever since. You never knew when you'd need a pocket knife. Like now.

In five long steps, Richard strode across the room, stabbed the penknife high into the wall and slashed down through the paper. It wasn't easy — the paper was thick and waxy — but the knife was whetstone sharp and Richard soon had a slit down to the floor.

Stepping through the rip in the wall, Richard found himself on the outside of the building and face to face with a very shocked Dominic De Vere.

"What the hell are you playing at!" Dominic all but shouted, looking at the tiny but vicious knife in Richard's hand.

Camille appeared around the side of the building — but she also kept her distance a little. If Dominic tried to bolt, she'd have him covered.

"I could ask you the same question," Richard said, increasingly irritated that Dominic had once again appeared in the middle of their investigation.

"What are you talking about?"

"What are you doing here?"

Dominic thought for a moment, collecting his thoughts. "But it's obvious what I'm doing here."

"Then perhaps you'd like to explain."

"It's simple. I saw, like, shadows inside the Meditation Space and it freaked me out. Because — you know — it's, like, a crime scene. Then I remembered! What if it was the killer and he'd come back to revisit the scene? You know, like killers are supposed to do. They return to the scene of their crime. So I thought to myself: if it was the killer inside the Meditation Space, maybe I could unmask him!"

Richard didn't believe a word of Dominic's explanation and he risked a glance at Camille. It was clear that she was just as sceptical.

"I didn't know you were the police, did I?" Dominic continued. "I just didn't want to be seen before I made my citizen's arrest." Dominic indicated the long rip that Richard had cut into the paper. "And now I'm going to have to repair this wall, aren't I?"

"Oh?" Richard said.

"You know, where you've ripped it," Dominic said, indicating the long slit in the wall.

"Yes, can I ask about that?" Richard said. "Because we've been wondering: what happens if one of these walls gets damaged?"

"You mean like when someone cuts through it with a knife?" Dominic said in a feeble attempt at sarcasm.

"Or they get damaged in a hurricane."

"Well, we've got spare rolls of paper in the basement under the hotel. But we've not had to replace any of the paper walls for nearly a year. Since the end of the last hurricane season, in fact. But I'll have to mend this wall now."

"I don't think you will," Camille said.

"Oh?"

"Because this is a crime scene. You can't go near it."

"That's very much been the thrust of what we've been saying," Richard added.

"Oh," Dominic said. "Right. I see."

"But there's another reason we don't want you fixing walls here," Camille continued. "And that's because we'd like you to accompany us to the police station so you can put Julia into a hypnotic trance."

Dominic was amazed by the suggestion.

But not as amazed as Richard was. Looking at his partner, he had to resist the urge to stamp his foot like a middle-aged Rumpelstiltskin in a suit. Camille had promised him she wouldn't do this!

For her part, Camille was avoiding her boss's stare as she waited for Dominic's response.

"And you're okay with that?" Dominic asked, surprised.

"Sure," Camille said. "Julia's asked for you specifically. She says she'll be able to remember the murder if you hypnotise her."

Richard was desperate to stop the madness, but he knew he couldn't countermand Camille's offer. Not now that she'd made it. This was because, of the very many self-imposed rules and regulations by which Richard led his life, the commandment that you never disagreed with your partner in front of a witness was one of the most unbreakable.

So it was through gritted teeth that Richard allowed Camille to lead Dominic over to the police jeep. Once

Dominic was in the back seat, Richard caught up with Camille before she got into the driver's side.

"What do you think you're playing at?" he hissed.

"I promise you, sir," Camille lied, "I had no intention of getting him into the station when we set out here, but seeing as how Dominic was clearly eavesdropping on us — and is the only person who anyone says ever disagreed with Aslan — I suddenly realised we should maybe bring him in, see how he is with Julia. After all, it's interesting that she asked for him, don't you think?"

Richard knew that what Camille was suggesting was totally unprofessional, and yet she was right about one thing. Here was Dominic again, turning up like a bad penny. And although nothing Julia said under hypnosis would ever be admissible in court, they could maybe use whatever she said as a jumping off point for their investigation.

Once back at the station, Richard was interested to see that while Dominic was pleased to see Julia, she was a touch awkward with him — which was odd considering that it was her who'd asked for Dominic's help. But then, Richard considered, from Julia's point of view she was about to go into a trance to try to remember the precise moment she'd committed a murder; it was perhaps unsurprising she was on edge.

As for Dominic, as far as Richard was concerned, he was his usual preening peacock self, even going so far as to warn the police that he might inadvertently put one of them into a trance, such were his powers. By this point, Julia was lying on the old mattress in her cell, Dominic sitting in a chair to her side, talking gently to her — and Richard, Camille and Dwayne were all crammed in behind. Fidel had also wanted to attend the hypnosis session, but Richard had insisted he stop trying to lift prints from the murder weapon so he could lift whatever prints he could from the two extra drawing pins Richard and Camille had just found at the murder scene. As a matter of urgency.

"You can feel a heavy, relaxed feeling coming over you," Dominic murmured to Julia as she lay on the bed, her eyes closed. "And as I continue to talk, that heavy relaxed feeling will only get stronger and stronger. And the deeper you go, the deeper you are able to go. And the deeper you go, the deeper you want to go, and the more enjoyable the experience becomes. Now you are resting comfortably in a deep, peaceful state of sleep."

Dominic looked up at Richard.

Clearly it was done. Julia was ready.

"We want to know what happened in the Meditation Space," Richard whispered as quietly as he could.

"Shh!" Camille said.

Richard was a little hurt. He'd never been able to whisper quietly, and he was sensitive to this unacknowledged failing.

But Dominic didn't seem too bothered by Richard's inability to whisper as he turned back to Julia.

"Okay, I'm going to ask you a few questions, and you're going to answer because you feel so safe, so secure . . . starting with, what is your name?"

"Julia Higgins," Julia said.

"And where have you been staying?"

"At The Retreat . . . happy."

Julia spoke in a quiet sing-song voice, almost like a child's. And Richard once again found himself thinking that if this was an act, it was a very convincing one.

"You're happy there?" Dominic continued.

"Happy."

"That's great. Well done. And what do you like doing at The Retreat?"

"Working. Meditating. Swimming."

"You went swimming today?"

"Yes. Swimming."

"And then what did you do?"

In her hypnotic trance, Julia frowned as she considered.

"It was the Sunrise Healing."

"What happened?"

"We talked. We drank tea."

"And then?"

"We lay down. And then . . ." Julia trailed off.

"What can you see?"

"I can see light. It's bright. All around me . . ."

"Well done. You're lying down. It's bright all around. But are there others in the room?"

Eventually: "Yes. I see people."

"Are they standing up?"

"No. They're all lying down. Like me."

"How many people?" Richard barked like a seal trying to get the attention of a passing oil tanker.

"Yeah," Dominic said altogether more smoothly. "Who else was there?"

Julia seemed to smile as she considered, and then she said, "Five people. Paul and Ann. Saskia. I like her. And that man Ben."

"She doesn't like him," Richard whispered.

"Shh!" Camille once again said and Richard briefly recoiled. That time surely he'd been quiet?

"And what about Aslan?" Dominic asked. "He's the fifth person, isn't he?"

"No. Aslan's not the fifth person."

Dominic and the police exchanged a quick glance. What was this?

"Surely Aslan's there?"

"No. There's a man there. Sitting cross-legged. White beard. White hair. But his name's not Alsan."

"Then who is he?"

"His name's David."

"What?" This time it was Dwayne who interjected.

"And there's blood everywhere. He's dead." Julia was beginning to panic in her trance. "Help me, I've killed David —"

"Julia, don't worry —"

"There's blood on the knife! He's dead! David's dead!"

Julia's increasing panic was too much for Dominic.

"You're waking up, Julia — you're coming out of your sleep — you're safe and you're waking up on my count. One, you're feeling calm." Dominic counted up to five — saying soothing words as he went — until he finally snapped his fingers and Julia woke with a panicked intake of breath.

Dominic grabbed hold of her shoulders. "You're safe."

Julia looked at Dominic — and at her surroundings — and began to relax, her head sinking back into the pillow as she regathered her composure.

"What did I say?"

"You did great," Dominic said, trying to be positive.

"But did I do it? Did I kill him?"

Dominic said, "I'm sorry, Julia . . ."

Julia squeezed her eyes shut in pain, her worst fears confirmed.

"But there was something else," Richard said. "You said the person you killed was called David."

Julia opened her eyes, puzzled.

"I'm sorry?"

"You said you could see only five people in the room. Paul, Ann, Saskia, Ben — but the fifth person was called David. Which I can't help feeling is a bit odd seeing as his name's Aslan."

"I did?"

"Very clearly. You said his name was David."

Julia was flummoxed.

"I'm sorry. I don't know why I did that. His name's Aslan. Of course it is."

A few minutes later, Richard had despatched Dominic with barely a "thank you" — which he'd been pleased to see had hurt Dominic's feelings — and he and his team were trying to work out whether they'd just got a new lead or not.

"Okay," Richard said. "So why did Julia just call Aslan 'David'?"

"Let me see if I can find anything online," Camille said as she went to her computer and fired it up.

"Man, I don't know," Dwayne said. "She's pretty, that girl, but she's crazy."

Richard turned to Fidel.

"How are you getting on with the drawing pins?"

"Well, sir," Fidel said, "the two drawing pins you gave me are just like the first one."

"How do you mean?"

"There's no thumb or fingerprint on the head of either."

"Really?"

"There's no print at all. It's either been wiped clean, never been used — which we know can't be true with the one you found in the pillar — or the person who used all three drawing pins was wearing gloves."

"Which suggests I was right. They were used by the killer to pin the knife to the pillar — or how else could they have wound up at the murder scene without any fingerprints on them?"

Delighted, Richard beetled over to the board and wiped out what he'd previously written about the drawing pins, updating the information.

"Oh, and Dwayne, have you been able to establish when the witnesses in the Meditation Space arrived on Saint-Marie?"

Dwayne picked up his notebook. "Sure have. And it's just like they told us. According to the airport, Julia got here nearly six months ago; Ann and Paul Sellars arrived a week ago; Ben Jenkins four days ago; and

Saskia Filbee only got in on the 4pm flight the day before Aslan was killed."

"Thank you," Richard said as he added this information to the board. Then, as he was finishing this task, Camille looked up from her monitor.

"Oh okay," she said, "I think you all need to see this."

"What is it?" Richard said as he, Dwayne and Fidel went over to see what Camille was up to.

"Okay," she said. "So I thought I'd start by typing 'David Kennedy' into a search engine. But it's no good, there are too many hits. So, seeing as Julia knows him, I typed in 'Julia Higgins' and 'David Kennedy', but still got nothing that seemed interesting. But then it occurred to me: 'Rianka' isn't a usual name at all, so how about I type in 'Rianka Kennedy' and 'David' and that's when I found it."

"Found what?"

"That Julia was right. The name of the man who was murdered wasn't Aslan. His real name was David."

This got everyone's attention.

"And better than that, according to the newspaper articles I'm reading here, there must be hundreds of people in the world who wanted to kill him."

"You're kidding me?" Dwayne jumped in. "Hundreds?"

"Because Aslan — or David Kennedy as he really was — was an ex-criminal."

"No way."

"Sure was. And a conman at that. He ran a Ponzi scheme."

"And what's one of those?" Fidel asked.

"According to this," Camille said, pointing to the newspaper article she was reading on the screen, "it had something to do with leasing artworks to businesses. I'm just trying to work it out. But it was twenty years ago . . . he was accused of stealing over two million pounds from a whole bunch of people . . . and he was convicted and sentenced to serve seven years in prison. Hang on."

Camille scrolled down the article until her mouse hovered over a picture of a plump man in his late thirties with a shock of black hair, dressed in a smart business suit. He was beaming as though he didn't have a care in the world.

They all looked at the photo of the man.

"Doesn't look anything like him," Dwayne said.

The team looked at the photo some more, and it was true. At first glance, the man in the picture bore no resemblance to Aslan.

"But this photo was taken twenty-one years ago," Camille continued. "Before his hair went white."

"And he grew a long white beard," Richard added. "I mean, to all intents and purposes, he has no face now — it's just white hair, a nose, a pair of eyes and a tanned forehead."

"And he's lost a hell of a lot of weight since then," Dwayne added.

"But yes, look at the eyes," Richard said. "You know what, it is him! He's got the same eyes."

As they all considered the changes that twenty years could wreak on a body, the picture began to make more sense. It really was a plump and besuited Aslan

Kennedy attending his court hearing. Only, his name — according to the article — wasn't Aslan. It was David.

Just as Julia had said it was.

They all looked up as they heard a woman's voice coming from the cells.

Julia was calling for them.

CHAPTER
FIVE

The police went through to the back rooms and found Julia holding onto the thick iron bars, deeply agitated.

"I think I've worked it out!" she said.

"Worked what out, Julia?" Richard asked.

"Why I thought Aslan was called David." The police shared a look. "Only he doesn't look anything like him, that's why I didn't notice. And anyway, I was only a baby when it happened."

"When what happened?" Camille said.

Julia took a moment before she answered.

"Well, the thing is, if Aslan is who I think he is, then you should know, he's a criminal. And years ago . . ." Julia briefly lost her way before summoning up the necessary courage to continue. "Okay, so years ago, my dad had some spare cash and he invested in an art scheme. He was an estate agent — he didn't have much to spare, but he put it all into this get rich scheme. Run by a man called David Kennedy — I can't believe I didn't notice the surname. But I don't suppose the name Kennedy is that uncommon . . ."

Julia trailed off.

"Keep talking," Richard said, unable to keep a sceptical tone out of his voice. This was all proving rather convenient for Julia, wasn't it?

"Apparently, this David Kennedy needed capital to buy works of art. That's the way Mum tells the story. And once he'd bought a load of oil paintings, he'd then lease them to businesses. After all, businesses need paintings on their walls. And they're apparently prepared to pay top prices for the best artists. So Dad gave David cash to fund his business, David bought some paintings — and together they watched the rental money on the paintings start to roll in. Again, this is Mum telling the story."

"But it was a con, wasn't it? A Ponzi scheme," Richard said.

"That's right," Julia said, impressed with Richard. "It turned out that David wasn't buying any paintings at all, he was just taking the money he was given."

"Hang on," Dwayne said. "How does that work?"

Richard turned to Dwayne. "Well, it's kind of obvious. Say you give me a hundred thousand pounds in cash because I say I can buy an oil painting with it — and then we can both make money from leasing it out so that businesses can hang it on their walls."

"Okay," Dwayne said.

"But I don't buy any painting with the money you give me, I just take, say, eighty per cent of the money for myself."

"You take eighty grand?" Dwayne asked.

"That's right. And I spend that how I like. On fast living. Fast cars. But remember, there's still twenty

grand of your original investment I've not touched —
because I've not bought a painting with it — and here's
the clever bit: I wait six months, and then I give you ten
grand of it back and say you've just made a ten per cent
profit on your hundred thousand pounds investment.
And six months later, I then give you the remaining ten
grand and say you've just made another ten per cent."

"Wow." Dwayne was clearly impressed. "Now that's
my kind of con."

But Fidel had already seen the flaw in the system.
"But, sir, what happens now you've spent your eighty
grand and given the other twenty back to the investor?
Haven't you run out of money, and you've still not
bought a work of art?"

"Quite so," Richard said, "and that's why Ponzi
schemes are also called pyramid schemes. Because the
whole thing relies on ever more layers of people
investing so that money can keep flowing up the
pyramid and the conman can continue to pay out
apparent returns while creaming the majority of the
cash off for himself. But the point about Ponzi schemes
is that there always comes a point when the crook at the
top of the pyramid simply runs out of people he can
touch up for cash, the money stops flowing, and the
collapse is always stunning."

Camille was looking at Julia with sympathy in her
eyes. She'd seemed to live every moment of Richard's
description.

"You're right," she said. "Dad gave David everything
he had. Not at first. But by the end of the year he'd
remortgaged the house and taken out loans so he could

104

invest even more. He'd also told all of his friends how much money he was making from David. The following year, when David was arrested and the scheme collapsed, Dad discovered he'd lost everything. Our house. His job. His friends. He'd been an estate agent and now he was a laughing stock who'd just been declared bankrupt and had his house repossessed. Then, just before Christmas, Dad went into the woods, in his car. He ran an exhaust pipe up . . ."

"He took his own life?" Camille asked, horrified.

Julia nodded. This was her pain. Her sorrow.

"I'm so sorry," Camille said.

The police looked at Julia a moment, but Richard was still puzzled.

"Are you saying you didn't know any of this before Dominic hypnotised you?"

Julia looked at Richard and nodded once, seemingly as upset by the thought as him. "But it means I've got a motive to want him dead after all. Doesn't it?"

"And it's why you killed him?"

Julia looked appalled at the idea, but she knew what the truth was. "Yes. I killed him because — at a subconscious level — I must have known his true identity."

Richard wrinkled his nose a bit.

"Then can you tell us where you got the carving knife from?"

This gave Julia pause. "What?"

"Where did you get the carving knife from that you used to kill Aslan? Or David as your subconscious knew him to be."

Julia thought for a long moment before answering. "I don't know."

"You still don't know?"

"No."

"But if you're prepared to admit to murder," Richard said, failing to hide his irritation, "and now to having a motive, why won't you also tell us where you got the carving knife from?"

"I'm sorry. It's because I don't know where it came from. Or how I got it into the Meditation Space."

Richard shuddered a little before regathering his strength.

"Alright, Julia, then tell me this, and I want you to think very carefully before you give your answer: if I said 'drawing pins' to you, what would you say?"

Julia was entirely baffled. "I'm sorry?"

Richard was undeterred. "If I said 'drawing pin' to you, what would you say to me?"

"I don't know what you're talking about."

Richard looked at Julia and tried to work out what was going on. After all, why would she admit to only some elements of the murder, but not others? And there was something else that Richard was beginning to realise.

"Then can I ask — because now I know you had a motive to kill Aslan — can you tell us how you ended up on Saint-Marie?"

"How do you mean?"

"Because I don't believe in coincidence, and this takes coincidence to a whole new level."

"It does?" Julia asked, confused.

"If you're saying you didn't consciously know that Aslan Kennedy caused your father's suicide twenty-odd years ago, then can you explain how on earth you just happened to be on the other side of the world and inside a paper house with Aslan Kennedy at the precise moment he was killed?"

This gave everyone pause.

"That hadn't occurred to me."

"Julia, how did you choose The Retreat for your holiday?"

Julia took a moment before answering.

"But that's the thing," she said. "I didn't."

"What?"

Everyone looked at Julia.

"I didn't choose The Retreat. I was offered a holiday here for free."

"You were? How do you mean?"

"I was chosen as a competition prize winner."

Richard and Camille exchanged a glance.

"Go on," Richard said.

"Well, there's not much to say. It was just one of those envelopes that arrive through the post. You know, it said 'You Have Won a Prize' on the front. I opened it, and it was from this place on Saint-Marie called The Retreat. It said I'd filled in a form online and had been entered into a monthly prize draw, which I'd won. They were offering me an all-expenses-paid holiday as my prize. I didn't believe it at first. These things are never real, are they? But it looked so authentic, I decided I'd phone the number that was listed and just check. And when I called, I got through to a guy who said his name was Aslan and he confirmed I'd won a free holiday to Saint-Marie."

"It was Aslan you spoke to?"

"Oh yes. And it was true. The flight tickets arrived, I came out here — this was about six months ago — I had a wonderful holiday, and I just fell in love with the whole place. And Aslan was so kind. So welcoming. When my week's holiday was up, I asked if I could stay on."

"Rianka told us you now help out in the office."

"That's right. Just a couple of hours a day. And in return, Aslan let me have a guest room for free, I can attend whatever sessions I want — and they've even been giving me a weekly salary. Not much, but enough to get by."

"And at no time did you know you were getting all this from the man who'd caused your dad's suicide?" Richard asked, still amazed at what he was hearing.

Julia bit her lip as she considered what to say, and Richard had a sudden memory of being taken pheasant shooting by his dad when he was ten. His father didn't shoot that often and Richard had always hated it. The damp woods, that feeling of rain down the back of his raincoat. And he and his dad had come across a rabbit that was cowering, ravaged with myxomatosis. His dad had told Richard to shoot it with his .410 shotgun. Up to this point, Richard had managed to avoid ever actually killing anything in his life by pretending he was just a bad shot. But when his dad, by that stage a Detective Inspector in the West Midlands Police, told him to shoot the rabbit at point-blank range, he knew

108

he had no choice. He had to shoot the rabbit. But he didn't. He couldn't. And, in disgust at his son's lack of backbone, Richard's dad had trodden on the rabbit's head with his size twelve police boots himself and stamped the life out of it.

But that's the image that now popped into Richard's mind as he considered Julia. She was looking as forlorn as the poor rabbit from his childhood.

"I'm sorry," she said eventually. "I had no idea who Aslan really was. Not until Dominic regressed me just now."

Rianka was in The Retreat's office when Richard and Camille found her.

"Mrs Kennedy," Camille said kindly.

"Oh?" Rianka said as she looked up from her monitor somewhat listlessly.

"Don't worry. We only have a few questions."

It was clear that Rianka had been crying, a balled-up tissue in her hand. While she took a moment to compose herself, Richard gave The Retreat's office a quick once-over and decided he liked what he saw. Unlike the folk-tattery of the rest of the hotel, here was neatness and order. The shelves were lined with files all neatly labelled, there was a schedule on the whiteboard that had quite obviously been written up with the help of a ruler, an entirely different shelf only contained staplers, a hole punch, reams of paper and other critically important stationery, and — above all else — Rianka was working at a desk that was entirely clear apart from her keyboard and monitor. Richard saw

109

three differently coloured bins lined up next to each other and his heart gave a little leap of joy: there was even a clear recycling policy.

Right then, Richard thought to himself, that was surely long enough.

"Rianka," he said, "we'd like to know a bit more about Aslan's past."

Rianka looked puzzled by the question, and then Richard and Camille saw the moment when the penny dropped.

Rianka's face fell.

"You know. Don't you?"

Richard and Camille waited, knowing that silence was their most eloquent response. After only a few seconds, Rianka got up, went to the door to the room and closed it.

"Look, I'll help you in whatever way I can, but I don't want you to think Aslan was a bad man."

"Even though he went to prison for stealing millions of pounds?"

This stopped Rianka in her tracks. After a moment, she returned to her desk and sat down.

She looked at the police.

"Okay. What do you want to know?"

Richard pulled out his notebook and clicked out his silver pencil.

"For starters, what was your husband's real name?"

"David Kennedy," Rianka said.

"And did he go to prison for running a Ponzi scheme?"

110

"Yes. He was given a seven year sentence. He was released after three years. That was about eighteen years ago."

Rianka was being as matter-of-fact as she could, but Richard could see that this was still painful for her.

"Then tell me, did you know what he was up to at the time?"

Rianka took a deep breath. She shook her head.

"No. I only met him three months before the whole thing collapsed."

"How did you meet?" Camille asked.

"It was a bar. In Mayfair. And he just swept me off my feet. It was all fast cars, champagne, hotel suites — a whirlwind romance — and within a month we were married. In Chelsea Registry Office — and I was wearing a designer dress we'd bought only that morning from the Old Brompton Road. Looking back, I think he already knew the whole thing was about to collapse and he was looking for stability. That's why he proposed to me. But that was also what he was like in those days. Impetuous. Always making snap decisions. And I know it'll be hard for you to believe, he was almost an innocent."

"He was stealing millions of pounds, that's hardly the behaviour of someone who's innocent."

"No — of course — I don't deny he was a criminal, but have you ever put your hand in the biscuit tin promising you'll only take one biscuit?"

"No," Richard said, only for Camille to kick his chair leg.

"Of course," he corrected, recognising what was expected of him. "All the time."

Rianka looked at Richard, in accord. "Because it never stops at one, does it? You take a second biscuit. And then you take another — and another. Don't you? And before too long you realise you've taken so many, you might as well keep going until they're all gone. That's what I think Aslan was doing when he stole from all those people — because don't get me wrong. He was a weak man, I now realise. But there was no malice intended. He took money from all those people because he realised he could. He was like a child with his hand in the biscuit tin."

"And you really had no idea what he was up to?" Richard asked.

"None of us did."

"So when did you find out?" Camille asked.

Rianka looked at Camille, ashamed.

"When the police came to our suite at The Savoy and arrested him. That's how crazy those days were. We didn't even have a home. We just lived in a suite at The Savoy." Rianka frowned as the hot shame of her memories flooded through her. "That moment when I answered the door and saw two men standing there in suits. I thought they were from hotel management."

Rianka looked at Richard, prepared to face the truth. "But that's when my life came crashing down. When I discovered that everything my husband had told me was a lie. That there was no art business. That he wasn't this great success. He was a crook who had stolen millions of pounds from hundreds of innocent people.

112

People who'd trusted him. I was so angry, you have no idea. We'd only been married three weeks!

"I felt so cheated. I'd given my heart to a crook. I couldn't believe it. By the time of his trial, I couldn't face it. I scraped together the last of my money and left the country, I didn't care where I went, I just had to get as far away from him as possible. I felt so ashamed. So hurt.

"I went to South America at first — staying in cheap hostels where I knew no one — and where no one knew me. I got a job working in an orphanage. But I was just getting through the days. You know? And all I kept thinking was, the man I'd loved was a crook. A hateful crook. When I discovered he'd been convicted and sent down for seven years, I decided I had to move on again. So I took the money I'd been able to save and went travelling. Just going from place to place. Not making friends, not doing anything, just waiting really. I didn't know what I was waiting for until I wound up on Saint-Marie and found I liked it here. But that's no surprise. There's something about this island that's special, isn't there?"

Camille smiled in agreement.

"And seeing as I liked it here, I got a job working in the office of the Bay Cove Hotel and I found I was good at it. And, little by little, I started to piece my life back together. Partly because my work was giving me back some of my self-esteem, but, if I'm honest, it was Saint-Marie itself. Whether it's the people — or the quality of the air — or the light — but I felt like it was the island that was healing me as much as it was what I

113

was doing. After a year or so of this, the manager at the Bay Cove asked me if I'd take over the running of the whole hotel, and I realised something about myself. David had so hurt me, I didn't ever want to put my future in the hands of anyone else ever again. And I'd already seen that there was an old derelict plantation house that was going for a song. So I went to the banks, asked to borrow a frightening amount of money, and I couldn't believe it when they agreed. I opened The Plantation Hotel only nine months later and I'm proud to say it was pretty much a success from the start. This is what I was meant to do. This is where I'm meant to be."

"And your husband had nothing to do with it?" Camille asked.

"No way. He was in prison. And as far as I was concerned, he could stay there for the rest of his life."

"So how did you and he get back together?"

"I'd been running the hotel for three years when this man arrived one day by foot. He'd walked from the airport. And he had no luggage. I recognised him at once. It was David. In a plain T-shirt, jeans and old trainers. I didn't know what to say or do, but he said that he was sorry for what he'd done — that he loved me, he'd always loved me — and that he'd changed. I didn't believe him. How could I? He'd caused me so much pain. But he'd come all this way, he didn't have any luggage, I couldn't just send him away, could I? So I let him stay as a guest for a couple of days and tried to ignore him. But the thing was, it was clear that he had changed. He'd obviously been through a lot while in

114

prison. And a couple of days turned into a couple of weeks. And a couple of weeks, into months.

"Because you have to believe me when I say Aslan was an innocent. He was. So when he saw what I was up to here, he started to get involved in the life of the hotel. And he'd clearly been developing the spiritual side of his nature while he was in prison. He was hugely knowledgeable. He started going to these meditation sessions in Honoré. And doing yoga.

"It wasn't long after that he changed his name to Aslan. I didn't quite trust him yet, but his sincerity was heart-breaking. He so clearly wanted to be a better person. And . . . well, the thing I never thought could ever happen again started to happen. I started to fall back in love with him. This simple soul, happy to spend all day in meditation, happy to give himself over to the problems of others. And the thing that really sealed it for me was he was no longer interested in money at all. He didn't spend it. Didn't ask for it. He was happy to live a simple life of service helping others. And I know this is strange, but the thing is, we were still married. You know, technically. A year to the day after he'd arrived on the island, I took him back and I have to be honest, it was the best decision I've ever made. Because he wasn't David any more. He was Aslan. The lion-hearted."

Richard looked long and hard at Rianka.

"*That's* what it means?"

Rianka was confused. "I'm sorry?"

"The name, Aslan, it means lion-hearted?"

"That's right. It's an African name. And my husband's been Aslan to me for nearly fifteen years now. We've grown old together. Who he was before . . .? That's not who he is now. Who he's not been for a long time."

Camille said after a suitable pause, "Then can you tell us a bit about the competition Julia won to come out here?"

Rianka sighed, clearly trying to work out where to begin. "I'm sorry, I should have told you all this before, shouldn't I?"

"It's alright," Camille said. "You were in no state to volunteer information."

Rianka was grateful for Camille's words. "A couple of years ago, Aslan told me he felt he'd had more luck than he deserved. Finding me again, finding his true calling. And he came into this office one day and asked me, did I think he looked anything like the man he'd once been? And I have to say, with his robes, his white hair, his tanned skin — and the way he was now lean like he'd never been before — he didn't look anything like the man he'd been twenty years before. And then he asked me if I'd let him use some of the profit the business was making to give free holidays to the people he'd wronged in the past.

"He had to ask me for permission, you see, because Aslan had no money of his own. He'd always insisted that I keep sole ownership of The Retreat. He said he had to prove to himself and to me that he was no longer interested in money. I paid him a salary of a thousand dollars a month, but he barely touched it — and at the end of each month, his bank automatically gave whatever money was left over to a local orphanage. Honestly, you have to believe me. That's how much he'd changed. And now he was trying to find a way of helping those he'd taken advantage of.

"If I'm honest, I thought that inviting the victims of his Ponzi scheme out for free holidays was a terrible idea. But Aslan was nothing if not persistent and he kept working on me — telling me no one would recognise him — and saying he had to do something for those he'd stolen from. He still had a list of their names, and he said he wouldn't stop until he'd found them all and given something back to each and every one of them. Or their relatives if they'd since died. The way he put it, it was about karma. He'd taken from them and now he had to give something back. In the end, I agreed."

"So you invented a fake 'You Have Won a Prize' competition," Richard said.

"That's right. I figured we'd need some pretext to get people out here without them realising what was going on. Hold on." Rianka went over to the other desk in the room and pulled out a pile of colourful flyers from a drawer. She handed them over to Richard and he could see that they featured lots of photos of The Retreat accompanied by an enticing blurb: "You Have Won a Prize".

"Aslan designed the flyers himself."

Richard looked at the picture of a smiling Aslan on the back of the flyer.

"Weren't you worried someone would recognise him as David Kennedy, the man who stole from them?"

"Aslan insisted it was twenty years ago. He didn't look anything like his old self. It would never happen."

"And what did you think?"

Rianka paused a moment. "I wasn't so sure. I mean, I didn't think anyone would recognise him — not really — but what if they did?"

"You were worried."

"A little. So I made Aslan promise me, he'd only have one person from the past out here at a time."

"How do you mean?"

"Aslan just wanted to send the flyers out to everyone he'd ever stolen from, but I was worried that even if they didn't recognise him, they might get talking among themselves and put two and two together. After all, this is a place where you're encouraged in any kind of healing session to talk about key events from your life. I didn't want two or three people one day discovering that they were all here on a free holiday and that they'd all lost money in the same art-lease scam decades ago. So I always made Aslan promise that he'd only ever send out one flyer at a time, and only have one guest here on a free holiday at a time. He never liked me saying it could only be one person at a time, but he knew I was right. If it was going to work, it was the only way."

"And that's how Julia ending up getting her invitation six months ago?"

"That's right. Aslan had felt particularly terrible when he'd discovered that her dad had committed

118

suicide because of what he'd done, so when Julia asked if she could stay on, he was happy to offer her a job. We needed help in the office anyway . . ." Rianka trailed off, the inevitable thought finally occurring to her. "You don't think she worked out who he was? Do you?"

"It's still too early to say for sure," Richard said. "But does this mean that while Julia was with you, Aslan stopped inviting other people out for free holidays?"

"Yes," Rianka said. "That was the condition I imposed on him when he offered Julia a job. While she was here he had to promise he'd invite no one else out on a free holiday."

"And he was happy to agree to that?" Richard asked.

"Of course," Rianka said. "It was common sense. Look I can show you." Rianka turned her monitor around a little and Camille went to look over her shoulder as Rianka indicated the screen. "This is the database of all of the guests who are staying with us, and the staff know that if a person's name has an asterisk by it, then that guest is staying here for free. And since Julia started working for us, we've not had anyone else staying for free."

"Would you mind?" Camille asked, indicating the mouse to the side of the computer.

"Of course," Rianka said, moving the keyboard over so that Camille could check over the names of the guests for herself. While Camille did this, Rianka looked back at Richard, worried.

Tears started to well up in Rianka's eyes again.

"This was what I was always worried about," Rianka said. "That someone would uncover the truth of

119

Aslan's past. But Julia . . .? I thought she liked him. She was always so nice to him. So nice to us both."

Looking at Rianka's screen, Camille said, "Sir, I think you should see this."

"What's that?" Richard asked.

Camille indicated the screen. "Julia isn't the only person with an asterisk next to her name."

Rianka didn't quite understand what Camille was saying. "How do you mean?"

"In fact," Camille said, "there are three other names here, each with an asterisk by their name, suggesting they're here as part of the 'You Have Won a Prize' competition."

"There are? But that can't be possible."

"But who are they?" Richard asked with a creeping sense of foreboding.

Camille said, "They're Paul Sellars, Ann Sellars and Saskia Filbee."

Richard and Rianka were stunned.

"No!" Rianka eventually said. "Aslan promised me. No one else while Julia was staying with us."

"I'm sorry," Camille said. "But it says here that Paul, Ann and Saskia were all here on free holidays."

"What about Ben Jenkins?" Richard asked. "Is there an asterisk next to his name?"

"No," Camille said. "He's here as a normal fee-paying guest."

Camille turned the monitor so that Rianka and Richard could see for themselves.

"Aslan . . ." Rianka said to herself in horror. "What have you done . . .?"

In the list of hotel guests, the names of Paul Sellars, Ann Sellars and Saskia Filbee all had asterisks next to them — just as Julia's name did. But did that mean that they'd all lost money to Aslan twenty years ago?

Luckily for Richard, he knew there was an easy way to find out.

He could ask them.

CHAPTER
SIX

While Camille went looking for Paul, Ann and Saskia, Richard sat out on the verandah and waited as patiently as he could, which wasn't very patiently at all.

As his foot beat out a restless tattoo on the tiles, he could see the Meditation Space clearly in the middle of the lawn — just as Rianka had done on the day of the murder — and he could see how difficult it would have been for anyone to approach it without being seen. It really was marooned in the middle of a vast lawn.

Richard could see a few guests in white robes walking through the garden, and others sitting on sun loungers down on the private beach, but the place was noticeably less busy than it had been on the day of Aslan's death. No wonder, frankly, but Richard didn't blame those who'd decided to stay on despite the murder. Their holidays had cost too much. And Richard supposed that it had helped that the self-confessed killer was already behind bars in Honoré Police Station.

But was Julia the killer, that was the question? Or was it one of the other four?

Richard found himself wondering why a load of Brits would go to the ends of the earth just to go to a health farm. After all, if you wanted to lose weight, you could just try eating less food. And if you wanted to swim in the sea, Britain was an island nation for heaven's sakes! There was sea galore — and even in land-locked Leicestershire, where Richard grew up, he'd only ever been a few hours' drive from the wide open beaches of Norfolk. Not that he'd admittedly ever been to them. Not with his phobia of sand.

He was mopping his brow with his hankie as Camille led Paul, Ann and Saskia over.

Paul wasn't very happy.

"I don't understand," he said. "We've already given our statements to your officer here, what do you want with us now?"

"I'm sure this won't take long," Richard lied easily.

"It had better not."

Richard took a moment to wonder why Paul was so irked at having to help the police again.

"Very well," Richard said. "Could the three of you tell us how you ended up choosing The Retreat for your holidays?"

"Well, that's easy enough," Paul said, apparently relieved by the question. "Ann and I won a competition."

"You did?" Saskia said, surprised.

"That's right," Ann said, breathlessly and then proceeded to fill them all in on the background. They'd got a letter out of the blue that said she and Paul had won a prize. It was something to do with a form they'd filled in online, and they'd won an all-expenses trip to a health farm in the Caribbean.

Saskia was surprised to hear this.

"But that's how I ended up here as well," she said. "I also got a letter saying I'd won a prize."

Richard and Camille shared a glance. Bingo.

Saskia explained how the covering letter had told her to ring a number in the Caribbean, which she'd done, and she'd ended up speaking to a man who called himself Aslan — and he explained how she'd won a free, all-expenses holiday in the Caribbean.

"And it was definitely Aslan you spoke to?"

"Of course. Who else could it be?"

"But I spoke to him as well!" Ann said, acting as if she and Saskia now shared a bond that would unite them forever. "And he was so nice, so friendly. He told me we'd won a week's holiday in the Caribbean."

"When was this?" Richard asked.

"How do you mean?" Ann said.

"When did you receive the letter?"

"I don't know," Ann said, turning to Paul.

He patted her hand, happy to help. "About six weeks ago, I'd say," he told the police.

"That's right," Saskia said. "That's when I got the letter. Six weeks ago."

"Then why did you choose this particular week to come out here?" Richard asked.

Paul and Saskia both said that this was the first week they were offered, and they were happy to take it.

"After all," Saskia said, "how often do you get given a free holiday in the Caribbean? I jumped at the chance."

Richard decided it was time to find out if the reason why these three were at The Retreat was the same as the reason why Julia was originally invited out for free.

"But then," Richard said easily, "you all recognised Aslan when you got here, didn't you?"

This threw the witnesses.

"How do you mean?" Saskia eventually replied.

"Aslan Kennedy. You recognised him when you got here. Of course you did. Don't worry, I know you're not otherwise involved."

Still nothing from the witnesses. Richard could see that none of the three had the first idea what he was talking about.

"Very well," Richard said, again trying to hide the importance of his line of questioning behind an easeful manner, "then what would you say if I told you that Aslan wasn't his real name?"

Nothing from any of them.

"In fact, his name was David Kennedy."

Still nothing. But then Richard saw Ann's face register shock while her husband and Saskia were still looking nonplussed.

"You don't mean Aslan was . . . what? Are you really saying . . .?" And then the truth of it struck home and both hands flew to her mouth in horror. "Oh my god, it could have been! Paul, did you realise?"

Paul still had no idea what his wife was talking about. Or was pretending he had no idea, Richard thought to himself.

"What on earth are you talking about, woman?"

"Aslan Kennedy wasn't Aslan Kennedy, he was David Kennedy — the man who took our money!"

Paul continued to look nonplussed. "What on earth —" And then he got it, turning to the police in amazement.

"No," he said. "That's not possible."

"But you admit it?" Camille asked. "You were one of the people David Kennedy stole from twenty years ago?"

Ann looked full-square at the police, happy to give testimony. "We were."

"So was I," Saskia said in a quiet voice, utterly amazed, Richard noted. "But that wasn't him."

"I'm sorry, but it was," Camille said.

Saskia had been standing, but at this revelation, she went to a nearby chair and sat down on it, the strength seeming to go from her legs.

Richard could see that the bafflement of the three witnesses seemed entirely heartfelt.

Paul, though, was still puzzled by what Saskia had said. He turned to her and said, "You were caught up in all that as well, were you?"

Saskia nodded slowly, still a bit too overwhelmed to use words.

Paul turned back to the police. "Then can you tell us what on earth's going on?"

"Of course," Richard said. "But first, can you all tell me how much money you lost to Aslan Kennedy — or rather, David Kennedy, as he was — twenty years ago?"

Paul turned to his wife for confirmation. "It was about ten grand, wasn't it?"

"It was twenty thousand pounds," Ann said, clearly amazed that Paul had forgotten the exact amount.

"And it was his art-leasing scheme you invested in?"

"That's right. Or what we thought was an art-leasing scheme," Paul said "The whole thing was a scam. Or so we later found out when the police arrested him. We never saw a penny."

"And was it the same for you, Saskia?"

"Pretty much," she said a touch tremulously. "I gave him fifty thousand pounds."

Richard was surprised that the figure was so large. After all, Saskia wouldn't have earned a huge amount in her job as a temporary secretary.

"And where did you get those sorts of sums from?" he asked her.

"From an inheritance," Saskia replied. Richard picked up an odd vibe from Saskia as she said this, but he couldn't quite place what it was.

"I see."

Richard turned back to address the group. "But all three of you agree, you all lost money to David Kennedy twenty years ago — and you're all here on a free holiday because David — or Aslan as he became — sent you literature saying you'd won a free holiday. But you're also all saying that none of you recognised that David was now Aslan?"

Ann, Paul and Saskia looked at each other, as unable to believe this as the police were.

"It would seem so," Paul said.

"But I don't understand. Why did he invite us?" Saskia asked.

"We aren't sure," Richard said. "Rianka said it was because Aslan felt guilty for his actions in the past. So he was trying to make amends to those he'd wronged. So can we ask one more time: did any of you recognise Aslan Kennedy for the man who stole from you twenty years ago?"

"No," Paul said forcefully, and it was clear he was speaking for the other two as well.

"Are you sure?" Richard asked.

The three witnesses all looked at Richard. Absolutely.

"But now you know," Camille asked, "how do you feel?"

Saskia looked at Camille. "How do you mean?"

"The man who stole fifty thousand pounds from you has just been murdered. By the only other person in the room he'd also stolen from."

"What?" Paul asked, stunned.

"Julia was just like the three of you," Camille explained. "She was invited here for a free holiday because Aslan had stolen from her in the past."

"But that's not possible," Paul said. "Julia can't have even been alive when that man was running his scam."

"You're right," Camille agreed. "She was a baby at the time. It was her father who gave David all his money. He lost everything and apparently committed suicide soon after."

"Poor man," Ann said, almost to herself. This was the first time that Richard had seen Ann be anything less than her usual on-the-surface flamboyant self. He had to remind himself that there was a thinking feeling person under the kaftan after all.

"Then let me ask another question. How well do you all know each other?"

"I'm sorry?"

"For example, have any of you met before this holiday?"

"No," Saskia said.

"Then have any of you met Julia before?"

"No. The first time we met Julia was on this holiday."

"And I didn't meet her until the morning that Aslan was killed," Saskia said. "Remember, I only arrived on the island the afternoon before he was killed."

"Yes," Richard said, "I've been wondering about that. Because you all say you don't know each other — and I know you all came out at different times — and yet all of the people on this island who Aslan once stole from were in the Meditation Space with him when he was killed. Can any of you imagine how that came about?"

"No," Paul said, "except for the fact that we didn't choose to be there."

"You didn't?" Camille asked.

"No," Paul continued. "It was explained to us when we got here. We could sign up for any of the courses on offer apart from the Sunrise Healing. There was a charge for everything else, of course, but the Sunrise Healing was a special treatment that Aslan offered for free — and it was always his choice who attended."

Ann said, "We were told that most people got to attend at least one of the Sunrise Healings, but we weren't to be offended if Aslan didn't choose us. He didn't offer the course to everyone."

"Aslan would only hold it with people he thought would benefit from it," Paul finished.

Richard was puzzled. "You're saying it was Aslan who chose you?"

"That's right," Ann said.

"But why on earth would he choose the only four people on the whole island who had a grudge against him and then lock himself in a room with them all at the same time?"

The witnesses had no idea, but then, Richard had to consider, he could just as easily ask: why on earth had Aslan invited four of his Ponzi victims out to The Retreat all at the same time? What was Aslan playing at?

Camille's mobile phone started to ring, and she moved off to one side to take the call.

Paul looked at Richard. "But I don't understand. Why are you questioning us?"

Now it was Richard's turn to be puzzled. "How do you mean?"

"Because if you're saying Julia's dad killed himself after losing money to Aslan, then clearly that's all there is to it. I know she's been here for months. She must have worked out Aslan's real identity and decided he deserved to die just like her dad had died. It's understandable. But I imagine she knew that if she killed him, her motive would soon be discovered. So she worked on Aslan, got him to invite the three of us out to the Caribbean at the same time and then she also made sure that he chose us all to be in the Meditation Space with her that morning. That way, when she killed him, she'd know that the scene would

130

be confused by the presence of three other people all with the same motive as her."

Against his better judgement, Richard was impressed with Paul's logic. What he was saying made sense, if it wasn't for the fact that Julia wasn't right-handed and therefore almost certainly hadn't been the person wielding the knife. They'd just have to wait on the autopsy report to confirm whether the killer struck right-handed or not.

And there was the small matter of the argument Saskia overheard the night before Aslan was killed. Because if Julia was the killer, how come it had been a man threatening Aslan that he wouldn't "get away with it"?

Camille returned to the group, putting her phone back into her little leather handbag as she did so.

"Ann Sellars, would you accompany us to the station, please?"

Panic slammed into Ann's eyes.

"I'm sorry?" Paul said on his wife's behalf.

"We'd like your wife to accompany us to the station."

"Certainly not," Paul said firmly. "If you've anything to say to Ann, you can say it to her right here and now. In front of me."

Camille looked at Ann, but she was still rooted in panic to the spot. Camille looked at Richard and he raised an eyebrow. It was Camille's call.

"Okay," Camille said. "Ann, one of our officers has been able to lift seven fingerprints from the handle of the murder weapon. Four of them belong to Julia Higgins, but they're prints from her left hand — and we believe the killer was right-handed. Whereas the other three prints we've been able to raise from the handle of the murder weapon all belong to you. And they're all from your right hand."

Ann was stunned. Unable to speak.

"What's more, we already know that the killer held the knife with the blade pointing downwards so he or she could strike down into the victim's neck and back, and the prints we've been able to lift show that you were holding the knife in a way that is consistent with a downwards stabbing motion. Can you even begin to explain to us why this is?"

Everyone looked at Ann as she slowly crumbled. And Richard noticed an odd look slip into Paul's eyes. It was almost a look of respect. As if he was reappraising his wife.

Ann turned in desperation to her husband. "Paul, you've got to help me." Paul continued to look at his wife, fascinated. "Paul, don't look at me like that, you know I didn't do it! I couldn't have done it!"

Ann's panic was becoming overwhelming, and Richard began to wonder. Was Paul actually enjoying her pain?

"Wait!" Ann said in a sudden spasm, standing up as she did so. After a few more moments of fevered thinking, she then turned back to Camille. "Oh god, it's so simple! Sorry, it's just I was so worried — I couldn't work it out — but I have, I'm sure I have."

Richard was more sceptical. "You can explain how your fingerprints have just been found on the knife that was used to kill Aslan Kennedy?"

Ann stood as straight as her plump body would allow.

"I can. And better than that, I can also explain how my fingerprints got on the murder weapon that way round." Ann shook out her shoulders as though to prepare herself for an oration and Richard had the sudden revelation that Ann had almost certainly been involved in amateur dramatics at some point in her life. "Because I'm not the killer. Of course I'm not!"

Yup, Richard thought to himself. Ann had got her mojo back.

"But now you mention it," she continued, "there *is* a carving knife I've held, and it was the night before Aslan was killed. So if it turns out that that's the knife that was used to kill him, well then that explains why my fingerprints are on it."

"I see," Richard said. "So what knife would this be?"

"Well! As you no doubt know, this is a retreat for the spirit as well as the body. And we're always encouraged to help out with community chores. It says in the blurb that it helps develop tolerance and understanding."

"It also gives Aslan free labour," Paul added.

Ann ignored her husband. "Paul thought it was a disgrace. But I thought we were already having a free holiday, the least I could do was do a couple of things to help out. And you know what? I enjoyed it. It made a difference doing a few chores because I was choosing to do them rather than because I had to," Ann said pointedly at her husband. "Anyway, the night before Aslan was killed, I helped with the washing up after dinner."

"You did?" Richard asked.

"Only for half an hour or so, and I dried lots of different pots and pans — I remember doing those — but I also dried various kitchen knives and put them back into their wooden block. And that's the thing, the wooden block I put the knives into was on a shelf. The only way you could get the knives in was if you slotted them in with a downwards motion."

Richard looked at Ann, amazed. He needed to clarify this.

"You're saying the murder weapon has your fingerprints on it consistent with a downwards stabbing motion because you dried the murder weapon the night before it was used and put it away in a wooden block such that you used a downward stabbing motion?"

"That's it exactly!" Ann said.

A few minutes later, Ann was leading Richard and Camille into The Retreat's kitchen, Paul and Saskia following. As it was early afternoon, it was empty as they entered, just a neon blue fly-zapper high on the wall and the hum of refrigeration units. Richard was quietly impressed with what he saw. The cooking ranges were all top-end, there were copper pots and pans arranged on shelves or hanging from neat pegs — and the far wall was dominated by three simply enormous glass-fronted fridges.

It reminded Richard that he really had to do something about the pocket-sized galley kitchen he had in his shack. And that in turn reminded him that he also had plans to terminate his relationship with his

134

lizard as well — but he had to put all such thoughts to one side for the moment. Instead he turned to Ann.

"So where is this knife block?"

"I'll show you," Ann said, heading over to one of the ranges. "Ah, here we are."

She indicated a metal shelf to the side of a range that had on it a large wooden block that contained various knives.

Richard realised that what Ann had said made a kind of sense. Even he — who was much taller than Ann — would have used a stabbing grip to slot the knife down into the carving block on the shelf.

"I knew it!" she said, turning with triumph to look at Richard. "It's got holes for six knives in it, but there are only five knives in there now, aren't there? And I bet you won't be able to find the sixth knife anywhere in this kitchen — or even in this house. And that's because the knife I washed up is clearly the knife that Julia then used to commit murder."

Trying to ignore Ann's look of triumph, Richard had to conclude that Ann's explanation of how her fingerprints had ended up on the murder weapon was at least partly plausible. After all, any killer would know that leaving their fingerprints on the handle of the murder weapon would almost certainly be a one-way ticket to prison. By this logic, of course, neither Julia nor Ann were likely to be the murderer as they'd been the only two people foolish enough to get their prints on the murder weapon at all.

But there was something else Richard had to concede about Ann. Like Julia — although for wildly different reasons — Ann just didn't feel like a killer. Her personality seemed entirely to be surface. There were no hidden depths. Unlike her husband, Paul, Richard thought to himself. He'd clearly briefly relished the idea that his wife was a killer. But why? Because he didn't like his wife? Or because he was the real killer and was now trying to get her convicted for a crime she hadn't committed? Either way, there was no doubting that Paul was a far better "fit" as a killer than poor, dim, ditzy Ann.

Richard felt a surge of frustration wash over him. One of the five people who'd been in the Meditation Space with Aslan was the killer, but which one of them was it?

Not for the first time, Richard had a strong feeling that he was missing something about the case. Something fundamental. But it was more than that, Richard realised, because he was increasingly of the opinion that there was a shadowy presence on the edges of the case. Someone he couldn't quite see, but who was still influencing events.

And this person was the real killer. And they were manipulating him. Manipulating them all. That's why Julia had ended up confessing to the murder; why Ann's prints were now on the murder weapon; and why four out of the five people who'd been with Aslan when he was killed had all lost money to him in the past. And once again, Richard found himself thinking back to the Meditation Space. Why on earth had the killer chosen to commit murder in broad daylight, inside a building made of translucent paper, while the door was locked from the inside, and while there were four other witnesses who could have witnessed the moment of murder?

It was almost as if the killer was throwing down a challenge to Richard. Was he clever enough to work it out?

The door swung open and Ben Jenkins barrelled into the room, full of bonhomie.

"Aye aye, I wonder what's going on here . . .?"

"Excuse me, sir," Camille said, "would you leave?"

"And miss whatever you're up to? No way."

"I'm sorry?" Richard said.

"Don't be. I've paid for this holiday — so I reckon I can come into the kitchen of the hotel whenever I like. Unless you have a problem with that?"

Richard looked at Ben and realised that Ben was right. Not that he could come into the kitchen as and when he chose, but that he had indeed paid for his holiday. Which was interesting, if only because the other four people in the murder room with the victim hadn't.

Richard watched Ben go over to a metal bowl that contained a pile of fresh fruit. He plucked himself up a crisp green apple.

"Doesn't look to me like you're getting very far with this case, Inspector," he said, before taking a bite out of the apple with a crunch.

Richard decided that enough was enough.

"Tell me, Mr Jenkins," he said, entirely politely, "what would you say to me if I told you that Aslan's real name was David Kennedy?"

Ben wasn't too fussed as he finished his mouthful.

"I'd say I'm not that surprised. Aslan was never going to be his birth name, was it?"

"But did you know that Aslan was, in reality, David?"

"Nope."

"Have you ever heard of a David Kennedy?"

Ben seemed to think for a moment, but Richard thought he saw the tiniest flicker of indecision.

"No. Name doesn't mean anything to me."

"Then tell me, what do you know about Ponzi schemes in general, Mr Jenkins, and art-lease Ponzi schemes in particular?"

Ben thought for a moment — but, once again, Richard decided that unless he was very much mistaken, Ben Jenkins was hiding something.

"No idea," Ben eventually said. "But Ponzi schemes are like those pyramid cons, aren't they?"

"That's right."

Richard remembered what Camille had said after she'd taken his statement.

"Tell me, Mr Jenkins, have you ever had a brush with the law in the past?"

"No," Ben said, still chewing on his mouthful of apple.

As Richard held Ben's gaze, he had a sudden revelation. If he was looking for someone at the heart of the case who was manipulating them all — the real killer — then what was more surprising? That four out of the five people in the murder room with Aslan all shared the same motive to want Aslan dead, or that the fifth person — Ben Jenkins — didn't?

And then there it was: the briefest flicker of fear in Ben's eyes, and Richard knew in that moment that Ben was lying to him.

Ben looked away, embarrassed, and Richard's heart gave a little leap.

"Alright, then," Ben said, trying to cover the moment in bluster. "As you were."

Ben wandered out trying to look nonchalant, but Richard knew the truth now.

Ben wasn't an innocent. He was connected to Aslan's murder somehow.

Richard just had to work out how.

CHAPTER
SEVEN

The following morning, Richard was brushing his teeth in the tiny en suite shower room of his shack and still musing on Ben's possible involvement in the murder. He knew the moment Ben had looked away was an admission of guilt — of some sort — and there was still the matter of the man who Saskia heard arguing in Aslan's office the day before he was killed. What if that had been Ben? But if Ben was the killer, why on earth did he want Aslan dead?

Richard caught a sudden movement out of the corner of his eye, and he jumped in fear like a suddenly yanked marionette, biting down on his tongue in the process.

It was Harry the Lizard scampering down the tree that grew through Richard's front room.

As Richard's heart tried to calm itself and his eyes watered at the screaming pain in his tongue, he struggled to work out what he found more irritating, being hounded by a lizard who wouldn't leave him alone, or having a tree grow through his front room.

At a deeper, more honest level, Richard of course knew that it was perhaps him with his china washbasin, toothbrush and smart pyjamas that was encroaching on the tree's personal space far more than the tree was encroaching on his, but it didn't change the fundamentals of the situation. There was a tree that grew through his floorboards and disappeared into the roof — and frankly, as far as Richard was concerned, it was an affront to all known standards of decency. Let alone building regs.

What Richard couldn't understand was why someone would build a house around a pre-existing tree rather than just chop the bloody thing down and throw it away first. Or, better still, kill two birds with one stone and cut the tree down and use the planks from it to *then* build the house.

But then, at least the tree was always there — where he expected it to be. It didn't jump into his eyeline at inopportune moments with its arms and suckers flapping and then, just as suddenly, run off again.

As Richard rinsed his mouth of menthol froth, Harry the Lizard watched on, his little chest rising and falling with each breath — and a certainty began to form in Richard's mind. The shack wasn't big enough for the both of them. So he was going to get rid of his lizard.

And he was going to get rid of the creature permanently.

Before he arrived at work, Richard slipped into the local hardware store hoping no one would see him. It wasn't that he felt embarrassed trying to buy lizard poison, far from it — it was a home-owner's inalienable right to dispose of vermin in whatever way they saw fit — but, as he flicked through the ancient boxes of various poisons, he also knew he didn't much want to have to explain exactly what he was up to — as even a cursory glance at the relevant website made clear, Richard's lizard was a protected species.

"Good morning, Richard," a mellifluous voice purred nearby and Richard looked up with a start only to find himself staring into the face of Selwyn Patterson, the island's Commissioner of Police.

"Oh. Good morning, sir."

Selwyn saw that Richard was holding a tatty box emblazoned with "RAT ATTACK KILLS ALL RATS (GUARANTEED TO KILL 100% OF ALL RATS)" across its front.

"Not planning a murder, are you?" Selwyn asked with a deep chuckle.

"Of course not!" Richard said, laughing so suddenly that he now knew he looked as though he was indeed planning to commit a murder.

"So what are you up to?"

"Oh, you know," Richard said with increasing desperation. "Just browsing."

"Browsing in the poisons section of a hardware store?"

"That's right, sir. Just browsing." Richard got out his hankie and wiped at the sweat at the back of his neck. "Hot isn't it?"

"Only, I saw you acting furtively over here, and I thought to myself, that man is up to no good."

"You did, sir? But I'm not being furtive."

"I think you are, Detective Inspector."

"Oh, I wouldn't say that."

142

"Then why are you wearing a pair of sunglasses inside?"

Richard took a moment before he answered.

"Oh, these, sir?" Richard lifted the dark shades he'd been wearing as if he'd only just noticed they were on his nose.

"Yes. Those."

"Well, the thing is, when I put them on this morning I thought they were my Reactor shades, sir. You know, the sort that are shades outside in the sun and stop being shades when you go inside, but they're not those shades, are they? Now I'm looking. They're the shades that stay shades even when you're inside."

Selwyn gently took the other box Richard was holding from him and read what it was called: "COCKROACH KILLER!!!"

"I understand Aslan Kennedy's been murdered," Selwyn said.

"That's right, sir." Richard was acutely aware that he was now having a conversation while he was holding a box of poison called *Rat Attack* and his Commissioner of Police was holding a box of poison called *Cockroach Killer*. This was not how Richard had expected the day to develop.

"I always went to The Retreat once a year," Selwyn continued. "For a detox. I liked both Rianka and Aslan. Him in particular."

There was a moment while Selwyn looked at his Detective Inspector.

"Well, don't let me stop you from your browsing."

Richard smiled milkily. "Good day, sir."

"Good day, Inspector."

With a smile and a tip of his peaked cap, Selwyn ambled off with all the urgency of a well-fed bear who knew it was hours still until lunch.

Richard gave his boss a few minutes' head start, and then he too bustled out into the sunshine and started off for the office, not noticing — because he never noticed — just how beautiful the town of Honoré was.

It sat nestled in between sweeping mountains and the sparkling sea, and was full of ramshackle houses, bars and shops — all colourfully painted, even if the paint on most of the buildings had peeled and faded from the constant, blistering sunshine. In fact, the only building in the whole place that wasn't at all run-down was the Catholic church that sat towards the mountain-side of the town, its tall tower and red-tiled roof seemingly looking down on the rest of the town like a benevolent parent watching carefully over a wayward child.

It was a town where people went about their business when they had to, but for the rest of the time were happy to hang out and chat or share a drink. "Liming", the locals called it. And one of the locals' favourite topics of conversation when they met up was their eccentric and, they believed, quite mad Detective Inspector, Richard Poole.

But ever since Richard had exposed a local policewoman as a double killer, the people of Honoré had taken Richard to their hearts and had been looking out for him. Helping him cross roads when he kept looking for traffic driving on the left; or explaining which local foods on a menu contained unadvertised

144

seafood or spices; or tolerating his tirades when shop owners decided to shut up a few minutes before advertised closing times.

They were entirely forgiving. They even liked him.

And Richard had no idea.

Mind you, as his team might have reflected later that morning, he didn't make it easy.

"Come on, you're supposed to be the island's brightest and best, what are we missing?" Richard hectored from the whiteboard.

"Hey, Chief," Dwayne corrected. "I never said I was the brightest, and I certainly never said I was the best."

"Look," Richard said. "A man goes into a room constructed of paper and wood that's otherwise marooned in the middle of a huge lawn — only a few shrubs nearby. Five other people go in with him. There's no one else inside before they arrive, no one else arrives or leaves while they're there. And it's the victim himself who locks the room down from the inside.

"They then all sit down on prayer mats and drink tea for a few minutes. And then, having drunk the tea, they lie down — apart from Aslan, if Julia's testimony is to be believed, as he apparently chose to do his 'healing' sitting up, cross-legged. But the key point is, the others were all lying down — their eyes hidden behind eye masks, their ears muffled by sounds of the ocean's deep — for ten or fifteen minutes, which is the brief window of time in which we know Aslan was brutally slain. All facts that prove just how improbable the murder is."

"You keep saying that, Chief, but why? It happened," Dwayne pointed out.

145

"I know, Dwayne, but think about it. If you were going to kill me, how would you go about doing it?"

"What?"

"Come on, Dwayne. I know it's somewhat macabre, but just humour me. If you were going to kill me, how would you go about doing it?"

"Well, first I'd check out what was playing at the cinema tonight."

"I'm sorry?"

"You're asking how I'd kill you."

"That's right. Not that you've ever thought about it before of course."

Dwayne looked at his boss and answered very carefully. "Not that I've ever thought about it. But — and I'm just plucking this from thin air, you understand — if I had to do it, the first thing I'd do is sort out my alibi for the time of the murder. And that's where the cinema comes in, because I'd make sure I watched a film today that I knew would also be on tomorrow night at 10pm, say. Then, having already seen the film, the next day I'd go to the cinema and buy a ticket for the 10pm screening and go in to watch it. But here's the clever part: because if you grew up on the island, you'd know you can still get out of the cinema through the old projectionist's booth, so I'd slip out of the building during the film and come down to your beach. Now, you're generally asleep by nine, nine-thirty, aren't you, Chief?"

Richard was looking increasingly wan. "Yes, Dwayne."

"And your locks aren't worth spit — not to someone with my skills. So I reckon I could get into your house unseen and unheard and kill you in your bed before

146

heading back to the cinema where I'd slip back inside, and wait for someone else to discover the body. Because the thing is, if anyone asked where I was at the time of the murder, I'd not only be able to say I was in the cinema, I'd be able to prove it with my detailed knowledge of the film I'd already seen the day before."

Richard looked at his subordinate a long moment. "Not that you've ever thought about it."

Dwayne realised he'd maybe revealed more than he'd meant to. "That's right. Not that I've ever thought about it."

"But, sir," Fidel asked, "why do you want to know how Dwayne would kill you?"

"Because, Fidel, Dwayne's right — if a little too specific for comfort — because if you're planning to commit a murder, the first thing you do is sort out an alibi. If you can. And yet with Aslan's death," Richard said, going to the board, "we've clearly got a premeditated murder — the knife pinned to the pillar in the corner of the room proves this — but the killer doesn't bother to sort themselves out with an alibi. In fact, they not only fail to make it look like they were elsewhere at the time of the murder, they actually make sure they're locked inside the room with the victim and a load of other witnesses when it happens. It just doesn't make sense. Why would you premeditate to commit murder in front of a load of potential witnesses?"

This hung in the air a moment.

"And why was Aslan killed inside a paper house set in the middle of a lawn? Because, of all of the places to choose to kill someone, why there? What are we missing?" Richard looked at his team's blank faces and sighed. "Come on, we've got to be making better progress than this! Fidel, how are you getting on with the kitchen knives?"

The day before, Camille and Richard had put the knives and knife block they'd retrieved from The Retreat's kitchen into evidence bags, and Fidel had been lifting prints from them ever since.

"Well, sir, the murder weapon that was used to kill Aslan is the same brand and design as the rest of the knives here. It's also the right size to fit the sixth slot."

"So you're saying that the murder weapon came from that block of knives?"

"Yes, sir. But I've also been able to lift a number of fingerprints from all of the knives that were still in the kitchen, and they've only been touched by one person."

"Let me guess," Richard said. "Ann Sellars."

"That's right, sir. Which is consistent with her drying the knives with a tea towel and then putting them away."

"And how do the fingerprints on the handle suggest she was holding the knife handles?" Richard asked.

"It's consistent with her stabbing the knife down into the slots of the wood block. But there's more, sir, because I also rang Rianka and she confirmed that she'd seen Ann doing the washing up the night before her husband was murdered."

"So that's a dead end," Richard said as he updated the whiteboard. "Ann can explain how her fingerprints were on the murder weapon after all."

Camille came and stood by her boss.

"What do you think?" she asked.

148

"I don't know," he said, "but I'll tell you what I keep coming back to. Why on earth did Aslan invite four Ponzi victims out to Saint-Marie at the same time?"

"I know what you mean," Camille said. "It's pretty risky."

"So either Aslan wilfully set up the circumstances of his own murder — which I find unlikely," Richard said, "or someone convinced him to change his policy and start inviting more than one Ponzi victim at a time. So the question is, who on the island knew about Aslan's 'You Have Won a Prize' scheme and the fact that he was really David Kennedy?"

"Well, that's easy, sir. It's Rianka and no one else."

"And yet," Richard said, "I can't imagine why she'd risk having a load of Ponzi victims all out at The Retreat at the same time. If word got out that Aslan was an ex-criminal, it could be the end of the business."

"Unless it was Rianka who killed Aslan," Dwayne offered.

"Of course," Richard agreed as he looked at the board, "but I just don't see how she benefits from her husband's death. And, remember, she was outside the Meditation Space when it was locked down. Only one of Saskia, Julia, Paul, Ann or Ben can possibly be our killer. It's one of them who must have known that Aslan was really David Kennedy. And one of them who somehow nobbled him so he ended up inviting all of the Ponzi victims out to the Caribbean at the same time."

"Then it has to be Julia Higgins," Fidel said. "Of those five, she's the only one who's been here long enough to have found out Aslan's real identity."

"I know," Richard said. "Paul Sellars had the same theory. That only Julia could have discovered who Aslan was in time to implement a plan to kill him. But somehow I think that's too easy."

"Too easy?" Camille asked.

"Because can't you feel it?" Richard asked. "There's someone behind the scenes here. Someone who's so devious we can only infer their existence from the shadow that's cast by their actions, but I'm telling you this much: I don't think Julia's our killer. She's too young, too . . . what's the word?"

"Beautiful?" Camille offered, an eyebrow raised.

"No, Camille. Facile. She believes in hypnotherapy, she's a hippy dippy loon. I don't think she's sharp enough to pull off a murder this meticulous. Just as Ann wears her heart on her sleeve — and then covers it in diamanté jewels. She's so big and blowsy, I can't imagine she'd carry out a murder like this any more than Julia would. What we're looking for here is a spider. Someone who spins a web and then waits in the shadows for the victim to be caught. And if I were guessing, I'd say that could only be one of Ben, Paul, or Saskia . . . but which one is it?"

Fidel joined Richard at the board. "So you're saying you don't think that either Ann or Julia is our likely killer."

"I don't think so. Neither of them has the right temperament for a murder this manipulative. And remember: Julia's left-handed. In fact, why haven't we had the autopsy report on Aslan's body yet?"

150

It still irked Richard that he'd been posted to an island in the Caribbean so small that it didn't have a single forensics lab on it. They had to do all of the forensics work themselves or send anything more complicated "off island" for the labs on neighbouring Guadeloupe to get back to them. It was no way to run a case, but Richard knew there was nothing he could do about it. It was a bit like life itself. You just had to soldier on.

"I rang them first thing this morning," Fidel said. "They've not booked it in yet."

"Very well," Richard said with a sigh. "Dwayne, if Julia's innocent, then I think that Paul's theory is correct, our killer must have worked out Aslan's real identity long before they arrived on the island. There wouldn't have been time to plan and carry out a murder like this otherwise. So I want you to get on to the various phone companies both here and in the UK. I think we'll find that one of the people in the Meditation Space has been in touch with Aslan — or The Retreat — a number of times over the last few months. Someone's been planning this a long time. Maybe we'll find the answer in the suspects' phone records."

"Yes, sir," Dwayne said.

"And, Fidel, I want you to do the same with Aslan's laptop. Maybe our killer's been in touch with him via email."

"Yes, sir," Fidel said.

"As for you, Camille, can you please get on to the labs on Guadeloupe. I want to know why they haven't carried out Aslan's autopsy yet."

"Yes, sir," Camille said.

After a couple of phone calls, Camille reported back that she'd been able to reschedule the autopsy for later that afternoon — and she also made sure the pathologist knew that he was to call them with a preliminary report the moment it was completed. But in chasing the lab on Guadeloupe, she'd managed to get hold of the toxicology tests that had been carried out on the suspects' blood and urine samples, and on the residues of tea that they'd all been drinking that morning.

"Really?" Richard said, eagerly.

"And you're going to like it," Camille said, handing over the report fresh from the office printer.

Richard scanned through the document at speed, gathering the salient details.

"You're right about that, Camille," he said. "According to this, the tea they were drinking was drugged."

"It was, sir?" Fidel asked.

"They found traces of gamma-hydroxybutyric acid in it."

"But what's that?" Dwayne asked.

"I'll look it up," Camille said, returning to her computer.

Richard carried on reading and, turning the page, saw the results of the blood and urine tests the paramedics had carried out on the witnesses.

"And better than that, not only was there gamma-hydroxybutyric acid found in the tea the witnesses drank, trace elements of it were also found in all of the witnesses' blood. That's Paul Sellars, Ann Sellars, Saskia Filbee, Ben Jenkins . . . and also Julia Higgins."

Richard looked up from the report, puzzled.

"But that's good news, isn't it?" Dwayne asked.

Richard looked at the board, his brow furrowing. He'd always half hoped that the tea had been drugged, and so was delighted to discover that his hunch was right. After all, they'd all said they'd felt groggy when they'd heard Julia start screaming, and it helped explain why the killer had been confident enough to commit murder in front of so many potential witnesses: the others were under the influence of drugs at the time. But it didn't make sense that Julia had also been drugged. Did it? Not if she was the killer. Richard wasn't able to finish off his train of thought, as Camille called over from her desk.

"Okay, I've got it here," she said, indicating her monitor. The team crowded around Camille's desk to see. "Gamma-hydroxybutyric acid is better known as GHB."

"And what's GHB?" Fidel asked.

"Of course!" Richard said without having to refer to the screen. "It's like Rohypnol. Or ketamine. It's a date-rape drug popular on the club scene. It causes wooziness and compliance."

"You know all this?" Dwayne asked, sceptically.

"You walk the mean streets of Croydon long enough, you come across pretty much everything, Dwayne. But GHB is perfect for slipping into a pot of tea if you wanted people's deep sleep to be deeper than normal. And better than that, if my memory is correct, GHB is

153

odourless, colourless and tasteless. Really it's the perfect drug to have put in the tea."

Camille had been following everything Richard said on the fact sheet she was reading on her computer.

"That's about right, sir," she said. "It says here, GHB can produce drowsiness, disorientation, and reduced consciousness."

"And that's what I don't understand," Richard said.

"What's that, Chief?"

"Because how come Julia also had GHB in her system?"

Richard's team looked at him, nonplussed, so he harrumphed — irked that he'd have to explain it to them. "Because if she's our killer, I don't think she'd have wanted to drink a dose of a sedative just before taking a knife to Aslan Kennedy."

"Oh," Dwayne said. "I see."

"And there's something else," Richard continued. "Because, look at all the effort our killer's gone to. Getting hold of a sedative well in advance. Getting hold of a knife that already had Ann's fingerprints on. Setting it in the Meditation Space before it was needed. Working out the angles in the murder room so that the perfect pillar was chosen to hide the knife behind; and then pinning the knife to the wooden pillar with drawing pins that the killer made damned sure didn't have any of his or her fingerprints on. So, after all this incredible preparation, are we really saying that Julia then risked everything by taking a good glug of sedative before committing murder — wielding the knife five times apparently with her 'wrong' hand, remember —

154

and all before deciding to scream her head off in a way that guaranteed she wouldn't get away with her crime?"

Richard was pleased to see that his team could see the logic of what he was saying.

"But this I do buy," he said, wanting to ram his point home. "We have our real killer. It's one of Ann, Paul, Saskia or Ben. And it was him or her who pinned the knife to the pillar beforehand. Him or her who drugged the tea in the pot. And it was him or her who made sure that while everyone else was taking a sip of drugged tea, they left their tea well alone. For the moment, at least. And this person isn't our tie-dyed Julia. This person is organised, ruthless, and supremely clever. And then when everyone else is woozy as hell and lying down with their headphones and eye masks on, the real killer gets up, gets the knife from the hiding place, kills Aslan, returns to their prayer mat and only now do they drink down their cup of drugged tea. They then put on their headphones and eye mask again and wait for someone else to discover the body, a process that's made altogether simpler for the killer because Julia not only discovers the body first, but in her hopped-up confusion, she thinks that she's the killer."

Everyone looked at Richard.

"Hopped-up?" Camille asked, amused.

"Yes, Camille," Richard said, going back to his desk. "Hopped-up. You know, high on drugs."

Despite his team's obvious amusement at his expense, Richard was pleased he'd got his point across so effectively and, later that afternoon, when the report finally came in from Aslan's autopsy, it seemed to confirm everything he'd said.

The victim was killed by five "sharp force injuries" — which is how the autopsy referred to the knife wounds in Aslan's neck and back. The first two wounds went into the right side of the neck, the second strike of which severed the carotid artery. Then, the next three strikes travelled down the victim's shoulder and into his back as the body toppled forward.

The report was unequivocal. To carry out all five injuries — and considering the angles of the wounds in Aslan's neck and back — the killer was standing behind the victim and wielding the knife right-handed.

Having read the report, Richard looked at his team.

"You know what? I'm fed up of playing into the killer's hands. I think it's time to push back."

"You want to release Julia?" Camille asked.

"We'd have to, anyway," Fidel said, and everyone turned and looked at him. "We're coming up to the thirty-six hours we can hold her without charge. So either we charge her with murder, release her, or apply to the Commissioner for an extension to hold her without charge. And I don't think he'd grant one. Not the way the evidence is stacking up."

"So how about we send the murderer a message?" Richard said. Everyone looked at him. "Because if we release Julia, the person who actually killed Aslan will realise that we're widening our nets again. And maybe that will put a bit of pressure onto them."

"Because when people feel pressure," Camille agreed, "they make mistakes."

156

"Precisely," Richard concluded — and he could see that his team agreed with him.

Half an hour later, Richard was showing a bemused Julia out of the police station onto the verandah outside.

"I don't understand." Julia couldn't have looked more forlorn if she tried. "I know what I did."

"But that's the thing, Julia, we now know you were drugged on a mind-altering drug at the time. I don't think you do."

"I killed him, I know I did."

"You really must stop saying that," Richard said, unable to keep a spike of irritation out of his voice.

"But I must have done."

"No, Julia, you only think you did. The facts suggest you're just mistaken."

Julia looked at Richard with hope in her blue eyes.

"You really think so?"

"You were drugged and confused. You got up and you saw the blood. By the time you knew what was going on, you'd picked up the knife. That's why you started screaming. You couldn't believe what you were seeing. You're not the killer."

A fat tear rolled down Julia's cheek.

"Please, don't cry."

"No, I'm not crying. I'm happy. Is it really true?"

"It would appear to be so."

"Then you've saved my life! Thank you!"

Julia flung her arms around Richard and buried her head into his neck, squeezing tight.

Richard did his very best impression of a plinth.

When Julia didn't let go, Richard raised his arms and sort of touched her slender waist with the cloth of his jacket that encompassed his forearms. And then he realised how it would look, a Detective Inspector hugging a beautiful young woman in a lime-green pro-drugs T-shirt who'd recently been suspected of murder, so he took half a step back.

"There there," he said awkwardly. "You can go now."

Julia looked at her saviour, and smiled.

"Thank you."

"Seriously. Just doing my job."

With a last little smile, Julia turned and left down the stairs that led to the yard. Richard watched her every step until she was lost in the street market outside the station.

"Ahhhhhh," Richard heard from behind him and he froze.

And then he heard a few sniggers. He turned.

Camille, Dwayne and Fidel were all watching through the open window behind him and had clearly witnessed the whole encounter.

"My relationship with the witness just then was entirely professional."

"Sure, Chief," Dwayne said.

By way of answer, Richard strode imperiously back into the station. And, ignoring his team's smirks, he updated the whiteboard. Because with Julia out of the frame, that left only four other people who'd been locked in the Meditation Space with Aslan when he was murdered.

One of Ann, Paul, Saskia or Ben was their killer, but which one of them was it?

The Murder
Five guests go for a swim
Paul hands out robes
Aslan prepares the tea
5 guests + Aslan go into Meditation Space
Aslan locks it down from inside
Drink tea — all cups turned over
10–15 minute window for murder, (8.00–8.10/8.15).
Right-handed killer!

Investigation / Leads
WHY KILLED IN PAPER HOUSE?
3 x drawing pins in the Meditation Space. Used to pin the murder weapon to a pillar. No prints on any of them
Tea drugged with GHB, a sedative
Who was in Aslan's office the night before @6pm shouting "You're not going to get away with it"?

Outside the Meditation Space

Rianka Kennedy
Wife
Has no idea who'd want Aslan dead

Married to Aslan when he was David — but left him when he was convicted
Took Aslan back 15 yrs ago when he came to the island

Dominic De Vere
Ex-hypnotherapist. Now handyman
Sacked by Aslan
Argued with Aslan
Caught returning to Scene of Crime

Inside the Meditation Space

Aslan Kennedy
Victim
Everyone says he's nice
Real name is David Kennedy
Ex-conman — ran art-lease Ponzi scheme, stole £2m
Went to prison 20 years ago, served 5 yrs

Julia Higgins
Worked at The Retreat last 6 months
Confessed to murder — but GHB in blood — and lack of real motive — and LEFT-HANDED . . . she's innocent

Ann Sellars
Housewife
Married to Paul

160

Arrived on island 7 days before murder
Lost £20k in Ponzi scheme
Her fingerprints are on the murder weapon — but
she washed the knife the night before

Paul Sellars
Arrived on island 7 days before murder
Handed out the white robes
Pharmacist
Wife alibis him for argument, at 6pm
Wife Ann lost money in Ponzi scheme

Saskia Filbee
Single, 45 yrs old
Here on her own. Says she arrived night before
Heard argument in office night before — at about
6pm — a man, but couldn't identify him
Lost £50k in Ponzi scheme

Ben Jenkins
Property developer. Portugal. Brush with authorities before?
Arrived on island 4 days before murder
No alibi for time of argument at 6pm
No connection with Aslan / David / Ponzi scheme
. . . so far

For the next couple of days, Richard was unbearably
grumpy. He tried to move the case on, but it wasn't
going anywhere. Fidel was unable to find any incriminating

emails on Aslan's computer, and definitely nothing that suggested that any of their suspects had been in touch with him in the preceding months. As for the telephone records for the four remaining suspects, when they came in they didn't show any suspicious activity either. Both Saskia and Ann had said that they'd rung The Retreat six weeks before when they'd first got the literature telling them they'd won a free holiday, and both of these phone calls were listed on their records. As far as the police could work out, none of Ann, Paul, Ben or Saskia had phoned Aslan or The Retreat at any other time, before or since.

And yet, Richard was sure, the killer must have been in touch with Aslan. Somehow. Nothing else could explain the sudden arrival of so many Ponzi victims in the Caribbean all at the same time. And the fact that they'd all been lined up in the Meditation Space at the precise moment that Aslan was killed.

As for Richard's hunch that Ben was more involved than he was letting on, that didn't seem to go anywhere, either. Dwayne had been digging into Ben's life in Portugal and discovered that he'd moved there in 1999. He worked those first few years as a plumber, and then, in 2002, he bought his first property, a holiday rental in a village called Guia. By 2004 he owned four other such holiday villas, and by 2007 he'd got fourteen and had packed in the plumbing business entirely.

"At current count," Dwayne said as he summed up the situation for his boss, "he owns thirty different properties across southern Portugal, he lives on his own in a residence on the first hole of the championship golf course at Vilamoura. And I'm telling you, Chief, in all that time he's had no brushes with the law, the tax authorities, or anyone else I can find. In short, his credit history's clean, his company checks out, he's lived at the same address for the last eight years, there are no gaps in his employment history. He's cleaner than clean."

This had just irritated Richard. He was convinced he'd seen a flash of fear in Ben's eyes, so maybe they'd been looking in the wrong place? Richard instructed Dwayne to go back to the 1990s and even earlier if he could — to when Ben was living in the UK — and see what he could dig up.

And it wasn't just the murder case that was infuriating Richard. Because he'd finally plucked up the courage to buy some rat poison and smuggle it back to his shack, but the question was, could he now really act as judge, jury and executioner on Harry the Lizard? After all, as a policeman, Richard's job had only ever been to identify behaviour worthy of punishment. He'd never had to hand out a sentence before. Let alone a sentence of death.

And the more Richard dithered about delivering the *coup de grâce*, the more he felt the very tangible presence of the box of poison in his house. He'd be surfing UK news sites on his laptop — or doing the crossword in his chair — and he'd suddenly remember the box of death that he'd hidden behind the J-cloths under the sink in his kitchenette.

It must have been how killers felt before they'd disposed of the body, Richard found himself thinking. The only difference between him and a proper killer being that he was managing to wind himself up into paroxysms of guilt before he'd even committed a crime. Not that it was a crime, he had to keep reminding himself. Only he paid the rates on the shack — he wasn't obliged to share it with anyone.

On the third day, Harry scampered into the shower with Richard and he was finally stung into action. Grabbing up a towel, the soap still in his hair, Richard thudded across to his kitchenette — too irritated to remove the sand that was by now sticking to his wet feet — and he grabbed up the packet of poison.

This was it. The lizard was going to die. And Richard had the means of despatch in his hand. He was Ozymandias. He was the Bringer of Death. But then he noticed a caption on the side of the packet: "MOST VERMIN DIE OUTDOORS", and it briefly troubled him.

No one should have to die on their own. Not outdoors.

Not even a lizard.

Richard found his resolve evaporating as quickly as it had arrived. He put the box back under his sink and washed his hands but, as he did so, he started to berate himself. He was such a wimp. He didn't want the lizard in his shack, but if he couldn't get rid of it, how could he even begin to achieve anything else in his life?

"You alright, Chief?" Dwayne asked later on that morning when Richard was at work.

"Sorry?" Richard looked up from his desk, distracted.

"You seem quiet. You alright, there?"

Richard realised he hadn't been paying attention, and he looked at the concern on Dwayne, Camille and Fidel's faces.

"Of course I'm alright," he said, irritably. "Why are you all looking at me like that?"

"Because I said the Metropolitan Police's case files on Aslan's original conviction have just arrived and you didn't seem to hear me."

Richard jumped to his feet, delighted finally to be able to learn more about Aslan Kennedy's original multimillion pound con from the past.

Unwrapping the package, Richard and his team discovered a thick green hanging file stuffed full of paperwork that had yellowed around the edges from old age. Here was Aslan's photo — or David, as he was back then — his original statement, the notes of the arresting officers, the case against him — and witness statements by the dozen. Richard pulled out three pages of typed notes at the end of the document.

"Now this is exactly what we've been looking for."

"What is it?" Camille asked.

"A list of all of the people who invested in the Ponzi scheme — and how much money they invested. Fidel, would you check the witnesses' names off on this list? In particular, just double check that Ben Jenkins's name isn't there. Or a Jenkins of any sort."

Fidel quickly scanned the list. "I don't see a Jenkins here," he said.

"You don't?"

"But that's hardly a surprise, is it, sir? After all, Aslan put asterisks next to the name of everyone who was here as part of the 'You Have Won a Prize' competition. And there wasn't an asterisk next to Ben Jenkins's name."

"I know," Richard said, "but what if it was a relative of his who invested? Because if everyone else in the Meditation Space lost money in the Ponzi scheme, then what's Ben's connection?"

"Okay, sir. But you should know, the list's organised by surname and there aren't any surnames here that begin with the letter 'J' at all. There's a Daniel Higgins — I'd imagine that was Julia's dad. It says here he invested £47,000 in April 1994; and £85,000 in September; and £100,000 in February 1995. That's a lot of cash."

"Nearly a quarter of a million pounds. No wonder he was desperate," Camille agreed. "Poor man. Are the other witnesses there?"

Fidel soon discovered that Ann Sellars lost £20,000 in January 1995 — just as she'd told them — and that Paul Sellars wasn't listed at all. Again, just as he'd said. But it was when Fidel looked up Saskia's name that he got a shock.

"Sir . . . you should see this," he said.

"What is it?"

Fidel looked at the rest of the team. "Saskia told us she lost fifty thousand pounds to Aslan, didn't she?"

"That's right," Richard said. "Giving her a pretty big motive to want Aslan dead if you ask me."

166

"You can say that again," Fidel said. "But it was a bit more than fifty thousand pounds she lost."

"It was?" Camille asked.

"According to the case file here, she lost ten times that."

"What?"

"Saskia Filbee lost five hundred thousand pounds to Aslan — but told us it was significantly less."

Richard looked at Fidel, a jolt of excitement running through him.

Why on earth had Saskia lied to them?

CHAPTER
EIGHT

While Richard and Camille waited in the grand hallway of the hotel for Saskia to come down from her upstairs bedroom, Richard found himself checking over the cork noticeboard that was by the main entrance.

It was covered in handwritten notes, schedules and adverts for courses, seminars and various therapies guests could sign up for — including Pilates, Yoga, Massage, Water Aerobics, and Aromatherapy. It all reminded Richard a little too much of the college noticeboards he used to look at when he was at University. Back then, he'd stand in front of the mess of papers pinned to the board and marvel at the busy lives everyone else seemed to be enjoying. He'd wanted to join in with this social whirl of clubs and hobbies, but he didn't know how to — the notices always seemed to be written in a private language he didn't understand. To this day he still didn't know what Korfball was.

"You wanted to see me?"

Saskia clipped down the main staircase and Richard once again found himself noticing how sensibly dressed she was. Today, she was in a pair of white cotton trousers, a tan-coloured top and a wide-brimmed straw hat. Fresh-faced, clean and simple — that's how

Richard found himself categorising Saskia as she approached.

"Yes," Richard said. "We just wanted to follow up on our interview with you the other day."

"Of course," Saskia said, and indicated a clutch of wicker chairs that stood by the main door. "Shall we sit down?"

As they went to the chairs, Richard remembered that Saskia was a career secretary. She was probably used to coping in lots of different social situations. So what was the best approach? Softly-softly?

Camille smiled kindly for Saskia's benefit and said, "Can you tell us how you ended up investing in Aslan's art-lease scheme?"

"Of course," Saskia said.

"No," Richard said. "Just tell us why you lied to us."

Saskia looked surprised.

"I'm sorry?"

"Because you lost half a million pounds to Aslan — or David Kennedy back then — but you lied to us that it was only fifty thousand." Richard leant forward a little so his next point would carry suitable emphasis. "So either you start telling us the truth, Saskia, or we can carry on this conversation down at the police station."

All of the colour had drained from Saskia's face, but Richard refused to break eye contact. He knew it was mean, giving anyone other than a career criminal both barrels, but this was a murder inquiry, it was no time for needless niceties.

"I . . ." Saskia said, frantically trying to find the thread of her thoughts. "Well . . . Look, I didn't mean to lie to you. And it's not really lying anyway."

"It isn't?" Camille asked kindly.

"Well, it is a lie. It's just it's one I tell myself — and I've been saying it to myself so long . . ."

Camille touched Saskia's knee and smiled sympathetically as though she understood everything Saskia was about to say already. For his part, Richard tutted — Saskia was still a suspect in a murder inquiry, no one should be touching her knee — but, luckily for Richard, he made sure he only tutted silently in his head so he didn't get any looks from his partner. He'd learnt that lesson long ago.

"Why don't you tell us everything?" Camille offered.

Saskia looked at Camille and knew that that's what she'd have to do.

"Well, the thing is, I'm from London," Saskia said. "North London. A place called Barnsbury Park. And I didn't have any brothers or sisters. My mum was a housewife, but Dad worked on the railways and was a union man. You know? It's why we lived in Barnsbury, it was near Dad's train depot on the Caledonian Road. It was a brilliant childhood. I had my school and my friends, and these great big hulking men covered in dirt would come and visit in their filthy fluorescent jackets and sit in the garden smoking their roll-ups and talking politics with Dad."

Saskia smiled at the memory.

"I could have stayed on at school until eighteen, but Dad left school at fourteen — and I was desperate to

170

get on — so I left at sixteen and ended up getting a job as a secretary for the ladieswear buyer for a department store on Oxford Street. And I really enjoyed the work — and the friends I made — and I thought that that was what life was going to be like. Living at home, working in town, being happy. Then, just after I'd turned seventeen, Mum got diagnosed with breast cancer."

Saskia's eyes welled with tears as she explained how her mum had promised to fight the illness, but in the end, it had made no difference.

"By the time I'd turned nineteen, Dad and me had buried Mum in a cemetery just off the North Circular. And Dad was never the same after that. He retired from work and just sat in a chair. He lost weight. He wouldn't eat. He stopped inviting his friends around. He just shrank, and there was nothing I could do. Mind you, I wasn't much better. Just getting up and going to work. Just existing. We were like ghosts that year, Dad and me. Both in the same house, but barely speaking. Barely alive. And then the following winter, Dad got flu, it developed into pneumonia, he had to go to hospital and he just faded away. By the time I was twenty-one, I'd buried both my parents."

Richard was grateful when Camille said, "I'm so sorry," as he knew from bitter experience that he sometimes sounded sarcastic whenever he offered someone his condolences.

"Thank you," Richard said, nonetheless wanting to get on. "But how does this explain how you invested in Aslan's scheme?"

171

"That's easy," Saskia said.

Saskia described how her mum and dad had always lived modestly, but her dad had also put any spare money he had into the stock market. It wasn't much — he was only a train driver — but it turned out that, over the years, he chose his stocks well. What's more, although her dad worked by the rough-and-ready Caledonian Road, her parents' house was in nearby Islington. They'd bought it for a song back in the sixties, but it had gone up in value significantly in the intervening decades.

"After Dad died, I inherited everything, and by the time I'd sold the house in Islington and Dad's shares, I discovered I'd just inherited nearly £1.4 million pounds."

Richard and Camille were impressed, but Saskia ploughed on before she lost her nerve.

"And Dad had never let on. He'd always been proud of who he was — his working class roots — and I can honestly say I'd never known he had that sort of money. But there I was, aged twenty-one, with the best part of one and a half million pounds, and that's when I made my first mistake. You see, Dad's solicitor was an old family friend in Camden and he said that with that kind of money I should go to Coutts Bank in The Strand. They had a special department for what he called wealth management."

Saskia told the police how she'd felt out of her depth on her visit to the glass-fronted splendour of Coutts. And how she'd got into a tangle with a well-dressed businessman in the revolving doors. He'd introduced

172

himself as David Kennedy, they got talking — and she liked him. He was attractive, witty, self-deprecating.

"Within the hour, we were having lunch at his club in Mayfair."

"He picked you up?" Richard asked, amazed.

Saskia reddened in embarrassment.

"He was so charming," she said. "And he made it sound so easy. His club was around the corner in St James's, could he buy me lunch — that's what he said. It's the least he could do having nearly knocked me to the ground."

"And you agreed?" Camille asked as delicately as she could.

"This was a different world to me. Coutts Bank? A private club with doormen and oil paintings? I didn't know what I was doing."

"How soon after meeting David did you tell him you'd just inherited one and a half million pounds?" Richard asked a lot less delicately than Camille had asked her own question.

"That first day," Saskia said. "The second martini. It was just after he'd said how he was making a mint from his art-lease business. And he was so charming. So believable. Before the end of lunch, I'd tried to hand over ten thousand pounds to him as my first investment."

Richard was stunned. "You gave David Kennedy ten grand the same day you met him?"

"Oh no, he was cleverer than that. He turned me down. He said I'd only just met him. I was still

173

emotional after the discovery that I'd inherited so much money. I should wait."

"How clever of him."

"And it made me all the more desperate to invest. So I met up with him a week or so later, and this time I told him to bring all of the figures with him. They were very impressive. Of course they were. They were made up. But he explained how top-end companies wanted art to put on their walls, and how he paid next to nothing to artists to make canvases with big blocks of colour. But the key thing he told me was that he had to make sure that he charged a fortune to the companies who wanted to lease the paintings. It was reverse psychology, he said. He even called it a confidence trick, that's how clever he was. After all, if he tried to lease the art at a low price, the big multinationals wouldn't want the paintings on their boardroom walls, but as long as he kept the prices high — and he wore the right clothes and talked the talk — it was just a licence to print money."

"He sounds quite businesslike about it all," Richard said.

"Oh, he was businesslike alright. He was utterly focused when it came to stealing money."

Richard glanced at Camille, knowing they were thinking the same thing. After all this time of people saying how New Age Aslan was, here — finally — was someone who was prepared to say he had a streak of ruthlessness. And what could prove his ruthlessness more than the fact that he loitered outside swish London banks trying to pick up wealthy single women?

"But he wasn't leasing any paintings to anyone. That's what I found out when his case came to trial. He'd just pretended to be my friend to get to my money. And that's what hurt so much. I thought he and I had become really good friends."

"You fell for him," Camille said.

Saskia dipped her eyes in shame.

"Of course I did. He was about twenty years older than me, but I just loved being with him. And I knew he liked being with me. Or so I thought. You have to understand. He was so glamorous. So rich. I had to see him every couple of weeks, and then, one night — after we'd had another great evening at his club, I couldn't help myself. I threw myself at him."

"What happened?" Camille asked.

Saskia was full of self-reproach. "He was a perfect gent. He said he liked me a lot, but he'd recently started going out with someone else — in fact had fallen in love — and he'd just asked this woman to marry him. It was better if we stayed friends. And the stupid thing was, him turning me down like that just made me believe in his integrity even more."

Richard and Camille exchanged a look. It was interesting to see just how canny Aslan had been — and just how well he'd understood the psychology of a young woman like Saskia. But then, he'd managed to con two million pounds out of people, it was perhaps no surprise that he'd been so adept at manipulation.

"Then can you tell me," Richard said, "how did you manage to hand over so much money?"

"That first month, I invested fifty thousand pounds in his scheme. Or thought I had. Of course, there wasn't a scheme, it was all a con — but a few weeks later David told me I'd lucked out on my timing and I could claim my first dividend from the investment."

"How much was it?"

"Five thousand pounds."

"An immediate return of ten per cent."

"And I was hooked. As he knew I'd be. Three months later, I got another cheque for five thousand pounds. I couldn't believe my luck, and before I'd even cashed this next dividend — or what I thought was a dividend — I'd written him a cheque for one hundred thousand pounds. That also gave me great returns — or apparently gave me great returns — and by the time he was arrested six months later, I'd given him half a million pounds. That's the whole truth."

Richard and Camille considered Saskia a moment.

"Didn't it occur to you that that was an awful lot of money to give to someone to buy paintings?"

"I didn't know what I was doing."

"Or that there was no way a load of paintings could have generated those sorts of returns?"

"*Nothing* occurred to me. And if I'd left it there, maybe I'd have recovered."

"But you didn't?" Camille asked.

"No way. Because after he was arrested, I was so angry that he'd betrayed me. So I went to see some fancy lawyers, and they told me I had a good chance of getting some of the money back. After all, the cash David stole from us all was never recovered. It had to be somewhere. So I had a team of forensic accountants working for me — private investigators — and lawyers firing off letters to various offshore banks and David's solicitors demanding access to his financial papers."

"And all to no avail?"

"It turns out that the only bigger crooks than criminals are lawyers. Within five years, I'd spent the best part of half a million pounds trying to get back the half a million pounds David had stolen from me. Thank god I had the sense to get a house for myself before I'd completely run out of funds."

Saskia took a moment to compose herself before facing her final humiliation.

"But there's no getting away from it. My dad left me nearly one and a half million pounds and all I've got to show for it twenty years later is a two-up, two-down in Walthamstow."

"Thank you," Camille said, although Richard couldn't see what his partner was thanking the witness for. After all, they could have wasted a lot less time if Saskia had just told them the truth from the start.

"You know," Saskia said, "it took me years to get over it. That what my dad had worked his whole life to achieve, I'd thrown away in a few years. That's why I told you I'd only lost fifty thousand pounds. Because in my head I tell myself that that's all I ever gave him. It's the only way I manage to get up in the morning, I pretend that that's all I lost."

Richard decided that he'd allowed Saskia to have too much control of the conversation.

"Saskia, did you kill Aslan Kennedy?"

Saskia was horrified. "No!"

"But you knew he was David the moment you got here, didn't you?"

Saskia's face froze as guilt slammed into her eyes. Richard and Camille shared a quick glance and Richard was briefly thrilled to see that Camille was impressed with him. This was a rare moment indeed.

"After all," Richard said, emboldened by Camille's approval, "you've already admitted that you and Aslan had been good friends back in the day, of course you recognised him the moment you saw him. Even including his long hair and white beard."

Saskia was getting increasingly strung out. "I promise you. I only got to the island the night before he was killed — and I didn't see him when he was inside his office being shouted at."

"But you told us you saw him leave the office immediately afterwards," Richard said. "You told us he looked distressed."

"I only saw him for a second," Saskia said, "you have to believe me. And I didn't realise he was David Kennedy. I didn't even realise who he was when I saw him properly for the first time the next morning."

With his thumb and forefinger, Richard pinched the woollen fabric of his suit just above his right knee and lifted it an inch to try and relieve the heat in his legs. It didn't seem to make any difference, but it at least gave him a moment to consider what Saskia had just said.

"I think you're lying."

"I'm not, you have to believe me."

"You recognised him the night before."

"I didn't."

"You recognised him and decided he had to die."

"No!"

"So you got a knife from the kitchen and set it in the Meditation Space. But tell me, where did you get the GHB sedative from?"

"No — wait, you have to believe me, I didn't recognise him!"

"But Saskia," Richard said, calmly, "if you're so innocent, why aren't you telling me the truth?"

"I am, I promise you. I've told you everything."

"But you haven't, because you've not mentioned your second meeting with Aslan the night before he was killed."

Saskia was shocked into silence by this assertion, so Richard continued, "Because we know that Aslan chose the people who attended his Sunrise Healing sessions personally, so how exactly did he choose you without you and he having a conversation at some point the night before he was killed?"

"That's the thing," Saskia said, eager to correct Richard's misapprehension. "The receptionist explained it all to me when I checked in. The list for the Sunrise Healing had already been published and my name was on it even before I'd got to the hotel."

"How do you mean, the list had already been published?" Richard asked.

Saskia got up from her chair and headed over to the cork noticeboard on the wall, explaining as she went. "Apparently, each night — just before tea — Aslan wrote up the names of the people he wanted in the next day's Sunrise Healing in one of those spiral-bound notebooks. She explained that you didn't have to attend, but that if I didn't go I'd maybe not get offered a second chance."

Richard and Camille went over and joined Saskia by the board.

"Are you saying you found out you had to attend the Sunrise Healing because your name was on a list?"

"That's right. The notebook should be here. Oh . . ."

Saskia trailed off, and Richard and Camille could see that she was pointing at an old nail that was sticking out of the wooden frame of the board.

"It's not here," Saskia said.

"It isn't?" Camille asked.

Saskia turned to the police. "I don't think so. Maybe I'm mistaken."

"But you're sure it was there the night before Aslan was killed?"

"There was a notebook. On this nail. A spiral-bound notebook with all of our names written out in blue pen. 'The Sunrise Healing' it said at the top. 'Aslan Kennedy invites' — that's how it started, I remember that much, and then it was a list of our names. Mine, Julia's, everyone's . . ."

"Hang on, you're saying that the list that chose who'd be in the Meditation Space the morning Aslan was killed was handwritten?"

"Yes."

"And it's no longer on its nail?"

"That's right."

180

"Then can you tell me, did you by any chance recognise whose handwriting it was?"

"I'm sorry. I'd only just arrived — I've no idea who wrote the list — I presumed it was Aslan — but it was definitely handwritten. And it was definitely here . . ."

Richard summed up for all three of them.

"But if it was Aslan who wrote out the list, then how come it's now missing? He was hardly in a position to remove it after he'd been killed, was he?"

As Richard was speaking, a couple of guests entered the front door with Rianka. Seeing the police, Rianka finished talking to the guests and then came over to join them.

"Can I help at all?" she asked.

Camille said, "We're looking for the notebook Aslan used to announce who would be doing the Sunrise Healing with him."

"Well, it's here . . ." Rianka said, indicating the board before she realised it wasn't. "It's supposed to be here. It's always here. It's a little reporter's notebook. You know, with a curly metal top. You flip the pages over . . ."

"But now it's missing?" Camille clarified.

Rianka was quite clearly at a loss for words.

"Then can I ask," Richard said, "was it always Aslan who chose the people who attended the morning session?"

"Of course. Or rather, he'd ask people first if they wanted to attend during the day — and then he'd put their names up on the list by supper that night."

"He didn't ask me first," Saskia said.

"He didn't?" Rianka was confused.

"No. The first I knew about it was when I saw my name on the list here. Not that the list's here any more."

Richard caught Camille's eye and knew they were both thinking the same thing. Because if the handwritten list was missing, then it had almost certainly been removed because it was incriminating. And that suggested that it was perhaps the murderer who had handwritten the list. Which made sense, Richard thought to himself. After all, they'd been trying to work out why on earth Aslan had chosen only Ponzi victims for the Sunrise Healing, and here was evidence that suggested that perhaps he didn't.

Maybe it was the killer who'd written out the list that filled the Meditation Space with Ponzi victims the morning that Aslan was killed. And who'd subsequently removed the incriminating notebook afterwards. In fact, Richard realised with mounting excitement, it was possible that if they could find the notebook, they'd be able to identify the handwriting of the list and therefore reveal the identity of Aslan's killer.

With Saskia's permission, Richard and Camille went to her room to search for the missing notebook. As Richard looked for it, he couldn't help but notice that Saskia had regathered some of her composure. If she'd lied to them about anything, she was hiding her nerves well. What's more, Saskia's hotel room was so neat and tidy — and she'd brought so few clothes with her — that they were able to establish that she'd not hidden the missing notebook anywhere in only a few minutes.

Then, with Rianka's permission — and her pass key — Richard and Camille went on to search Paul and Ann's bedroom. Paul and Ann were down on the beach, so the police were able to work unimpeded — but it took well over half an hour because, although Ann had come on holiday with three suitcases stuffed full of clothes, the suitcases were now empty and their contents were scattered all over the room. But, again, neither Richard nor Camille could find any reporter's notebook.

As for Ben, he was in his room and he tried to stop Richard and Camille from searching it.

"You can't come in here without a warrant."

Richard could see how worried Ben was, but he knew he had the law on his side. As the police had the hotel owner Rianka with them, all they needed was her permission to search the room and then they wouldn't need a warrant. Seeing how Ben was so reluctant to let the police in, Rianka was happy to give her permission, but although Richard and Camille spent over an hour searching — their every move watched over by Ben like a hawk — they weren't able to find anything incriminating in Ben's room, either.

Richard hadn't necessarily expected to find the missing notebook in Ben's room — if Ben was their killer, he would have destroyed it by now — but Ben's manner still puzzled Richard. If Ben had nothing to hide, then why was he now so on edge about the investigation?

Even though the police couldn't find the missing notebook in any of the four suspects' rooms, Richard then wondered if the killer had maybe removed it from the board and hidden it somewhere much nearer. After all, the hallway was stuffed with any number of oriental ornaments, bookcases and other nooks and crannies a notebook could have been hidden behind — or inside.

This time, Richard and Camille were joined in their hunt for the notebook by Fidel — although Richard was cross to discover that Dwayne was refusing to leave the station to help with their search. He apparently had a lead he wanted to pursue, but Richard imagined he just didn't want to leave his desk. So Richard asked if Rianka would help Fidel identify places to look in the kitchen — the nearest room to the noticeboard — while he and Camille tried to find the notebook in the hallway.

"So what do you think?" Camille asked her boss quietly, as she went through a pile of old flyers in a little oak dresser underneath the noticeboard. "Could Saskia be our killer?"

This gave Richard pause as he looked through a shelf of well-thumbed travel books and guides to Saint-Marie.

"She's certainly got a motive," he said. "Aslan stole half a million quid from her. And she definitely tried to hide that motive from us. So, normally I'd say yes, she could be our killer . . ."

"But?"

Richard sighed.

"But everything about this murder is preplanned, isn't it? The knife being placed in the Meditation Space beforehand. The fact that the killer must have got hold of the GHB drugs beforehand — and known there was a tea ritual that allowed the GHB to be administered. I don't see how Saskia could have carried out such a site-specific murder less than twenty-four hours after touching down on the island for the first time in her life."

"I know what you mean," Camille said as she went back to looking for the notebook.

"Because if she's our killer," Richard continued, "she also managed to doctor the list for the Sunrise Healing *before* she could possibly have known such a list even existed."

"You're right. Everything suggests that Saskia was manipulated into being in that room just as much as everyone else was. So if we're ruling Julia out because she is left handed — and I agree with you when you say Ann's too slapdash to have carried out a murder this organised — then maybe we should now rule Saskia out because there's no way she could have written out the list of names before she'd even touched down at the airport."

"I tend to agree," Richard said.

In truth, although Richard agreed with everything Camille was saying, it didn't mean that he even remotely ruled any of the witnesses out. This was because of the peculiar way he had trained himself to think about all of his cases.

When Richard had been at Cambridge University, he'd studied History — mainly because he felt it was his patriotic duty to learn everything about the history, culture and peoples of the British Isles — but it had been a toss-up at the time as to whether or not he should have studied Science. And, although he hadn't read a single history book since leaving University, Richard had continued to be an avid reader of science books.

In particular, he had long been fascinated by the infinitely strange world of quantum mechanics — where the impossible-to-believe was often entirely routine. And he'd found one experiment — Scrödinger's Cat — that was even useful in his criminal investigations.

Back in the 1930s, Schrödinger had invented a thought experiment to illustrate the inherent absurdity at the heart of much of quantum mechanics. In it, he said that you could put a cat inside a locked box with a vial of cyanide that had either killed the creature or not, but — according to the rules of quantum mechanics — the cat was, in fact, neither dead nor alive until the box was opened and the cat was observed.

Although the experiment was purposefully supposed to be a paradox, this was exactly the intellectual position that Richard always tried to take with every clue, every fact, every lead — and every witness — he encountered when he was running a case. Everything was true and not true both at the same time; and every witness was always both innocent and guilty — again, both at the same time, until proven otherwise. In effect, Richard was sceptical of *everything* he was told, and tried to keep all possible outcomes open at all times.

So he was happy — as Camille was suggesting to him now — to rule Julia, Ann and Saskia out as possible

186

murderers, but that didn't mean he'd actually ruled them out. Not definitively.

"Which means," Camille continued, "we're left with only Paul Sellars or Ben Jenkins as our possible killer. Aren't we, sir?"

"It would seem so," Richard agreed, while also keeping the option in his mind open that he wasn't in fact agreeing.

"And it's interesting that they're both men, seeing as Saskia overheard a man in Aslan's office the night before shouting at him 'you're not going to get away with it'. Isn't it, sir? But which of those two is our most likely killer?"

"Of those two?" Richard thought for a moment. "I'd say Ben, wouldn't you? He's definitely worried about something. If we could just discover what it was. And I'm sorry, it's too convenient for him that of the five possible murderers, he's the only one of them who doesn't appear to have a link to the victim at all."

There was a creak from a floorboard at the top of the staircase and Richard and Camille whipped their heads around. Someone was upstairs eavesdropping on their conversation.

"Hello?" Richard called out. "Who's that?"

There was a clatter from above as the person who had been listening made a run for it, and, before Richard could react, Camille was already taking the stairs two at a time and vanishing onto the upstairs landing.

Richard didn't know what to do. Should he also give chase? Or wait here? In the end, he decided that discretion was the better part of valour and he'd guard the bottom of the stairs in case whoever had been listening in to them tried to make a bolt for it back down the stairs.

A minute later, Camille returned, out of breath.

"Whoever it was got away," she said.

"But there was definitely someone up there?"

"Definitely. The door to the corridor was closing when I got up onto the landing — but when I got through to the corridor, there was no one to be seen."

"So you didn't see who it was?"

"Sorry, sir. Whoever it was was too quick."

"Never mind," Richard said, frustrated.

Richard went into the kitchen where Rianka was still helping Fidel look for the notebook.

"Rianka, is the staircase out here the only one up to the floors above?"

Rianka looked up from where she'd been searching under a sink. "No. There's an old servants' staircase at the back of the house. And the door to the fire escape's normally left ajar as well. For the through draught."

"So there's two other ways someone could get down from upstairs. Apart from the staircase here. Is that what you're saying?"

"That's right. Why?"

Richard and Camille exchanged a glance, both thinking the same thing. Whoever had been listening in on their conversation could easily have got out of the building by now.

188

There was a slapping of bare feet on wood and they all looked around as Dominic came down the main staircase of the hallway whistling tunelessly to himself, a pile of clean laundry in a basket in his hands.

CHAPTER
NINE

Richard, Camille and Fidel all exchanged glances. Was it a coincidence that Dominic should appear at this precise moment?

Dominic slowed to a stop, a frown creasing his face.

"Hey. Why are you all looking at me like that?"

"Just wondering how long you've been upstairs?"

"What are you talking about? I've been doing my laundry."

"Is that so?"

"Yeah. The washing machines are all on the first floor. Rianka lets me use them. Tell them, Rianka."

"It's true," Rianka said. "Everyone who works here uses the laundry facilities."

"But how long have you been up there for?" Richard asked.

"I don't know. An hour?"

"And you were in the laundry room the whole time?"

"Yeah. And if you don't mind, I'd like to get past. I want to get all this home."

Dominic lifted up his basket of clean washing to indicate his *bona fides* before carrying on down the stairs and heading for the main door.

It was only once he'd reached the door that Richard had a sudden feeling that he'd just missed something important.

"Hold on a second there, Dominic."

Dominic paused by the door, and Richard looked at him. What was it? There was something about Dominic that had just spiked his interest, if he could just work it out. Was it something he'd said? Or was wearing? Richard tried to chase the thought down, but he knew — from bitter experience — that the harder he pursued it, the more elusive the thought would remain.

"What?" Dominic eventually asked.

Richard realised he had to say something.

"Tell me, if you had to get rid of a notebook — and get rid of it fast — how would you go about doing it?"

Dominic looked at Richard, puzzled for a moment, and then his face cleared.

"That's easy. I'd burn it in the furnace."

"The furnace?" Richard asked.

Dominic looked at the policeman as though he were stupid.

"Under the house there's a bloody great furnace for heating the hot water for The Retreat."

"There is?" Richard asked, turning to Rianka.

"Yes," she said.

"Can I go now?" Dominic asked.

"Of course. Thank you."

As Dominic left, Richard turned to Rianka. "Would you mind showing us the hotel's furnace?"

"If you want to see it," she said. "Of course."

Rianka led Richard, Camille and Fidel out of the front door and around to the side of the house where there were worn stone steps that led down to an open archway under the house. Going down the stairs, the police soon found themselves in a huge store room. And unlike the rest of the pristine, gloss-white building, it was dark and cobwebby and stuffed full of clobber piled pell-mell as it had accumulated over the years.

There was old furniture, posters from a trade fair advertising something called "Wellness", large cellophane bags of round pebbles, boxes of incense, flat-packed parts for a Swedish sauna, old rowing machines, and, by the far wall, an ancient furnace with hot water pipes running from and to it, a floor-to-ceiling pile of chopped wood to its side.

Rianka led them over to it.

"This is the original furnace for the house. We use it to heat the water for the guests."

Richard inspected the old cast-iron machine and was impressed with what he saw. This was more like it. Proper levers and valves. Proper engineering.

Rianka got up an old metal rod and opened the hatch so Richard could look inside. There was a thick layer of white ash inside, and quite a few remaining slivers of logs, their edges glowing into flame as the extra oxygen that now filled the furnace briefly revived them.

"Dominic loads it up with wood every morning and afternoon," Rianka said. "It's one of his jobs."

Camille called over from the far side of the room.

"Sir, I think you should see this."

192

Richard and Fidel went over to join Camille and she showed them how she'd found four rolls of white paper leaning against the wall. Each one was about twelve feet tall — the height of the Meditation Space — but, rolled up as they were, they were only about a hand's width across, and they were secured with thick rubber bands at the top and bottom of each roll to stop them unravelling.

"So what are you saying?" Richard asked. "These are the spare rolls of paper for the Meditation Space?"

"That's right," Rianka said, coming over to join Richard, Fidel and Camille. "If we lose any of the walls of the Meditation Space in a storm, we can repaper the building from our stock here."

Richard picked up one of the unwieldy rolls and inspected it. It was surprisingly light to hold — although, Richard realised, the rolls were of course only waxy paper, it was perhaps no surprise they weren't all that heavy.

"And are they all present and correct?" he asked.

"Yes," Rianka said. "We only keep four rolls spare. One for each of the four walls of the Meditation Space."

"And how often do you replace them?"

Rianka thought for a moment. "It's unlikely that we get through a whole hurricane season without having to replace the walls at least once. But we've had those here for some time. At least ten months I'd say."

"Dominic said the same thing," Camille said, turning to Richard.

Before Richard could comment, his eye was caught by a tiny green light on a shelf nearby.

It puzzled Richard because his subconscious was telling him that the light was important. But what could be important about a little green light? Richard went over to it and found himself looking at a shelf with an LCD monitor on it, various routers, and a whole spaghetti junction of cables going into a cabinet with server racks stuffed full of computing equipment. And there were also charging stations for at least twenty WiFi headphones. There were only a couple of headphones currently on their stands, a little LED in the earpiece suggesting that they were fully charged.

"Sorry, can I ask? What's all this?"

"Oh, that's the AV suite," Rianka said.

"The AV . . .?"

"Audio Visual. It's where we broadcast The Retreat's music from."

It took Richard a moment, and then he got it. "Of course! The whale music the witnesses were listening to when they all lay down."

Now Richard was looking at the cabinet of electrical equipment, he could see dozens of little green lights that were all winking at him and his subconscious continued to scream at him. There was something important about the lights, but what was it?

Richard decided there was only one way to track the thought down, and that was if he ignored it entirely. He turned to Rianka.

"Can you tell me how all this works?"

194

Rianka was a little puzzled by the question, but was happy to answer.

"Sure. Well, we've got WiFi routers placed over the whole Retreat and we broadcast meditation music twenty-four hours a day on them so that if anyone wants help in losing themselves — you know, when they're having a massage — or whatever — all they have to do is pick up a set of WiFi headphones and they can listen in without disturbing anyone else's peace."

"Seems a bit hi-tech," Richard said, somewhat disapprovingly as he picked up one of the WiFi headphones.

"We try to move with the times."

Now that he was looking more closely at one of the headphones, Richard could see that there was a little dial above the right earpiece. It was set to 3.

"Are these the various channels?" Richard asked as he put the headphones on.

"We broadcast on six different channels — and each one has a different emotional colour."

"Emotional colour?" Richard listened for a bit. "I see that channel three appears to be waves lapping on a beach."

"That's right."

Richard looked at Rianka, dumbfounded. "You broadcast the sound of waves lapping against a beach to people who might well already be on a beach listening to waves lapping against a beach?"

"I know," Rianka said, tolerantly. "But people seem to like it, and we're here to serve their needs."

195

Richard turned the dial, listened a moment, and then visibly shuddered.

"Oh god," he said.

"What is it?" Camille asked.

Richard looked at Camille, but in reality he was staring into a bottomless pit of despair.

"It's pan pipes, Camille."

Camille reached up and clicked Richard's headphones to another channel before he could cause any more offence.

"Oh. Now hang on. This is better. What is it?"

"It's channel five," Camille said.

"What's on channel five?" Richard asked Rianka.

Rianka smiled. "Nothing. We're not broadcasting anything on channel five at the moment."

"You're not?"

"We used to have a human heartbeat, but a few guests said they found it a bit creepy, so Dominic turned the channel off entirely a few days ago."

Richard took a moment to consider the WiFi set-up. Was it important? And then there were the rolls of spare paper for the Meditation Space. They, too, might have been important — but if all of the rolls were present and correct then it was hard to see how. If anything, they just confirmed once again that the walls of the Meditation Space hadn't been tampered with because here were the replacements, unused.

Richard took a moment longer to see if his hunch about the green light would reveal itself to him, but the mystery remained just that, a mystery. So he set off for the furnace again.

After two steps, he stopped stock still, frozen to the spot.

"What is it, sir?" Fidel asked.

"Shh," Richard said rudely.

Not caring that he risked making himself look ridiculous, Richard picked up his left foot a couple of inches and held it in the air a moment. The floor was tiled and Richard brought his foot down onto it with a gentle slap of leather undersole on ceramic.

"What are you doing, sir?" Camille hissed.

"I said, shhh," Richard responded just as vehemently.

He lifted his right foot a couple of inches off the ground and held it in the air. He looked at Camille and some sixth sense told him what was about to happen.

He lowered his right foot to the floor, but it didn't make a gentle slap this time, the noise it made was a little metallic click.

Richard smiled and tapped his left foot. *Blat*.

He tapped his right foot. *Click*!

Left, *blat*; right, *click*; *blat, click* —

"What are you doing?"

Richard dropped to his knees and started to scrabble at the double knot on his right shoe.

Camille and Fidel exchanged a glance of amazement. Richard was removing a shoe in public? This was unheralded.

With a slightly disturbing sucking noise, Richard yanked his right shoe off and stood up proudly, holding it in his hand.

"Ladies and gentlemen of the jury, I present to you, Exhibit A."

Richard slowly spun his shoe around so the others could see its underside.

There was a drawing pin stuck into the middle of the sole.

"What is that?" Rianka asked.

"I think it's a drawing pin," Fidel said, underwhelmed.

"It is indeed, Fidel."

Richard got down on his hands and knees and started to inspect the floor underneath the server rack. He couldn't find any other drawing pins, but the fact that he'd found one at all suggested to Richard that the killer might have been near the WiFi rack. After all, they'd found drawing pins at the scene of the murder, and now they'd found another drawing pin here. It couldn't be a coincidence.

"Very well," Richard said to Rianka once he'd got back to his feet, "I'd like you to shut the furnace down for us."

"You do?" Rianka said. "It'll be very inconvenient for the guests."

"Even so," Richard said. "The drawing pin on the floor here suggests to me that the killer maybe came into this room — and that might have been because he or she was burning the incriminating notebook in the furnace. Even if all we find in the ash is the metal spiral that held the notebook together, it would be instructive."

Rianka looked at Richard's intensity and sighed.

"Very well. I'll shut the furnace down and let the guests know."

"Thank you. Then, Fidel, this is now a secondary scene of crime."

Fidel couldn't stop himself from an involuntary shudder. "No, please, sir —"

"Which means I want you to seal it, search for any further clues that might identify the killer — in particular, any further drawing pins — and then I want you gathering up all the ash from the furnace once it's cooled down. Put it through a sieve or colander or some such. We're looking for the metal spiral from a reporter's notebook in amongst the ash. Or any charred bits of paper that didn't completely burn."

Fidel was defeated before he'd even started. "Yes, sir."

Richard considered, was that it? He turned and looked at Camille, and that's when it struck him: the thought he'd been chasing down all this time. What was special about the green lights here — and what he'd subconsciously noticed about Dominic as he passed them in the corridor upstairs.

"Rianka. Where does Dominic live?"

"I'm sorry?"

"Dominic, your handyman. If he was doing his washing in the hotel, that suggests he lives on site."

"That's right," Rianka said. "He's got the old plantation manager's cottage. It's at the end of the garden."

"In what direction?"

"Well, you go just beyond the Meditation Space," she said, "and then keep walking."

"Now isn't that interesting?"

Once Richard had got his shoe back on again — not an easy job considering how tight and sweaty his sock still was — and once he'd left Fidel and Rianka behind to shut the hotel's furnace down, Richard was soon leading Camille out into the blinding sunlight and across the lawn towards the Meditation Space. Following Rianka's instructions, they passed the wood and paper tea house and carried on walking away from the main hotel, down a slight incline, around a clump of bushes surrounding three palm trees, and then there it was: a small pink-tiled house at the far end of the gardens flanked on either side by rhododendron bushes.

Richard went up to the old door and knocked once on it before turning back to look at the house and gardens. The Meditation Space was well over a hundred yards away, but it was in a direct line between Dominic's house and the main hotel. On the morning of the murder, Richard could see it would have been possible for Dominic to walk from his front door all the way up to the back of the Meditation Space without anyone at the hotel seeing.

Even so, Richard had to concede that even if Dominic could have got that close to the Meditation Space, he still wouldn't have been able to get inside it without ripping through the paper walls.

The door opened and Dominic looked at the police.

"Oh. What do you want?"

"Just a quick question. May we come in?"

Dominic looked at them a moment longer. "Alright," he said, not exactly enthusiastically.

Richard pushed past with a fake smile and entered Dominic's sitting room. It had been painted white and was entirely minimalist. There was a joss stick in a jar on a little table; there were only beanbags to sit on; and on a windowsill there was a tower of wide, flat pebbles that Dominic had stacked in decreasing width so they formed a gentle pyramid. Richard wanted to push them over.

"I don't have long," Dominic said. "What do you want?"

"Oh, it's simple. I just wanted to know the exact nature of your relationship with Julia Higgins."

Dominic was surprised. But then, so was Camille.

"I'm sorry?"

"You and Julia. Why don't you tell us what's really going on?"

"What is this?"

Richard could see that Dominic had been unsettled by his question.

"Only, when Julia was in custody, she was wearing a distinctive top. Advertising illegal drugs. But that's not what's important about it, because it was also lime green. In fact, pretty much the bright green of the green lights on a load of WiFi routers. And, unfortunately for you, I noticed that precise — and rather distinct — colour in your washing basket."

As he'd been speaking, Richard had ghosted over to Dominic's basket of washing, and now he reached into it and pulled out the very same lime-green hash-promoting T-shirt Julia had been wearing when she'd been in the police cells.

Dominic looked at the T-shirt and Richard could see that he had no quick answer as to what it was doing in his washing.

"Don't worry," Richard said, pretending to be reasonable. "We know you can't be the killer. You were outside the Meditation Space at the time of the murder. But we do need to know the nature of your relationship with Julia Higgins."

"Alright," Dominic said, a little hurt. "I've got nothing to hide. But you're right. Julia and I used to be a thing."

"A 'thing'?" Richard asked.

"That's right."

"And what 'thing' would that be?"

"Lovers."

Richard looked at Dominic a long moment while he let this fact settle. He then pulled out his notebook and silver pencil. He clicked the pencil and a tiny needle of lead jumped out of the end of it, ready for spiking down onto the page.

"And when did your relationship start?" Richard asked.

"Within days of her getting here."

Richard started scratching in his notebook. "So that's six months ago."

"That sounds about right. Six months. Want a drink?"

"No." Richard was surprised that Dominic hadn't yet noticed that he had a new one-man nemesis and his name was Richard Poole. "How did you meet?"

"She was interested in my work."

"As a handyman?" Richard asked, unable to keep the contempt out of his voice.

"As a hypnotherapist. This was back when Aslan still let me practise. And she was receptive. Man, that woman was so receptive."

"To hypnotherapy?" Camille asked.

Dominic turned back to Camille. "There's an intimacy you develop if you explore someone's psyche together.

It's inevitable. Look, this has got nothing to do with anything — I don't even have to answer your questions."

"I know," Richard said, "but you will, as a concerned citizen be helping the police with their inquiries."

"Alright," Dominic said, and Richard noticed that he flicked a nervous glance at a door in the corner of the room as he said this.

"Very well," Richard said, now edging over to the door that Dominic had just looked at. "To start off with — just for the record — can you tell me a bit more about your relationship with Aslan Kennedy?"

"Well, that's easy. We didn't have one."

"You didn't?" Camille asked.

"No. I thought his beliefs were just cuckoo, you know? People aren't 'good'. They aren't always 'growing' and 'reaching for the light' — that's how Aslan thought of everyone. As basically spiritual."

"Whereas you don't?"

"Hell no," Dominic said. "People have secrets that aren't even known to themselves."

"Which is why you like hypnotising people."

"Damned right. It's only when you access the dark underbelly of someone's subconscious that you discover what really makes them tick."

Richard considered Dominic's words a moment before continuing.

"We've heard that you and Aslan argued," Richard said. "Is that right?"

"Argued? Sure. Why?"

"Because," Richard said, "apart from you, we can't find anyone else who Aslan argued with."

"But that's not true," Dominic said, puzzled. "Aslan argued with everyone."

"He did?" Richard asked, not believing Dominic for a moment.

"Of course he did. And I'm telling you, he could have a foul temper on him if you pressed the wrong buttons. You just ask Rianka. She had to put up with the worst of it. Because he was stubborn. Man, but Aslan was stubborn. Once he'd got it into his head that he was going to do something, there was no shaking him."

"For example, his decision to sack you," Richard said.

Dominic frowned. Like a teenager who was being told off by his parents.

"Sure," he eventually said. "But it wasn't for the reasons you're thinking."

"And what reasons do you think I'm thinking?" Richard asked.

"That it was a professional disagreement. That maybe he disagreed with how I went about my business."

"That's what Julia told us."

"Of course she did," Dominic said with a superior manner. "She never got it."

"Then why don't you tell us? Why was it?"

"Alright," Dominic said, as though he were about to reveal an amazing secret. "If you want to know, Aslan sacked me as The Retreat's hypnotherapist because he was jealous of how I was getting on with all of the guests. There was only one guru allowed here at one time and that had to be him. That's why he demoted me. He was jealous of how popular I was."

204

Still puzzled, Camille asked, "But after he sacked you, you stayed on as the handyman?"

"Sure. I didn't have anywhere else to go. And I was having too much of a good time with Julia to leave this place. But that was then."

Camille picked up on Dominic's clarification.

"How do you mean, 'but that was then'?" she asked.

Dominic took a moment before he replied, and then he sighed and said, "Okay. So Julia came round this morning and told me it was over. You know. Between us. In fact she said she'd spent her time in your cells thinking. And she said she had to stop running. It was time to go home."

"And by home . . .?"

"She meant the UK. That's why she told me she and I had to break up. She brought back some of my stuff. Including a few of my clothes like that T-shirt."

"I see. And how did you feel when she dumped you?" Richard asked.

"She didn't dump me."

"Oh. Sorry." Richard read back over his notes. "I thought that that is what 'it was over' meant."

"Sure. And it does — but there was no dumping. She told me we were done, that's all. She was going home."

"And yet, it was still you she wanted to see when she had to be hypnotised."

"Of course. That's my skill. With her at least. But anyway, that's why I've got that T-shirt. And why I washed it today. Is there anything else?"

"Just one more thing. Why do you keep glancing at this door here?"

It was true. The more Richard had edged closer to the door in the corner of the room, the more Dominic had continued to flick nervous glances in its general direction.

"No reason," Dominic said, lying.

"Oh okay."

As Richard said this, he pushed the door open and went into the room next door before Dominic could stop him. And what Richard found in there was everything he'd felt was absent from Dominic's pristine room next door. There was a mess of old plates of food, old bottles of beer, overflowing ashtrays — but, best of all, the place was littered with test tubes, beakers and a Bunsen burner attached to a gas bottle; retort stands and rubber pipes; and various brightly coloured bottles of household cleaner, many of them cut open and entirely empty.

Although it was a complete mess, it was also quite clearly a functioning chemistry lab for the brewing of exotic drugs and mind-altering substances. Richard was rather pleased with himself when he recognised a rig for fractional distillation.

"Everything here is legal," Dominic was quick to say as he followed Richard in. "It's all bought over the counter — or grown organically."

Richard picked up a bottle of bleach. "What do you do with this?"

"Very little. It's hydrogen peroxide. To be used sparingly. Look, I'm interested in the mind — about accessing memories, feelings, emotions we suppress. Nothing I brew in my home is illegal. This is just about creating potions that give you legal highs — or loosen your grip on reality."

"Is this really why Aslan sacked you?" Richard asked, picking up some dirty test tubes that were lying on a table and smelling their crusted contents. "Because you were drugging the hotel guests?"

"No way," Dominic said. "All this is for personal consumption only. When I hypnotised the guests, I did it naturally. Like you saw me do with Julia."

"Is that really so?" Camille asked. "Have you never used any of these mind-altering chemicals on her?"

"No way," Dominic said, affronted. "You just ask her for yourself. But then, Julia never needed any help going into a trance, she could pretty much regress at will. Like you saw her do in the police station."

Richard said, "And you reckon that all of the ingredients you've got here are legal?"

"One hundred per cent. I know what I'm doing."

"Then can you tell me what you know about GHB?"

"I'm sorry?"

"GHB." Richard clarified, "Gamma-hydroxybutyrate."

Dominic thought for a moment.

"I'm sorry, I don't know that one."

"Really?"

"Sorry. No idea."

Richard looked at Dominic and decided that he was almost certainly lying. After all, it was hardly credible to believe that someone who created homemade mind-altering drugs didn't. Either way, it was his duty as a serving police officer to make sure that all of the ingredients in Dominic's lab were legal.

"I'd like to make a list of all of your ingredients here."

Dominic was shocked. "What?"

"Don't worry, it won't take long. We can photograph all of the evidence *in situ* with our phones."

"What? Why?"

Richard looked at Dominic. "To make sure you've not been breaking the law."

There wasn't much Dominic could say to that. His shoulders slumped.

"Alright. Take photos of whatever you like. But you should know. I think I was burgled last week."

This got the police's attention. "You were?" Richard asked.

"Yeah. It's not normally this messy. Seriously. But last week, I came back from work and I could tell someone had been searching through my lab."

"Do you know if they took anything?"

"I couldn't tell."

"You couldn't?"

"No. I don't really keep a proper list of what I've got here, but it was just a feeling. Someone had been through everything and maybe had taken some stuff."

Richard and Camille exchanged a glance, not believing a word that Dominic was saying.

"Did you report this burglary to the police at the time?" Camille asked.

Dominic had the good grace to look bashful as he explained that seeing as he didn't know what — if anything — had been taken, he hadn't bothered to go to the police.

It was in that moment that Richard decided that Dominic had almost certainly been making GHB in his home lab — had just guessed that it related somehow to Aslan's murder — and he was now trying to cover for himself by inventing a burglary so that if any of his GHB turned up as part of the investigation later on he'd be able to blame the phantom burglar.

But that meant that Dominic was perhaps a bit more quick-witted than Richard had previously given him credit for. Either way, Richard knew that his next step should be to inventory all of the chemicals they could find here and see if Dominic had the ingredients to make doses of GHB.

There was a clatter from next door, a voice shouted "Chief!" — and then Dwayne bombed into the room. He saw the homebrew chemistry lab and his eyes widened in wonder. "Wow."

"What are you doing here?" Richard asked.

"Sorry. I went up to the house, found Fidel searching some room underneath it — man, but that's a tough job you've given him."

"A job you might have offered to help him with."

"And not tell you what I've just found out?" Dwayne looked at his boss, delight in his eyes. "Because I'm telling you, I think I've worked out who our killer is."

"You have?"

"Who is it?" Camille asked.

"Not in front of a witness," Richard said. "Dominic, would you go next door and shut the door behind you as you go?"

Dominic tried to look affronted as he indicated his homebrew chemistry lab. "But what if you try to plant evidence on me?"

"Just go next door, would you?" Richard said, exasperated. Really, Dominic was like a surly teenager sometimes, he thought to himself.

Once Dominic had finally left the room and closed the door behind himself, Dwayne went in close to Richard and Camille, keeping his voice low as he filled them in on his breakthrough.

"Well, Chief, you were right to make me look into Ben Jenkins's time in the UK before he went out to Portugal," Dwayne said. "Because it turns out that he's been in prison. And he wasn't locked up for just any crime either, he was convicted of Wounding With Intent back in 1996. But get this, because this is where it gets good: he served the second year of his sentence in 1997, and guess where he was banged up?"

"Don't tell me it was Brixton Prison," Richard said.

Dwayne beamed. "Got it in one."

Camille was amazed. "Why's that important?"

Richard turned to her. "Because in 1997, Aslan Kennedy — or David Kennedy as he was then — was serving the last year of his prison sentence. Also, by a startling coincidence, in Brixton Prison."

Camille looked at Dwayne in wonder. "You're saying Ben Jenkins and David Kennedy were both in the same prison at the same time?"

"But it gets even better," Dwayne said. "Because, for that last year David Kennedy was in prison, he and Ben Jenkins shared a cell together."

210

"You're kidding me!"

"Then we've got to go and interview him at once."

"And that's where we have a problem. Because I've just been up to his room and the door was already open. It's completely empty. None of his things were there. So I went downstairs and spoke to the receptionist who said that Ben Jenkins had settled his bill and checked out half an hour ago."

"He did?" Camille asked.

"Where did he go?"

"The receptionist didn't know. He didn't even order a taxi, he just paid his bill and walked out of the front door with his suitcase. That's the last she saw of him. But she did say this: he was in such a rush to settle up and go, he didn't even turn around as he left when she offered to get him a taxi."

"But I don't understand," Richard said. "We've still got his passport, haven't we?" All of the witnesses had had to hand in their passports immediately after the murder to make sure they didn't try and leave the island.

"Locked up safe and sound in the safe at the station."

"Then where does he think he's going?" Richard asked. "Dwayne, get on to the ports and airports — and hire boats — whatever you can find both legal and less legal, I want Ben Jenkins's photo circulated and fast. That man is not getting off Saint-Marie, okay?"

Dwayne looked at his boss and saluted.

"Yes, sir!"

CHAPTER
TEN

While Fidel continued to search for drawing pins and burnt notebooks in the hotel cellar, and with Richard photographing all of the ingredients in Dominic's chemistry lab, Dwayne and Camille tried to track down Ben Jenkins. For his part, Dwayne went out on the road to the airport and nearby harbours to get the word out: if anyone saw a man answering to Ben Jenkins's description trying to get off the island, they were to call the police. As for Camille, she went back to the station to see if she could uncover any more leads that could explain why Ben Jenkins had suddenly done a runner.

"So what have you got?" a hot and bothered Richard asked Camille as he returned from The Retreat later that afternoon with a smartphone full of photos of the ingredient labels from Dominic's lab.

Camille explained that according to the court records Dwayne had been able to dig up, Ben had had a disagreement with a local garage owner back in 1995. Ben had said that he'd been sold a second-hand car that had had its odometer tampered with, but the local garage owner denied it. When Ben discovered that the car had in fact been clocked, he went to the garage owner's house and beat him viciously with a baseball bat.

Ben had already been done for criminal damage twice before — he clearly had a history of violent behaviour — and when the judge came to convict him, she gave him six years.

He was imprisoned in Brixton Prison, just as David Kennedy had been, and it was in Ben's second year that the two men shared a cell. At the end of that year, David was released — and one year later, so was Ben.

But everything else they'd learnt about Ben still seemed to stack up. He hadn't got into trouble with the authorities in Portugal since moving there after he left prison; and Camille couldn't find any record of Ben having been to Saint-Marie before.

"Then what about contact between Ben and Aslan?"

Richard guessed that it must have been the killer who'd persuaded Aslan to invite all the Ponzi victims to the island at the same time. Therefore, if Ben was the killer, there should have been evidence somewhere that he had been in touch with Aslan at some point over the last few months.

Camille said, "I've gone through Ben's mobile phone records again. And his landline in Portugal. He's made no phone calls to Saint-Marie and received no phone calls from Saint-Marie. And I've been through The Retreat's phone records and, as far as I can see, there have been no phone calls to any kind of Portuguese number."

"Then what about emails?"

"Fidel's already been through Aslan's laptop. There was no email trail from any of the witnesses, let alone Ben Jenkins."

"Then what if Aslan's deleted the email trail?"

"Then maybe it's still on his service provider's server . . .?"

Richard considered what his next steps should be. Trying to get the local service providers to release their customers' emails was nigh-on impossible, even with a warrant. However, it was worth a try.

"Very well," he said. "You keep going through whatever phone records you can find. Anything strange — or you can't explain — presume it's a lead and track it down. I'll see what I can get from Aslan's service provider."

"Yes, sir."

For the next few hours, Richard and Camille tried to find the proof that Ben had indeed been in touch with Aslan, but to no avail. Aslan's email service provider wasn't interested in helping Richard, and Camille continued to find no evidence of Saint-Marie numbers that Ben had dialled or received from Portugal, either from the records of his mobile phone or his landline in Vilamoura.

It was one of those sultry afternoons when the clouds seemed to gather thick in the sky and press down, presaging torrential rain, and Richard had difficulty staying focused on his task. As he sat at his desk, marking out the passing minutes with each drop of sweat that rolled down his forehead, his thoughts began to drift into a soupy dream state. He thought about his

214

lizard — about how much he had to get rid of him — how awful it had been bumping into the Commissioner — but, above all, his thoughts kept slipping back to images of Julia Higgins. Of her in her cut-off jeans and tight lime-green T-shirt in the cells. Of the look in her eyes when she went to hug him outside on the verandah. And how her golden hair seemed almost to be on fire when the sun caught it. Julia really was a delight, wasn't she? Richard found himself thinking idly, sweat now tightening his shirt collar to his neck. Unlike his partner, Camille, who, while by all accounts — and by all known biometrics — was beautiful, was too stroppy. That was her problem. Too feisty.

"Too bloody rude," Richard mumbled out loud, completely unaware of the look of surprise Camille shot him. "Pretty, mind. So pretty."

Richard slowly toppled off his chair and fell to the floor.

Camille was over to her boss in a second. "Sir!"

Richard lay in a crumpled heap, his chair spilt off to the side. Camille loosened the tie around her boss's neck before grabbing his collar and pulling it open, Richard's top two shirt buttons pinging off as she did so.

Richard was out cold, and Camille grabbed up an old case file from his desk and started wafting air at his face.

"Sir, wake up! You fainted. Sir! Richard!"

At the sound of his name, Richard's eyes fluttered briefly and he began to come round.

"Don't worry, you just fainted. It's your suit, sir. You shouldn't be wearing a woollen suit in this weather."

Richard's eyes opened properly and, without moving, he looked up at Camille's face. He then flicked a furtive glance at the floor and realised that he was lying down.

"Not again?" he said.

"I'm afraid so. I'll get you some water."

While Camille got her boss some cold water from the fridge, Richard got onto his hands and knees, his head still spinning. As he paused a moment to regather his composure, Richard had a memory of saying something out loud just before he fainted. He had a sixth sense that it was something to do with Camille, but what was it? After a moment longer of thought, Richard decided that it probably wasn't best to analyse any of the last few minutes of his life in any detail, and, grabbing onto the corner of his desk, he pulled himself back to his feet.

He swayed a bit, but he knew he was going to be okay.

"This bloody heat," he said.

Camille came over with a glass of water and handed it over. Richard drank it down greedily.

"But you can't do anything about the weather, sir. You can do something about your clothes."

"And go around looking like a tramp, Camille?" Richard said, pre-emptively irked. Now he was thinking about it, he realised that he was pretty sure he had indeed said something about Camille just before he fainted, but what was it? Oh well, it was gone now.

Richard righted his chair and sat down in it again.

216

"Thank you for saving my life," Camille reminded her boss to say.

Richard was trying to do up the buttons of his shirt as she said this.

"You've broken the buttons on my shirt," he said.

"I'm so grateful," Camille said as her next suggestion of what her boss might say, but Richard was back up and running.

"And how are you getting on with Ben Jenkins's phone records?"

"Hey, it's no problem," Camille said, going back to her desk so she could continue going through the witness's phone records. "But no luck so far."

"Then keep on looking," Richard said.

It was only a minute or so later — as Richard was once again checking to see if he'd had an email from Aslan's service provider — that it occurred to him that he'd maybe not thanked Camille for helping him out when he fainted. This made Richard feel bad. He should have thanked her. But the problem was, the moment had passed, hadn't it? It would be weird to say thank you now, all these minutes later.

A very hot and ash-smeared Fidel trudged back into the station holding a small cardboard evidence box.

"Ah, Fidel!" Richard said, glad of the interruption. "How did you get on in the hotel's basement?"

Fidel put the box onto his desk before turning to address his boss.

"Well, sir, I don't know what to think."

Richard resisted the urge to point out that this was no change, then.

Fidel explained that he'd searched the basement for any further clues and hadn't been able to find anything that seemed to be important. Not even another drawing pin — either by the router rack or anywhere else.

However, he'd been able to scrape through the ash of the furnace using an old metal colander Rianka had lent him. And the thing is, the contents of the furnace had of course been almost entirely white ash, but Fidel had found some charred paper.

Just as Richard had said he might.

There were six pieces in total — each one no bigger than a raffle ticket — they were almost entirely burnt — but they had clearly once been scraps of white paper.

"Do you think it's the remnants of the notebook that was taken from the noticeboard?" Richard asked eagerly.

"I don't know, sir, but I wasn't able to find the metal ringbinder that should have been there as well. If these pages came from the missing notebook."

Camille said, "Then maybe the killer burnt the paper while disposing of the metal ringbinder elsewhere?"

"It's possible, I suppose," Fidel said, not entirely convinced.

"Either way," Richard said going to the evidence box, "it's interesting that you found bits of burnt white paper in the furnace, considering how we were looking for bits of burnt white paper."

"Yes, sir."

"Were you able to make out any handwriting on them at all?"

Fidel explained that he'd not looked too carefully as he knew how fragile burnt paper was. Instead, he'd secured each piece in between separate sheets of non-toxic plastic — and then book-ended them with pieces of card he'd then wrapped in gaffer tape. The pieces were now ready either for unwrapping and processing in the station, or for sending straight on to the labs on Guadeloupe.

Richard knew a technique for developing photographic imprints to reveal what was written on burnt paper, but it was hugely time consuming and there were too many pieces of paper here for him to process them all.

"Fidel, can you please get these sent to the labs? I want to know if anything was written on them before they caught fire."

"Yes, sir."

"Oh," Camille said from her desk, and Richard and Fidel looked over.

"Problem?" Richard asked.

Camille took a moment before answering.

"I don't know. But I've maybe found something in the phone records after all. Not that it's got anything to do with Ben Jenkins."

"It doesn't?" Richard said, going over to join Camille at her desk.

"I don't think so," Camille said. "But look here: we know Ann Sellars rang Aslan six weeks ago. We've got her records here and we can see she dialled a Saint-Marie number." Here, Camille got out Ann's phone records and indicated the number that Ann had dialled in the Caribbean. She then got out The

219

Retreat's phone records and showed the record of the call arriving. "And when we look at The Retreat's phone bill, we can see the call coming in here, and it's a +44115 number."

"That's right," Richard said. "Ann and Paul live in Nottingham. 0115 is the dialling code from Nottingham."

"But that's the thing, sir," Camille said. "Because it's not the only time that The Retreat received a phone call from Nottingham. In fact, it was called three other times from a Nottingham number, and each of the phone calls lasted between ten and twenty minutes." Camille indicated The Retreat's records and Richard could see she was right. Someone else in Nottingham had rung The Retreat the day after Ann had rung, and the call had lasted twelve minutes. Then, a week later, there had been another call from the same number that was eighteen minutes long. And the last of the three calls had only been three weeks ago. It had been twenty minutes long.

Richard said, "Good work, Camille. So who's been ringing Aslan from Nottingham?"

"There's an easy way to find out." Camille picked up her office phone and dialled the number listed in The Retreat's records. "I'm calling the number."

Before Richard could stop her, Camille held up her finger for silence in the office.

"It's ringing . . ." she said, and then — after a few more moments of waiting — Richard heard someone pick up the phone at the other end.

"Hello," Camille said. "This is Detective Sergeant Camille Bordey of the Saint-Marie Police Force."

Camille listened for a moment, and then frowned, puzzled.

"What do you mean, you haven't informed the police yet?" she said into the phone.

Camille jammed the phone against the crook of her shoulder. As she grabbed up a scrap of paper, Richard handed her his precious retractable pencil — Camille smiled a quick thanks — and then she started making notes as she listened to the person on the other end of the phone.

"Really?" she said. And then, "No way. You're kidding me . . ."

Camille went on to explain that she was just doing background checks in relation to another crime, took the details of the person she'd been talking to, and hung up.

"What was that about?" Fidel asked, eagerly.

Camille was still puzzled as she checked over her notes. She looked up at Richard.

"That was a nice woman called Veronica Gibbs. She's the manager of the pharmacy where Paul Sellars works."

Richard said, "That was Paul's pharmacy?"

"It was."

"So why's he been phoning Aslan from his place of work?"

"And why so many times?" Fidel added.

"That's not what Veronica wanted to tell me," Camille said. "Because, according to her, she's been thinking of ringing the police for some time."

"She has?"

"She's long suspected that Paul's been stealing drugs from the store room."

Richard could tell from the look in Camille's eyes that this wasn't the end of the story.

"And not just any drug," Camille said. "It's something called Xyrax."

"But what's that?" Fidel said.

"Well, let's look it up and find out," Camille said.

Camille typed "Xyrax" into a search engine on her computer and got a result the moment she hit the return key.

"Well, well, well," she said. "You know what? It turns out that Xyrax is a trade name for a sedative you might have heard of called gamma-hydroxybutyric acid, otherwise known as GHB."

"No way," Fidel said, stunned.

Richard was no less amazed. "You're saying that Paul's boss suspects he's been stealing a drug that just happens to have been the very same drug that we found in the suspects' tea when Aslan was murdered?"

"Got it in one."

Richard and Camille were both waiting outside a pine-clad building at The Retreat as Paul and Ann emerged, having just had what Richard could see from the label next to the door had been an "Aromassage" session.

"Oh. Hello," Paul said a touch suspiciously as soon as he saw the police.

"We'd like to search your room again," Richard said, just as easily.

222

Ann was surprised by the request, but Paul was shocked. "Why? Rianka's already told us you've looked once, why do you need to look again?"

"Don't worry," Richard said. "That was looking for a notebook. We're looking for something else this time. It should only take thirty seconds."

Paul and Ann didn't have much choice, so they accompanied Richard and Camille back to the main house and up to their room. As they went, the other guests at the hotel kept looking at Ann and Paul as they walked in between Richard and Camille, and Richard could see how troubled Ann was by all their stares. After all, it was well known by now who Richard and Camille were, and why they were there. Being seen with the police was clearly making Ann deeply uncomfortable.

But not Paul. He just seemed irritated.

As they entered their hotel room, Camille went straight into the bathroom to start looking for any contraband Xyrax pills.

"What are you looking for?" Ann asked, worried.

"We're just pursuing a lead," Richard said evenly, "but in the meantime, let me tell you a story. Because we've known for some time that one of the people locked in the room with Aslan must be our killer. And, fortunately for us, we've found a cracking motive for four of you: Aslan stole money from you all in the past. And yet there's a paradox with this motive. Because, for anyone to have carried out such a meticulously planned murder, they must have known Aslan's real identity well in advance. At the very least, they would have had to come to the Caribbean with an idea that they already wanted him dead. So remind me, when did you both arrive at The Retreat?"

"I don't remember exactly," Paul said carefully, and Richard wondered if he'd already worked out where he was going with his story.

"Seven days before he was killed," Richard reminded Paul and Ann. "In fact, you were both due to finish your holiday and go back to the UK the afternoon that Aslan died. But the previous seven days was plenty of time to learn how bookings for the Sunrise Healing worked. Plenty of time to see how there was a tea-drinking ceremony. Plenty of time to see that guests sometimes did the washing up after meals, and that included the chance to dry the kitchen's carving knives. Tell me," Richard said, turning just as conversationally to Paul. "Did you kill Aslan Kennedy?"

"Of course not," Paul said dismissively, and Richard noticed how Paul was exuding an air of utter calm and composure, his balding pate still carefully supporting the threads of hair that so perfectly arced over from his left ear to his right.

But whereas Paul was composed, Ann most certainly wasn't. One moment she was sitting on the end of her bed, the next she was up and looking to see what Camille was doing in the bathroom, and Richard once again took a moment to marvel at the outfit that Ann was wearing. With her hair bouffed and her voluptuous body encased in an electric-blue jumpsuit that was elasticated at her wrists and ankles, Ann looked like Margaret Thatcher crossed with a flying squirrel.

224

"Stop fussing, woman," Paul said as Ann straightened the corner of a bedspread.

"No. Of course," Ann said, sitting down immediately, the bed giving a squeak of protest as it sank under her weight.

Richard turned back to Paul.

"Oh okay, then can you tell me why you've been in contact with Aslan so much over the last couple of months?"

Paul seemed puzzled by the question. "I haven't."

"You haven't?"

"That's right," Ann chipped in. "I was the only person who spoke to Aslan. And it was only a quick call. Just to confirm the details of the holiday."

"I know," Richard said to Ann. "You rang The Retreat on the fourth of May at 12.10pm for just over seven minutes."

Ann was surprised that the police could possibly have known this, but Paul was beginning to look at Richard a lot more carefully.

"That's right, we've been through your phone records, Mr Sellars."

"Then you'll know I've not been in touch with Aslan Kennedy."

"Not from your home, but you have from work."

While Paul remained a blank, surprise slowly registered on Ann's face.

"Three times in the last two months. The shortest phone call being twelve minutes; the longest, twenty minutes. Or are you denying it was you who phoned

Aslan on those occasions and for those lengths of time?"

Paul barely missed a beat as he said, "Look, it's not what it seems," as smoothly as he could. "I was intrigued by what I'd seen in the brochures we'd been sent, I was bored at work, so I rang up and spoke to this guy who said his name was Aslan. But I only wanted to confirm what was on offer. You know. The various remedies — and treatments — and whether they were all free or whether we'd have to pay for some of them."

"I'm sure it didn't take three conversations totalling over forty minutes to establish that everything would be free, Mr Sellars."

Paul paused a moment before giving his answer. "It did."

"No, I don't think so. So how about you tell me why you really needed to talk to Aslan Kennedy for so long?" Richard asked.

Paul gathered his thoughts, and then tried to soldier on. "Well, no, perhaps — if you put it like that. But the thing is, I rang him that first time to find out what treatments would be included in the price, but I really liked Aslan when I spoke to him and . . ."

Paul didn't quite have the heart to continue with the lie, so Richard decided to help him out. "So you rang him another couple of times just because you liked chatting to him."

"That's right," Paul said, before licking his lips.

"You're lying."

Paul took an in-breath to protest, but before he could speak, Richard said, "You recognised his voice that first time you spoke to him, didn't you? Or you recognised his face on the brochures you were sent for The Retreat. But either way, you knew perfectly well that Aslan Kennedy was really the man who'd conned you and Ann out of your money twenty years ago."

"No," Paul said.

"It wasn't a question, Mr Sellars, it was a statement of fact. Nothing else would explain the repeated calls — and not from your home where they could easily be traced. From your place of work. And before you consider continuing to lie, you should know that if you don't start telling me the truth I'm planning to arrest you on suspicion of murder."

"There's not much suspicion," Camille said as she entered from the bathroom holding a little white tub. "We have all the proof we need here," she said as she handed the tub over to Richard before turning back to Paul. "You see, your manager told us that someone's been stealing a sedative called Xyrax from your pharmacy."

Richard looked down at the tub in his hand and could see that there was no label, which suggested it hadn't been legally prescribed. But the lid was already off and Richard was able to pour some of the orange chalky tablets onto his hand. Each pill had XYRAX carved into its surface.

"So can you tell me," Richard said, "seeing as your boss says she's been suspecting you've been stealing Xyrax from work, what you're doing with a tub of unprescribed Xyrax in your hotel room in the Caribbean?"

Paul didn't even begin to know what to say, so Richard decided to help him out again.

"Because you should know, we now know the tea you were all drinking just before Aslan was brutally stabbed to death was laced with gamma-hydroxybutyric acid — which I don't need to tell you is the active ingredient of Xyrax."

As Paul's face fell, Ann stood up from the bed as though she'd been stung. "No! Paul, tell me it isn't true? You didn't . . .?"

Violence seemed to engulf Paul from nowhere as he spat at his wife, "Just shut up, would you? This isn't about you, not everything's about you!"

Richard could see how furiously bottled-up Paul was, so he discreetly nodded to Camille and she got his message at once.

Camille went and sat on the armchair next to Paul's.

"It's simple, Paul," she said calmly. "If you're the killer, you're welcome to carry on lying to us. That's okay. That's what killers do. They lie. But if you're innocent, you really need to start telling us the truth right now."

As Paul looked at the kindness in Camille's face, a little tear appeared in the corner of his right eye and he angrily rubbed it away with the palm of his hand.

Camille waited.

"Alright," he said eventually, only just keeping his emotions in check. "You're right. I don't know how, but I recognised Aslan's face the moment I saw it on the brochure we were sent. I didn't know who it was, I just knew that I recognised him if you know what I mean.

228

I've been a pharmacist my whole life. You get good at faces. And I had this niggle that I knew him from somewhere in the past.

"But I didn't let it bother me, I just kind of filed it away, and then — a few days later — it came to me. You know, obviously my subconscious had been working on it while I wasn't thinking and it arrived just like that, all in one go. He wasn't Aslan, he was David Kennedy, the guy who stole from us all those years ago. I couldn't believe it. What was he doing now running a health spa in the Caribbean? And above all else, why was he offering me and Ann a free holiday?

"So I rang him, you're right. And from work. I didn't want Ann knowing. After all, I wasn't one hundred per cent sure that he was in fact David Kennedy, but I asked him when he set up The Retreat, if he'd been in the hotel business his whole life — you know, that sort of thing. And I could tell he had a good idea I was onto him. It was there in what he wasn't saying as much as in what he did say."

"How do you mean?" Camille asked.

"Like he said he'd been at The Retreat since 2000, but he wouldn't tell me what he was doing before then. And he wouldn't say what exactly the competition was supposed to be that Ann and me had entered online and won.

"It took a couple of phone calls to be sure, but by the third one, I realised that the strangest thing of all was the way that Aslan — as he was now calling himself — always seemed to have time to chat with me."

"At which point, you stole the Xyrax from work as part of your plan to kill him."

Paul looked at Richard and shook his head slowly.

"That's got nothing to do with this."

"Even though the gamma-hydroxybutyric acid all of the suspects had in their bloodstream the morning Aslan was killed must have come from crushed up Xyrax pills that could only have come from you?"

Paul didn't know what to say to that, so Camille asked him much more gently, "Then tell us. If you didn't steal the Xyrax as part of your plan to kill Aslan, why did you steal it?"

Paul knitted his brows and Richard noticed that he'd started rubbing the palms of his hands together like a man in the middle of some kind of psychological trauma.

And for a long moment, Camille just held the man's stare.

Richard couldn't help but admire this quality in his partner. Because while he knew Camille to be almost infinitely irritating, he couldn't deny that she had the most uncanny ability to make others think she was kind, compassionate and someone you'd want to tell your problems to.

"Come on, Paul," Ann bullied, "tell them —"

"Because of her!" Paul's arm shot out as he pointed his finger accusingly at his wife. Ann was stunned by the accusation, but Paul hadn't finished.

"Because I live with this pointless woman, just look at her! She hasn't got a thought in her head, she believes everything she's told, and she talks and talks —

230

and talks! — the whole time. Have you any idea what that's like? Living with someone who just won't shut up? So yes, I took the Xyrax, it's a sedative — and have done for years because it's not addictive like valium — it just takes the edge off the constant barrage of noise. You know? Although you can't possibly know what it's like living with her!"

Paul was panting as he finished this tirade, and Richard finally managed to place Paul's supposed superior drawl from the earlier interviews. How he seemed to be hiding behind an entirely stand-offish manner.

Paul wasn't superior, and nor was he stand-offish. He was on sedatives.

"So yes, I'll admit to everything. I knew who Aslan was long before I came out here. And I've even been stealing Xyrax from work. But for my own use, you understand. If there was any trace of gamma-hydroxybutyric acid in the tea we drank during the Sunrise Healing, then I've no idea how it got there — because you've got to ask yourself: why on earth would I want to kill Aslan?"

"He stole from you," Camille pointed out.

"No he didn't. He stole from Ann — and now you know what I think of her — do you really think I'd cross the street for her, let alone commit murder for her?"

Richard looked over at Ann and saw that she was staring at her husband as though at a stranger, the tears rolling silently down her cheeks.

"And anyway," Paul said, with grim satisfaction, "if you're looking for someone who's known for a long time that Aslan was really David Kennedy, you need look no further than my wife."

Ann started to shake her head in horror. "No," she mumbled.

"Because if I could recognise David after all these years, I bet she did. She's got a better memory for faces than even I have. And she's always known about my Xyrax pills. Not how I get hold of them of course, but she knows that they're a sedative and why I take them. And the thing is, I wouldn't kill over twenty grand — not even if it were my money. Not after all these years. But Ann would, because it wasn't just twenty grand you lost, was it?" This last comment was aimed squarely at his wife. "It was your whole future David Kennedy stole from you when he took your money, wasn't it?"

Richard and Camille shared a glance, both of them knowing that as much as they were disgusted by the triumph Paul was showing at spiking his wife like this, they wanted to know more.

"It's not true," Ann said, aghast. "I didn't know Aslan was anyone other than who he said he was. And I didn't know Paul's drugs were a sedative, he's lying about that. He's always told me his pills were for his heart."

Paul didn't feel that he needed to rebut his wife, and Camille and Richard waited for Ann to continue, but she was clearly too lost in the pain of her husband's accusation.

232

"Then would you mind telling us how David Kennedy stole your future?" Richard eventually asked.

Ann finally tore her eyes from her husband and looked at the police.

"Very well. Twenty years ago, I was at music college. I'm a singer. Was a singer. A soprano, it's all I wanted to do. And I knew I maybe wouldn't make it as a professional, but I knew I had a chance. Paul's right. It had always been my dream to sing on the stage. Not be famous, you understand, but to be — you know . . . just that. A professional. And I'd saved and saved so I could do the course. Paul didn't understand what it was about. He never understood. He was off training to be a pharmacist. He had these big plans — not that he ever achieved them."

"Now look here," Paul started, but Ann wasn't having any of it.

"You've had your say, Paul Sellars, now it's mine," she said, standing imperiously as she did so and commanding the room. Having done so, she wafted over to the French windows, and Richard found himself wondering how much of the melodrama in Ann's life was real, and how much of it was "play-acting". Because now he'd learnt she'd always wanted to be on the stage, he found that he was finally beginning to understand her. Her flamboyant clothes, her larger-than-life persona; this was someone who was desperate for an outlet for their passions, but who didn't have one.

"You see, I only just had enough money saved to complete the course. And then a friend of a friend recommended this art-lease scheme to me. They said it

233

was a licence to print money. And I ended up handing over all my savings, all twenty thousand pounds I'd managed to set aside for the course. By the end of that first year, I discovered I'd lost everything. Every penny. I was devastated. This was it. My vocation, and I couldn't carry on." Ann took a moment to steady herself, the pain still clearly cutting her like a knife, and Richard was interested to see the anger in her eyes as she turned to look at her husband. "So I asked the college to hold my place open for me for a year because Paul said he'd get the money together for me to finish the course.

"But the following year I discovered that Paul hadn't been saving anything for me. The college couldn't hold my place open for two years and I had to let it go. And I know it doesn't sound like much, but this is all I'd ever wanted to do my whole life. I was that close . . . and that man took it from me."

Richard was surprised to see that Ann was looking at her husband as she said this.

"You mean, David Kennedy?" Richard asked, confused.

"No. He was a crook. I'd expect it of him. But Paul was my husband. His duty was to help me, and he never even lifted a finger."

Richard took a moment to let the tension dissipate between Ann and Paul. When it didn't, he stood up, signalling that the interview was coming to an end.

"Then one last question, Ann, if you don't mind. You see, looking at it from our point of view, Paul's right. If he recognised Aslan's true identity, it's possible that

234

you did as well. And despite you saying you didn't know what Xyrax was, I could well imagine a jury believing that you'd look it up and learn that it was a sedative. And, as you've just admitted, you had more reason than most to want revenge on Aslan Kennedy. As you readily admit, he took away your chance of ever being a professional singer. But my question to you is this, and I want the truth this time. How did your fingerprints get on the murder weapon?"

Ann looked at Richard as though he'd just betrayed her.

"But it's just like I told you. I did the washing up and put it away the night before. That's the last time I ever touched one of those knives."

"Even though you'd never done the washing up on any of the previous nights you'd been here?"

"Even so," Ann said, darkly. "Because there's something else you're forgetting. How can I be the killer? It was a man in Aslan's office the night before shouting at him that he wouldn't get away with it, wasn't it? Which makes me ask, was that you, Paul?"

Paul wasn't having any of this. "As well you know, I was with you on the beach," he said.

"You know," Ann said to the police, "I didn't say at the time, but I can't guarantee that Paul was with me the whole time. Not really."

"Oh?" Richard said, pretending that this was news to him, but he well remembered his first interview with the witnesses and the fact that Ann had seemed puzzled when Paul had said that his wife could alibi him for the whole afternoon.

"That's right," Ann continued. "Because every afternoon here, I've had a nap on the sunloungers after my afternoon swim — and the day before Aslan was killed was no exception."

"Stop talking rot," Paul said. "I was with you the whole time."

"But that's what I'm saying. I was asleep on my sunlounger for at least an hour — at about 6pm — that's when I've been having a doze every afternoon since we've got here. So if there was a man who was heard shouting at Aslan in his office at that time, it could have been Paul."

"You know," Paul said smoothly to his wife, "you really should have mentioned this before. Now it just looks like sour grapes."

Ann turned her back on her husband as she said, "But if you want me to, I'll admit it. I hated David Kennedy. Not because of the money he stole from me. Not really. But because of what I was doing with that money. And losing it meant I never got to follow my heart. But please believe me, I had no idea that the man running this hotel was him."

Richard looked at the two suspects and didn't even know where to begin. Because Paul was right, there's no way he would kill Aslan to revenge his wife. Not unless he was lying about his relationship with Ann, and that hardly seemed possible, did it? The animosity he was showing towards her was too real. Altogether too keen. And as for Ann, Richard could well imagine her recognising Aslan as David from the flyers — just as Paul now admitted he did — but if she were the killer, then why on earth did she allow her fingerprints to be found on the handle of the murder weapon?

Richard once again found himself feeling manipulated. What was he missing? Who was the killer?

Was it in fact Ann trying to get revenge on the man who'd stolen her future from her?

Or was it Paul who killed Aslan — either because he loved his wife after all and was wreaking revenge on her behalf? Or maybe because he hated her and was now trying to frame his wife for the murder? But that didn't seem possible, either. If you hate your wife, Richard found himself thinking, you divorce her, you don't commit murder to get her locked up.

Then maybe it was Saskia Filbee — because of the million pounds she lost to Aslan and the lawyers? But if she was the killer, how did she arrange it, seeing as she only arrived on the island the night before the murder — and after the list of names had been published for the Sunrise Meditation?

And then — finally — was it Ben, for reasons still unknown? After all, if he wasn't the killer, why on earth had he run away?

And who was the man who'd been threatening Aslan that he wouldn't get away with it the night before he was killed?

Richard realised that the whole case was at risk of unravelling, but, in truth, he didn't have even the first idea how much worse things were about to get.

Within the next twenty-four hours, the killer would strike again.

CHAPTER
ELEVEN

In truth, the police knew that if Ben really wanted to put his mind to leaving Saint-Marie, there'd be little they could do to stop him. A few hundred dollars to a local boat captain and you could be on either of the neighbouring islands of Guadeloupe or Martinique in a couple of hours.

But the police had to carry on as though they'd be able to find him, and the fact that they had his passport in custody was their one sliver of hope. Without his passport, it would be that bit harder for Ben to vanish.

That evening, Richard was in his shack and somewhat edgy. The rain that had been promised during the day had duly arrived as Richard had sat down to eat his tea of poached eggs on toast. He'd had to sit inside and mournfully push the watery eggs and floppy white toast around his plate while whole sheets of rain swept across his beach, unable to think over the thunderous clatter of rain on his tin roof. And then, the very moment that Richard had finished his eggs on toast, the rain had stopped and the sun had come out to boil him again.

Having done the washing up, swept the floor of sand, had his early evening shower, swept the floor again, got into his pyjamas and then decided that the floor needed a quick sweep, Richard had since been checking through the photos he'd taken of the chemicals and cleaning products they'd found in Dominic's house.

After all, just because Paul Sellars had a heap of Xyrax pills in his hotel room, it didn't mean that it was Paul's stock of Xyrax that had been used to drug the witnesses. What if Dominic also had the ingredients to make GHB in his lab? What's more, thirty seconds of research on the internet had shown that Richard's first instincts had been right: gamma-hydroxybutyric acid could easily be manufactured in a home lab. All Dominic would have needed was some butyrolactone, some sodium hydroxide, tap water, pH paper, and basic knowledge of GCSE chemistry. Dominic definitely had the chemistry knowledge — and the ability to make sodium hydroxide — but did he have the necessary butyrolactone in his lab?

For the last few hours, then, Richard had been identifying each cleaning product or chemical he'd photo-graphed in Dominic's lab, looking up its active ingredients on the internet, and then trying to work out whether that chemical could then be used to synthesise the butyrolactone Dominic would have needed to create GHB.

As Richard kept checking the ingredients in the photos he'd taken of the chemicals and cleaning products, he also found his mind wandering over Dominic's role in the case. After all, Dominic was the only person who'd not got on with Aslan — Aslan had even recently sacked him — and Dominic had also kept his relationship with Julia a secret. What's more, could

Dominic really be believed when he said that someone had burgled his chemistry lab the week before the murder? What was Dominic really up to?

Mind you, Richard had to concede, Dominic had never been inside the Meditation Space, so, if he were the killer, how on earth could he have done it?

It was boring work, and it didn't help that although it was nearly ten o'clock, it was still boiling hot. Richard had got all of the windows open, the old French doors were thrown open wide, but there wasn't even the hint of a breeze. It was one of those humid, still, tropical nights when the sweat would sit proud on Richard's skin and he knew he'd barely get any sleep. The only small mercy was that Harry the Lizard didn't seem to be anywhere, so at least Richard didn't have to come face to face with the physical embodiment of his lily-livered inability to act decisively.

And that's when he found it.

At first, the photo had seemed just as innocuous as all the others he had been looking at. The picture showed a spray-bottle cleaning product called "Wheel & Rim Cleaner" that had a photo of a sparkling car wheel on the front of it. The blurb on the bottle said, "Guaranteed to remove 100% of all rust!".

But it was when Richard looked at the next photo on his phone — which showed the bottle's active ingredients — that he realised he'd hit pay dirt. The cleaning product was listed as being 99.9% pure butyrolactone — which Richard knew was the last remaining ingredient Dominic would have needed to make gamma-hydroxybutyric acid in his home lab.

Which rather complicated matters, because Richard now had to consider: did the GHB that was used to sedate the suspects come from Paul's supply of stolen Xyrax? Or did it come from Dominic's home lab?

Richard's reverie was interrupted when he heard someone outside, and he looked up in surprise.

Julia Higgins was standing on his verandah.

It took Richard a few moments to process this information and then he jumped to his feet, nearly knocking his smartphone to the floor as he did so.

"Oh! Hello. Julia. What a surprise. Sorry you find me like this." Richard indicated his Marks and Spencer pyjamas, very sensibly striped with alternating bands of dark blue and maroon.

"Wow," Julia said in wonder. "This is the most beautiful house I've ever seen."

Richard looked about himself and wondered what on earth Julia was talking about. Thanks to a quick "once-round" with the broom only a few minutes before, the floorboards were at least mercifully clear of sand, but the furniture was so dilapidated that Richard had always presumed the place had been furnished from a charity shop's closing down sale — and, now that he was looking, Richard found himself once again remembering that he really should hire a skip to get rid of all of the tat that the previous owner, D.I. Charlie Hulme, had left behind.

"It is?" Richard replied, somewhat surprised.

"Yeah."

Julia stepped into the light of the room and Richard finally got to see that she was wearing what was frankly an indecently tiny dress. Made of the local madras — a bright yellow, green and red gingham — Richard realised there was probably more material in one of his favourite hankies, and as his eyes were drawn to Julia's tanned legs, Richard noticed in a panic that she was barefoot.

"Sorry, only I've only just swept the floor, would you mind not bringing any sand . . ."

But Julia didn't hear Richard's words as she stepped over to the old sideboard, reached up on tiptoes and pulled down a carved onyx head from the top of an old dresser.

"What's this?" she asked.

The carving was of a traditional Arawak tribal elder.

"I've no idea," Richard said, still panicking at the trail of sand Julia had left behind on the floor.

"It's beautiful."

Richard tried to look at the onyx head, but there were two problems with this. Firstly, it was a carved onyx head — why on earth would you look at one of those? — and, secondly, there was sand on the floor.

"Look, I'm sorry," Richard said, bustling over to the far wall, yanking his Dustbuster from its charging station and turning it on — at which point it started to emit a very loud and high-pitched drone. Getting down on his hands and knees, Richard stabbed at the sandy footprints Julia had left on the floorboards.

"You'd be amazed at how useful these things are," Richard called out over the banshee wail. "There's almost no space it can't get into. There we are. That's better."

Richard stood back up, pleased that he'd managed to restore order to his world. He then returned to the docking station and clunked the little vacuum cleaner back into place. Only then did he realise he'd maybe spoiled the mood of intimacy.

"Anyway," he said with a conversational tone he certainly wasn't feeling. "What are you doing here?"

"Do you want to go for a walk?"

Richard didn't really understand the question.

"I'm sorry?"

"Do you want to go for a walk?"

Richard was still flummoxed. "Where?"

Now it was Julia's turn to be taken aback.

"Along the beach."

"You mean . . . outside?" Richard was appalled at the thought, and then he indicated that he was only wearing pyjamas — while saying as breezily as he could "Unfortunately, I'm not really dressed for a night-time ramble."

"Come on," Julia said. "It's such a beautiful evening, I want to look at the stars."

And so it was that Richard found himself walking in his pyjamas and tan leatherette slippers across a white sand beach with a beautiful young woman who, by her own confession, wanted to go for a walk with him and look at the stars.

"So . . ." Richard said as a way of trying to find out what on earth was going on. After all, he couldn't help but notice that the person he was talking to — in the middle of the night — had recently been in a prison cell because he'd arrested her on suspicion of murder.

"Aren't they beautiful?" Julia said, looking up at the riotous sweep of stars that filled every inch of the sky.

Richard looked up at the night sky.

Very little in life held Richard spellbound in wonder — and stars were no exception. As far as he was concerned, they were just great big balls of gas that were a very long way away. But he had to admit to himself that he'd always liked looking at them, if only because they reminded him that the universe was ever-expanding — or at least was expanding for the moment — and one day, many thousands of aeons after he'd died, the whole thing would collapse back in on itself until everything that had ever existed was crushed down into a ball of almost infinitely small size.

The actual pointless futility of existence somehow made coping with its apparent pointless futility more manageable, he found.

Richard glanced at Julia and could see that she was now looking at him with an expression he couldn't read. It wasn't irritation — Richard knew how to decode that one well enough — or disappointment, or frustration. So what was it?

"I just wanted to thank you."

"Ah. Right. And why would that be?" Richard asked, still none the wiser.

"You never thought I'd killed him. Did you?"

This wasn't strictly true of course, but Richard had an instinct that now was not the time to get bogged down in the minutiae of the case. Even so, he couldn't let her believe a lie.

"Well, I don't know about that," he said as breezily as he could, "but I knew we hadn't got the full story. After all, you never seemed to know how you'd done it. Or where the knife had come from. Or why you'd done it, really. And then there's the fact that the wounds were inflicted by someone right-handed, which we knew you weren't . . ."

Richard stopped speaking as he realised that he was in fact getting bogged down in the minutiae of the case.

Julia smiled and pointed at a little tower of smooth pebbles further along the beach.

"Oh look," she said, "a wishing tower."

There was a local custom on Saint-Marie that if you wanted a wish to come true, you first collected a cluster of flat pebbles and made a tower out of them. You then made a wish, and if the spirits of the island willed it, your wish would come true. The tower which had been built a little way off along the beach was a pretty typical example, about a foot high.

As far as Richard was concerned, the whole custom of littering beaches with towers of stones was a health and safety nightmare — and whenever he saw any soupy-eyed youngster constructing one, he always wished he could make an arrest based on the criminal offence of whimsy.

"Yes," Richard said, unable to keep a note of disapproval out of his voice, "I saw Dominic had a similar wishing tower in his house."

At the sound of Dominic's name, Julia sighed.

"I should tell you," Julia said. "I broke up with Dominic."

Richard looked at her a long moment and then gave a quick shrug to indicate that he didn't really understand what this fact meant.

"Weeks ago. In my mind. I just hadn't told him. Or me for that matter. I still didn't know. But I *knew*, if you know what I mean. You know?"

Richard didn't of course, so he very carefully shook his head side to side in a nodding-in-agreement kind of a way.

"And being in that prison cell, I began to realise. I only came out here for a holiday. What was I still doing on the island? Dominic was never going to be long-term, being here was never going to be long-term. I was just . . . I think, if I'm honest, I was just running away."

"What from?"

"The future."

Oh god, Richard found himself thinking to himself, here we go again. "The future?"

"You know," Julia said, for once being entirely straightforward. "Getting a job. Using my degree. Because . . . all this?" Julia indicated the beach and the sea. "This can't be long-term."

She turned back to Richard. "I'm going back to the UK. Just as soon as I can."

"Which is obviously once the murder investigation concludes," Richard pointed out, as lightly as he could.

"Of course. That sea looks so inviting."

"I'm sorry?"

Julia took a few steps into the sea and let the water gently lap at her bare feet. Richard was, of course standing a yard or two further up the negligible slope of

246

the beach. It was bad enough being out on the sand in his slippers, but he couldn't risk them getting wet or salt-damaged in any way.

"The sea. Don't you just want to dive in?"

Richard took a tentative step nearer to the water's edge and indicated the expanse of sea as it glistened in the moonlight.

"But there are sharks out there," he explained.

Julia looked at Richard. "Of course. But they're out there."

Julia pointed further out to sea and Richard was once again struck by the collective insanity that seemed to grip otherwise rational humans when they declared a view of the sea beautiful even though it must, perforce, contain a quantity of sharks. Hadn't they realised? Sharks were like German U-boats. They could be *anywhere*.

"Come on, we could go in," Julia said.

Richard froze.

"I'm sorry?"

"We should go for a swim."

If he'd been wearing a suit, Richard would have straightened the knot of his tie.

"Don't tell me you've never been for a midnight swim?" Julia asked, amazed.

"I haven't been for a swim."

Now it was Julia's turn to be surprised.

"I'm sorry?"

"I don't even own a pair of trunks."

"What?"

"I don't . . . you know, I don't like swimming in the sea."

"But you've swum in the Caribbean?" Julia asked, amazed.

"As it happens . . . no."

"You've got a private beach here, and you've never felt what it's like to go swimming in that water?"

Looking at Julia's surprise, Richard began to realise how ludicrous his non-swimming policy must appear to others. He wanted to explain that the one time he went paddling in the sea, he'd trod on an anemone and ended up having to go to hospital to get a tetanus jab, but he had an instinct that maybe this wasn't the time or place for a lengthy speech on the inadequacies of what passed for the island's Accident and Emergency provision.

"Well, that's going to change," Julia said, decisively. "You're going for a swim right now."

Richard began to panic. "What? I am?"

"Come on, no one's around, you have got to go for a swim, it's like a bath out there."

"But I said, I don't own any trunks."

Julia looked at Richard as though he were entirely stupid.

"You don't need to wear trunks."

"I think you'll find that I do."

"You don't need to wear anything at all. Come on," Julia said, a look of delight in her eyes. "There's no one around. We can go skinny-dipping, just you and me!"

Time seemed to slow down for Richard at that moment. But it also seemed to speed up — and bulge in the middle — and all while Richard seemed to have an out-of-body experience where he was looking at himself on the beach talking to a beautiful young

248

woman who'd just suggested they both take their clothes off and go swimming together.

"What do you say?" Julia asked again, her eyes sparkling, as Richard just stood there like a statue of himself. "There's no reason to be inhibited, it's just our bodies. Come on, I'll go first. Then you can follow."

Julia reached down, clutched at the hemline of her skirt and was about to pull her dress up over her head when Richard's hand shot out and grabbed her arm.

"You can't do that!"

Julia looked at Richard, surprise in her eyes. She then began to realise that maybe this wasn't a trivial matter — or in any way fun — for Richard.

"I'm sorry," Richard said, "but I don't do this. You know, go for walks with beautiful women. Or have them offer to take their clothes off."

Richard couldn't have looked more confused, and Julia's heart went out to him.

"You're stressed."

"Seriously. You have no idea."

"At the thought of going swimming naked with me."

Richard bit his lip a bit. "Uh-um."

Julia thought for a moment and then smiled. She let go of the hemline of her dress.

"Hey, then it's alright. If it would make you unhappy."

Richard didn't say anything. His flight and fight mechanisms had both kicked in at the same time, and now he couldn't move.

Julia looked at Richard. "Maybe I shouldn't have come. But anyway . . . I just wanted to thank you. For believing in me. You're very lovely, you know that?"

After a moment, Richard's left hand wafted an inch from his body. It was all he could manage.

Julia leant forward and gently kissed Richard on the lips. A butterfly kiss.

She turned and walked away, and still Richard didn't move. He was too stunned. Not that his encounter had ended with a kiss — he hadn't even got to the bit in his memory where Julia gave him a kiss — he was still stuck on the bit where he told the beautiful woman not to take all of her clothes off in front of him.

Self-reproach filled Richard. Why was he such a stick-in-the-mud? Why was he so boring? Why couldn't he ever be spontaneous? What was he so frightened of? Where did this over-developed sense of propriety come from? He was a man, wasn't he? A red-blooded male. And single, to boot. He turned and called out before he could stop himself.

"Julia, would-you-like-to-go-for-a-drink-sometime?"

Julia stopped and turned, moonlight briefly flashing across her golden hair.

In the few hours Richard felt it took Julia to answer, he found himself remembering each of the three times in his life he'd asked a woman out for a drink. The first woman had said no. The second had barked a laugh and the one-word answer — "*You?*" — after which he'd felt so damaged by the experience that he'd waited nearly ten years before daring to ask anyone out again. And she'd said no as well.

That was fifteen years ago.

But as Richard looked now, he saw a smile appear at Julia's lips.

"I'd like that very much," she said.

And with that, Julia turned and walked off the beach.

Richard watched her go while his psyche was off doing cartwheels of joy across the beach. But then, he realised, he was a middle-aged man standing alone on a beach in the middle of the night wearing pyjamas and slippers. So he returned to his shack and went to bed.

But as he turned down the corner on his book of sudoku puzzles later that night and switched off his bedside light, Richard found himself smiling to himself in the dark. He was almost feeling optimistic.

The following day, Richard found that he was still feeling great. And so, while his team continued to try and track down Ben Jenkins, Richard found himself driving the police jeep at seventy miles an hour up to the highest promontory of Saint-Marie — a vertical cliff known locally as "Lover's Leap" — with an empty tin of shortbread biscuits from Edinburgh on the passenger seat to his side.

There were little air holes that Richard had stabbed into the lid with his metal compass.

His mother had sent him the tin of biscuits for his birthday present the previous year. Unfortunately, the tin hadn't arrived in time for his birthday as it had got lost in customs, and it had taken all of Richard's detecting skills — and the judicious flashing of his police warrant card to any number of officials — to track the precious gift down, but a short three months after it had arrived on the island, Richard had finally got possession of his birthday present.

That smell of butter and sugar as he'd popped the tin lid! It was the stuff that dreams were made of, and the forty-two consecutive days that Richard had been able to take a single shortbread biscuit with his morning cup of tea had been truly a Golden Age in the life of Richard Poole. And it wasn't just because of the quality of the shortbread — that had, of course, been excellent — it was also that feeling of homeliness Richard had got from looking at the picture of Edinburgh Castle on the tin's lid every time he had taken a biscuit.

Although Richard had no Scottish blood in his family, he was proud to call himself British and this enamelled painting of an ancient castle on a granite rock — a kilted bagpiper in the foreground — spoke to him, he felt, at a deep level.

But on the forty-third day, the supply of biscuits had run out — as Richard had always known would be the case even as he'd bitten into the buttery goodness of the first biscuit. But that was okay. Everything ended, whether it was life, the universe or a tin of shortbread biscuits. Richard had kept the empty tin, though. Of course he had. And, that morning, he'd used it to catch and trap Harry.

All it had taken was a bit of vim and vigour, and Richard had found that he'd been blessed with both the morning after his encounter with Julia.

In the end it had been easy. All he had had to do was put out Harry's cat food and mashed flies as usual and then wait crouched nearby with the tin ready. Only a few minutes later, Harry had skittered across the floor

252

to his food — as Richard knew he would — and he'd been able to pounce, slamming the upturned tin down on top of the unsuspecting lizard with a cry of "Aha!"

For a brief moment, Richard had panicked that he'd maybe banged the tin's edge down through the little creature's tail, but a quick search around the boundary of the tin's edge showed no evidence of a guillotined tail.

He had Harry trapped.

Richard hadn't known why it had taken him so long to realise that he didn't need to kill Harry to get rid of him, he just had to release him back into the wild. That's all. And releasing Harry back into the wild was even the right thing to do. Lizards shouldn't be domesticated.

And if the place he released his lizard was both a good few miles away from his shack and also near the highest cliff on Saint-Marie, well then, that was just one of those things.

But as Richard took the hairpin bends up to Lover's Leap with the occasional squeal of protest from the jeep's tyres, his thoughts weren't really on the lizard — and nor were they on the murder case — because he still couldn't get over the fact that a beautiful woman had tried to go skinny-dipping with him the night before. And just as impossibly, she'd then agreed to go out for a drink with him at some unspecified time in the future.

Bombing into the car park by Lover's Leap, Richard slammed on the brakes and the wheels briefly locked as the police jeep slid across the gravel and came to a stop with a judder.

Richard was briefly startled. He must have been driving much faster than he'd thought, but — equally — he didn't want to overthink what he was doing here. Not now he was a man of action.

Richard grabbed up the biscuit tin, stepped out of the jeep and was instantly buffeted by what felt like a violent gale. This high up, there was always a strong hot wind coming in off the sea and racing up the cliffs. As his suit jacket flapped and his tie flew out behind him, Richard pushed against the gale and carried the tin over to a grassy area nearby.

Crouching down, he popped the lid of the metal tin with his thumbs. He then very carefully eased the lid off and looked inside.

The shortbread tin was empty.

The lizard had vanished.

Richard looked inside the tin again, but there was no getting around it. The lizard was no longer there.

So where was he?

Cold dread began to trickle through Richard's body as he realised what must have happened. He looked at the lid he'd removed and oh so slowly turned it over so he was looking at the underside of it.

Harry the Lizard was holding on with his suckers and looking at Richard with what was a frankly insolent grin. Yeah, well, Richard thought to himself, that was the last time Harry would trick him.

Richard carefully lay the lid down on the grass so Harry could scamper off to his new life.

Only, Harry didn't move.

Instead, he just looked up at Richard with a cheeky grin.

Oh well, Richard thought to himself, Harry was hardly Richard's responsibility any more. He could just leave him here. But as Richard turned away, he realised that Harry was still standing on the underside of the biscuit tin lid. A biscuit tin lid that Richard liked looking at.

Richard's irritation spiked as he returned to the tin lid, pulled out his hankie, got back down on his haunches and started to waft it near to Harry's face.

"Shoo!" he said.

The lizard didn't move.

"Go on . . . skedaddle!" he said.

Harry looked up at Richard as though he was expecting to be fed.

"Look, you're a lizard, would you please leave me alone!"

Still nothing from Harry.

Richard decided that desperate times called for desperate measures. He carefully picked up the tin lid at the edges and gently tried to shake Harry off.

Harry seemed to hunker down and hold on as though it were a game.

"Oh come on!" Richard said, and shook the lid a bit harder.

Harry's suckers on his feet were equal to the task.

"Please, for the love of god, won't you just bugger off!"

And, as Richard said this, he flicked the lid as though he were shaking a sheet out, the lizard popped into the air — got caught by a gust of wind — and sailed off and over the edge of the cliff.

Richard watched the little green creature disappear from view.

"No!"

Richard was up and running, but he already knew it was too late as he threw himself to the ground just short of the cliff's edge. And, as he looked over at the vertiginous drop to the sea hundreds of feet below, Richard now knew what it felt like to be a murderer. He'd just killed a blameless lizard! And remorse filled his body.

Harry the Lizard emerged from a nearby clump of grass and scampered up Richard's arm and onto his head. Richard froze as he realised that Harry hadn't gone over the cliff edge as he'd first thought — and as he spun over to swat the lying and cheating creature away, Harry scampered down Richard's suit jacket and disappeared off into the long grass, his tail swishing happily behind him.

"Always have to have the last word, don't you?" Richard shouted out at his lizard's departing back.

Richard got back to his feet, dusted himself down, grabbed up the biscuit tin lid and returned to the jeep, and only then did it dawn on him. He'd done it.

He'd finally got rid of his lizard.

Richard was still feeling full of pep as he strode confidently into the office, firing out, "So have we found Ben Jenkins yet?" as he went straight to the board.

Fidel and Camille looked up from their desks.

"And a good morning to you, too, sir," Camille offered.

When Richard didn't say anything more, Fidel realised he hadn't answered the question he'd been asked.

"Not yet, sir," he said. "But Dwayne's still out spreading the word."

"Then tell me, have we been able to find out any more about him — or why he might have gone on the run?"

"I'm sorry, sir. And I'm checking both in Portugal and the UK. As far as I can tell, since leaving prison, Ben Jenkins hasn't even got so much as a parking ticket."

Richard shot back, "Then what about the labs on Guadeloupe? Have they worked out if there was any handwriting on the burnt pieces of paper you sent them?"

"I don't know, sir. They've not been in touch," Fidel said.

"Then get on the phone to them at once! I want that lab test given top priority and carried out asap."

Fidel sighed to himself as he picked up his phone to make the call. Richard was impossible at the best of times, but when he started snapping out orders, he could be insufferable. But Fidel also knew that Richard's "get up and go" moods tended to get up and leave him after a while. They just had to be ridden out like a tropical storm.

Richard turned his attention back to the board. What had they got so far? What were they missing? Who was their killer?

The Murder
Five guests go for a swim
Paul hands out robes
Aslan prepares the tea
5 guests + Aslan go into Meditation Space
Aslan locks it down from inside
Drink tea — all cups turned over
10–15 minute window for murder, (8.00–8.10/ 8.15).
Right-handed killer!

Investigation / Leads
WHY KILLED IN PAPER HOUSE?
3 x drawing pins in the Meditation Space. Used to pin the murder weapon to a pillar. No prints on any of them
Tea drugged with GHB, a sedative
Who was in Aslan's study the night before @6pm shouting "You're not going to get away with it"?
WHERE'S THE NOTEBOOK OF NAMES FOR THE SUNRISE HEALING?
Is it the burnt paper in the furnace in the cellar?

Outside the Meditation Space

Rianka Kennedy
Wife
Has no idea who'd want Aslan dead

258

Married to Aslan when he was David — but left him when he was convicted
Took Aslan back 15 yrs ago when he came to the island

Dominic De Vere
Ex-hypnotherapist. Now handyman
Sacked by Aslan
Argued with Aslan
Caught returning to Scene of Crime
Has drugs lab in his house — could have munufactured GHB

Inside the Meditation Space

Aslan Kennedy
Victim
Everyone says he's nice
Real name is David Kennedy
Ex-conman — ran art-lease Ponzi scheme, stole £2m
Went to prison 20 years ago, served 5 yrs

Julia Higgins
Worked at The Retreat last 6 months
Confessed to murder — but Xyrax in blood — and lack of real motive — and LEFT-HANDED . . . she's innocent

Ann Sellars
Housewife

Married to Paul
Arrived on island 7 days before murder
Lost £20k in Ponzi scheme
Her fingerprints are on the murder weapon — but she washed knife the night before
Had her dreams as a singer ruined when she lost £20k
Clearly hates her husband, Paul
Says she didn't recognise Aslan / David

Paul Sellars
Arrived on island 7 days before murder
Handed out the white robes
Pharmacist — who stole Xyrax from work
KNEW ASLAN'S REAL IDENTITY
Wife Ann lost money in Ponzi scheme
Hates his wife, Ann
Wife NO LONGER alibis him for argument at 6pm

Saskia Filbee
Single, 45 yrs old
Here on her own. Says she arrived night before
Heard argument in office night before — at about 6pm — a man, but couldn't identify him
Lied that she'd lost £50k in Ponzi scheme — she lost £500,000
Says she didn't recognise Aslan / David, but she was his friend . . . ! Maybe she did

Ben Jenkins
Property developer. Portugal.

Arrived on island 4 days before murder
No alibi for time of argument at 6pm
Served 3 yrs for Wounding With Intent and was
Aslan / David's cellmate in 1997 for 1 year
Lied that he didn't know him . . . ?
WHERE IS HE?

Every time Richard looked at the whiteboard, he felt an almost overwhelming sense of frustration. Six people go into a paper house. When the door is next opened, one of them is lying on the floor dead — so who of the other five people killed him? Richard felt as though he had a load of jigsaw pieces, but he couldn't even begin to put them together because they all came from different jigsaw puzzles.

And all the time he kept thinking to himself, just where was Ben Jenkins?

The man had a history of violence, he hadn't told the police he'd shared a cell with Aslan for a year, and now he'd done a runner. But then, if he was guilty of murder, why hadn't the police been able to find any communications between Ben and Aslan in the last few months? The killer had to have got Aslan to invite the Ponzi victims out at the same time — nothing else made sense — and yet none of Ben's phone records from Portugal, or Aslan's phone records or emails, showed there'd been any contact between the two men at all.

Unlike Paul Sellars, who had also — it turned out — been lying to them. Because, not only had he been in

261

contact with Aslan with regular phone calls over the last two months, Paul had even admitted that he'd always known that Aslan was in fact David Kennedy. And Paul had been stealing GHB — in the form of Xyrax — from his place of work. That couldn't be a coincidence, could it? But then, Paul was also right when he said he didn't have a motive to kill Aslan. It wasn't his career that had been ruined by the Ponzi scheme, it was his wife's; and it was her money that had been lost when Aslan was arrested, not Paul's.

If Paul was the killer, he'd have to have another motive. One that the police didn't yet know about. But what could it be?

But then, Richard found himself thinking, it was only when he was interviewing Paul that he'd discovered that Ann was maybe a hell of a lot more psychologically damaged than she'd ever let on before. And there was no getting away from it, the only right-handed fingerprints they'd been able to raise from the murder weapon's handle belonged to Ann. But why would she leave her prints on the knife if she really were the killer?

As for Saskia, she'd also lied to the police. And if losing half a million pounds was enough of a motive to want Aslan dead — and it was — wasting the rest of your fortune on trying to get the money back just gold-plated that motive. And out of all the available motives, Richard felt that Saskia's was still the most powerful. Losing a fortune like that — and after it had taken her dad so long to earn it — could drive anyone to murder. And yet, Richard had got no sense of present anger from Saskia when they'd last interviewed her. Yes, she was bitter — and ashamed — but Richard felt that Saskia had mostly put the past behind her. Unless she'd been tricking the police of course. But even if she'd come out to the island with the express intention of killing Aslan, just how could she have done it, seeing as she only arrived the night before he was killed?

It seemed to boil down to: Julia confessed to the murder, but couldn't have done it; Paul could have done it, but didn't have a motive; Ann had a motive — in which case, why were her prints on the murder weapon; and no one's motive was bigger than Saskia's, but she'd only arrived on the island the night before the murder. Saskia was the only one of the five who couldn't possibly be their murderer.

And none of this mattered, Richard knew, because it wasn't any of these suspects who'd just done a runner; that privilege belonged to Ben Jenkins, who — they now knew — had been Aslan's cellmate back in the day. So why had he run away? What was he so frightened of?

As Richard continued to worry and fuss at the board, he began to feel overwhelmed by the questions he still didn't have the answers to. How come Aslan had invited all of the Ponzi victims out to The Retreat at the same time? Who was it who'd been shouting at Aslan in his office the night before he was killed? And what did it mean when this man was heard saying "you won't get away with it"?

What's more, where did the GHB in the teapot come from? Was it from Paul's pills? Or was it a homebrew from Dominic's lab? Or — perhaps — did it come from some other source altogether?

And where was the notebook with everyone's names written out for the Sunrise Healing session? Who'd removed it from the board after Aslan had been killed? And why?

Also, while Richard had made no secret of how baffled he was that Aslan had been slain inside a paper house, he hadn't really been able to articulate just how much this fact had continued to irritate him. Because not only did it seem to overturn all the usual rules of murder — that premeditated killings happen in private away from possible witnesses — but it also, to Richard at least, seemed to be a personal challenge to him.

Aslan had died in a room that had been locked down from the inside, and the only five possible suspects were all locked inside the same room with him. And to make things easier, one of them was even left-handed, so that left only four possible suspects. As far as Richard could tell, one of Ben, Saskia, Paul or Ann was the killer — was laughing at the police — but which one of them was it?

As Richard continued to study the whiteboard, he hadn't noticed Camille sidle up to him.

"So tell me, how did you get on last night?"

Richard panicked, graphic images of his encounter with Julia flashing into his mind. Eventually, he managed to let out a "What?" like a duck quacking.

Camille was puzzled. "You know. Last night. How did it go?"

Richard felt himself blushing full scarlet. "What on earth are you talking about?"

"Going through the chemicals we found in Dominic's house," Camille said, looking at Richard's red face and neck. "What are *you* talking about?"

Richard pulled his hankie and mopped his forehead as he went over to his desk. "Sorry. It's this stupid weather. Just a hot flush."

"Then take your jacket off!"

Richard wondered if Camille was about to spill the beans to Fidel about his recent fainting fit, but, looking into Camille's eyes, he saw only compassion there. Even kindness. This only proved to Richard's mind that Camille was about to set him up for a bit of public teasing, so he quickly moved the conversation on by pretending to sort through his notes.

"Well, in answer to your question, Camille, there's no doubt that Dominic has all the ingredients to make any amount of GHB — and the knowledge, frankly, because I'm sure he was lying when he said he hadn't heard of it — but what I can't fathom is how he'd have administered it. Because you're right, he's able to have made the drug — and he's even possibly got a motive seeing as Aslan recently sacked him. After all, Dominic's stayed on as The Retreat's handyman, which is odd. Don't you think? So maybe he only stayed on so he could plan the murder of the man who sacked him? But even if that was so, our killer has to have been inside the murder room with Aslan — which we know Dominic wasn't — so he can't be our killer."

Richard was about to announce that they should switch their attention back to Ben Jenkins when he noticed Fidel deep in thought.

"What's that, Fidel?" Richard asked. "Have you got something?"

Fidel looked a little surprised at being called out. He took a moment before answering.

"Well, sir, it's something of a long shot, I'd rather not say."

"Don't worry, speak up. As long as the killer's still on the loose, there's no such thing as a stupid idea."

"Okay, sir, well, the thing is — I was wondering — you know, what if Dominic hypnotised Julia to commit the murder?"

Richard looked at Fidel. "No, I take that back. There is such a thing as a stupid idea."

"No — I know, sir," Fidel said, paddling fast, "but the thing is, I think there's a way he could have done it."

Richard looked at just how eager Fidel was and sighed.

"Very well," Richard said. "But only because it will take considerably less time listening to your idea than it otherwise would trying to stop you from telling me it."

"Thank you, sir," Fidel said. "So here's what I was thinking. Well, we already know how Julia drank the drugged tea along with everyone else."

"That's right."

"And we know that Dominic's a hypnotherapist who's been dating Julia."

"Also true."

266

"So how about a few days before the murder, Dominic puts Julia into a trance — like we saw him do with her when she was in the cells — and then he implants some kind of trigger-word? You know, and tells her that when she hears the trigger-word, she has to get a knife from behind a pillar in the corner of the room and kill Aslan Kennedy. Then, on the day of the murder, Dominic creeps up to the Meditation Space — unseen from the main hotel, say — and says the trigger-word through the paper walls . . . and Julia hears it and kills Aslan — although, now I'm saying it out loud, I can hear how stupid this sounds."

"Yes it is," Richard agreed, "but let's not let that hold us back, shall we? Instead, let's imagine you're right: Dominic waits until everyone's lying down, he creeps up to the Meditation Space unseen, and then he says the magic trigger-word, at which point . . . what are we saying? Julia heard it even though she was wearing headphones at the time? Or, I know! Maybe Dominic broadcast this trigger word on the spare WiFi channel we know he freed up a couple of days before the murder? And he somehow made sure that only Julia's headphones were tuned to the WiFi channel that was playing the recording of him saying the trigger-word over and over. Maybe that's how it was done?"

Fidel didn't dare say anything.

"But let's say Julia somehow hears this trigger-word. Are we then saying she gets up — now hypnotised — and goes to the corner of the room where she picks up a carving knife with her wrong hand — her right hand. But never mind, she's got the knife, she's improbably

267

holding it in her weaker hand, but now — through the power of hypnosis alone — she then strikes down into Aslan's neck twice, and into his shoulder and back three more times?"

Richard let this unlikely scenario hang in the air a moment.

"So thank you, Fidel, for your theory, but — just for the record — no one was hypnotised into killing Aslan Kennedy. And nor could Dominic be our killer, either. He may be involved — somehow — I don't deny it. Maybe because he inadvertently supplied the GHB — or maybe he's in cahoots with the killer — but the only person who could possibly have wielded that knife has to have been one of the people who was locked inside the room with Aslan! Okay?

"And on that subject," Richard continued, "it's Ben Jenkins who's now disappeared. Ben Jenkins who shared a prison cell with Aslan all those years ago. Can we at least agree that he's currently our prime suspect? In which case, we've got to find him before he gets off the island."

And by that afternoon, that's exactly what they did.

Dwayne found Ben Jenkins.

CHAPTER
TWELVE

It turned out that Ben had checked into one of the less reputable hostels down on Rue Cassini Beach — a place that didn't require a passport to get a room — and all had gone well for him until he'd tried to get a taxi to the Portuguese Consulate from a man who owed Dwayne a favour. The taxi driver had taken Ben's money, phoned Dwayne to find out where he was, and then driven Ben straight to Dwayne.

Ben had been none too happy to discover he'd just been stitched up by a taxi driver, and there'd been a moment when he'd maybe thought about making a run for it, but Dwayne and the taxi driver had dealt with people like Ben their whole lives, and — at the last moment — Ben had realised that the game was up. He wasn't going anywhere, so he allowed Dwayne to gather up his luggage and bring him into the station to "help the police with their inquiries".

After all, as Dwayne pointed out to him, the alternative was that he'd arrest him on the charge of murdering Aslan Kennedy.

Now, Dwayne dumped Ben's canvas bag onto the floor of the police station before yanking Ben over to

Richard's desk where Fidel had already lined up a chair for the witness.

"Here he is, Chief," Dwayne said as Richard looked up from his work.

"Thank you, Dwayne," Richard said. "Great work."

Dwayne beamed from ear to ear, but Richard was already taking in Ben and noticing how his hail-fellow-well-met bonhomie had vanished entirely.

"Fidel, lock the doors," Richard said. "I don't want Mr Jenkins bolting a second time."

Ben looked at Richard, glowering, and Richard stared back at him with exactly the sort of superiority that he knew would needle him further. Now for the olive branch.

"And Camille, come and join us, if you would."

"Of course." Camille brought over a little chair and set it up to the side of Richard's desk.

Richard surveyed his domain. Fidel had closed and locked the main doors and returned to his desk, Dwayne had already started rummaging through Ben's luggage looking for evidence — and Camille was sitting demurely on a chair to the side of his desk. Good. Richard took out the silver retractor pencil from his inside jacket pocket, clicked it once to get the lead out and put it gently down on his desk, ready to take notes.

First of all, Richard asked about Ben's background and his time in Brixton Prison. Ben didn't really want to talk about it, but Richard wasn't really that interested in being polite.

"Look," Ben eventually admitted, "that was back then, okay? Back when I had a terrible temper. I was

270

angry a lot of the time. But going to prison for what I'd done? That was the wake-up call for me, and I realised I had to change. I had to find another way. And that's when I got lucky. That first year I was in Brixton, I was made to share cells with a guy who'd been a conman."

"David Kennedy," Richard said.

"Yeah, and I'd expected him to be a bit of a geezer, but he wasn't anything like that. He'd already been inside a few years, and he was pretty quiet. But, when he looked at you, it was like he knew what you were thinking. And he spent all his spare time reading self-help books from the prison library. And religious books, too. In the year I was locked up with him, I saw him read the Bible, the Qu'ran, and the Mahabharata. All from cover to cover."

"You sound like you liked him," Camille said.

"Like him? He's the reason why I'm here today. It was him who taught me I had to accept responsibility for what I'd done. And he showed me how he was trying to retrain his brain. To reject his need for money. He said he had to find a different set of values." Ben shifted his weight in his seat, a little uncomfortably, but he made himself carry on. "If you must know, I found David one of the most inspiring guys I'd ever met. And I count that year I spent locked up with him in a cell as one of the most important in my life."

Richard flashed a quick glance over Ben's shoulder and caught Dwayne and Fidel's eyes. Dwayne shrugged, summing up the feelings of all of them. This wasn't quite what they'd expected Ben to say about his time in prison with David Kennedy.

271

Ben continued his story.

"By the end of the year, we both knew David would make parole and we had to say our goodbyes. That wasn't a good day. He'd become so important to me, and I knew I'd be saying goodbye to him forever. You see, David and I had decided we had to cut all ties with our past lives if we were ever going to make a fresh start. So I knew that once he'd gone, he wouldn't try to contact me, and once I got out — a few years later — I never tried to contact him. But then, I wanted to make damned sure it would be hard for me to keep up with my old life. That's why I moved abroad.

"I'd been a plumber before I got sent down and I kind of went to Portugal on a whim. It was a hot climate, it was popular with Brits buying up holiday properties on the coast, and I had this idea that if everyone needs a plumber — and they do — then a load of Brits in a foreign country would probably want a British plumber. I wasn't wrong. It was like a gold rush back then. Portugal couldn't build villas fast enough, and it was boom times for me. Within a couple of years, I'd got enough cash set aside to buy a rental property for myself. Within a few years, I had a few more.

"Since then, I've done pretty well for myself, as I'm sure you've been able to find out for yourself. But you have to believe me. The reason I got my life together — the reason I've done so well since — is all thanks to that year I spent sharing a cell with David Kennedy. That man changed my life."

Ben had come to the end of his story and Richard considered him a moment before continuing. He was a little put out by how in control Ben seemed. He was quite obviously vexed at being interviewed, but Richard felt he couldn't discern any of the fear he'd seen in Ben's eyes when they'd been in The Retreat's kitchen. Why wasn't he worried any more? Was it the fact that he was now able to tell the police the truth? Or was there some other reason why Ben was no longer worried about being a suspect?

"Thank you for that," Camille said, easily slipping into her assigned role. "Then can you tell us how you ended up coming to Saint-Marie, please?"

"And perhaps you can tell us," Richard said, placing his palms down on his desktop, "why you've just spent the last twenty-four hours on the run?"

Ben looked back from Camille to Richard, and sighed, but — again — Richard didn't pick up any of Ben's previous indecision.

"Look, you've got me wrong. I wasn't on the run, but I was evading you."

"And why was that?" Camille asked, as though Ben was a good friend who'd maybe made a choice in life that she didn't yet understand.

Ben gave his answer to Richard. "Because I tried to stay strong after Aslan was killed. I tried to believe you wouldn't come after me. But then there was that moment in the kitchen when I was eating an apple and I knew you'd guessed I was worried. Worried as hell. And then, the day after, you searched my room. It was like you were closing in. And then I was upstairs and I

273

saw you both downstairs, and I heard you say you reckoned I was your prime suspect."

Richard said, "It was you who was upstairs eavesdropping on us at the hotel, was it?"

"That's right." Ben turned to Camille. "And I just knew I had to get away, I had to get my head together. Work out what my options were."

"You knew how it would look, you trying to get away?"

"I knew how I already looked to you. What difference did it make?"

"Then can I ask," Richard said wearily, to make it sound like the question wasn't that important, "what do you know about the notebook that had all your names written out for the Sunrise Healing where Aslan was killed?"

Ben cocked his head, puzzled by the line of questioning. "How do you mean?"

"For example," Richard explained, "was it you who removed it from the board after Aslan was killed?"

Ben was puzzled. "No. Has it been removed?"

Richard looked over at Dwayne, who knew what his silence was asking of him.

"I've been through Mr Jenkins's luggage, sir, and there's no reporter's notebook here at all. Or anything incriminating as far as I can see."

With a quick nod of thanks, Richard turned back to Ben, but now it was Ben's turn to ask a question.

"Why are you interested in the notebook? It was just a list of our names. You know, the people who'd been chosen for the Sunrise Session the next day."

274

Richard decided to change the subject.

"Would it surprise you," he said, "if I told you that you were the only person in the murder room who hadn't lost money to Aslan Kennedy in his Ponzi scam twenty years ago?"

Ben was stunned. "What?"

Richard held Ben's gaze. "Of the five people who were locked in the murder room with Aslan Kennedy, you're the only person who he never stole any money from."

Ben's mouth opened to say something, but then it closed again. He was speechless.

"You see," Camille said, "Aslan had been inviting some of the people he'd stolen from in the past out here on all-expenses-paid holidays — as his way of making amends — but this was the first time he'd allowed four of them to be at The Retreat all at the same time."

"And we want to know how you came to be locked up with them all in the murder room when Aslan was killed," Richard finished.

Ben licked his lips. "I have no idea. You have to believe me. You see, this is exactly what I knew would happen. You don't believe me."

Richard looked at Ben and decided it was time to step up a gear.

"Damned right we don't," he said. "So, seeing as Aslan didn't invite you out here, can you even begin to explain how you ended up on the other side of the world in a paper and wood house at the precise moment that your ex-cellmate was brutally slain?"

Ben was taken aback. "How do you mean?"

"We know Aslan didn't invite you, so what are you doing here?"

Ben looked hurt, and thought for a moment. He then plucked at the light pink shirt he was wearing to let some air circulate, the heat clearly prickling his skin underneath — and Richard noticed beads of sweat on his forehead. Good. He was feeling the heat, literally as well as figuratively.

"Alright," Ben eventually said, "but what I'm about to say is going to sound like it's incriminating me. That's why I wanted to see my consul. I wanted to give my statement direct to someone who wasn't going to misrepresent my words."

"You think we'd frame you?" Richard said with a touch of needle.

"I don't trust the justice system in Europe. I definitely don't trust the justice system in the Caribbean."

Richard saw Camille, Dwayne and Fidel bristle at this, but he was quick to hold up a finger to silence his colleagues before they could speak. Instead, he smiled for Ben's benefit. The smile was entirely mirthless.

"Go on."

Ben shifted his weight again, still not happy. "Have you got a glass of water?"

"Of course," Richard said.

As Fidel brought over a glass of ice-cold water, Ben spoke of his life since leaving jail. How hard it was to put the past behind him; but how rewarding it was, too, even though he knew that no matter how hard he tried, he'd never really escape his past. And that's what had happened.

"About a year ago, I was contacted by this ex-con I'd known in Brixton. A guy I only ever knew as Ratty. He was called Ratty because that's what he was like. A rat. Anyway, I knew he'd got out soon after me and he'd tracked me down all these years later — god knows how — but he said he'd heard I was now making a mint and would I be interested in employing him for his financial services. That's what he called them. But when he got into the nitty-gritty, all I could tell was it involved moving money in and out of off-shore accounts faster than the authorities would be able to keep up with it, it seemed dodgy as hell. No better than money laundering."

"So what did you do?"

"I told Ratty to get lost. And you can check my bank accounts — my company accounts. I've been on the straight and narrow ever since I got out of jail. I can account for every cent I've earned, and every cent I've paid in tax."

Camille smiled. "Don't worry. We checked you out."

"Thank you," Ben said, but a little warily. "Anyway, so I was telling him thanks but no thanks on the financial services, but just before he hung up he said had I heard that my old mate David Kennedy was up to his old tricks?"

This got the police's attention. Even Fidel and Dwayne stopped what they were doing so they could listen in.

"I'm sorry?" Richard said.

"Ratty told me that David Kennedy had changed his name to Aslan, that he was pretending to be a Spiritual Guru out in the Caribbean and was on the con again."

The police all froze.

Eventually Richard said, "He said that, did he? That David was now called Aslan and he was conning people again?"

"That's right. Ratty said he knew the off-shore accounts David Kennedy had used back in the day, and not only were they active again, but he'd heard on the grapevine that he was up to his old tricks again."

"Did your friend Ratty say how Aslan was conning people?" Camille asked.

"No. And I didn't ask. He had to be lying. That's what I told myself. But the thing is, I couldn't get it out of my mind. What if I was wrong? What if David had really gone back to his old ways? So I went to the internet to see if I could find anyone called Aslan working as a guru in the Caribbean, and there he was. At first I didn't see how it could be David. He looked nothing like how I remembered him. But if I imagined David fifteen-odd years older, much more tanned, having lost a lot of weight — his hair having gone completely white, and also having grown a long white beard . . . well, then maybe it was him. But I'm telling you, I wasn't sure.

"But the website had an email address, so I sent him an email — you, know, just saying hello from an old friend — and he replied within about a minute saying he didn't know who I was and telling me not to make contact again. I'll be honest. I was shocked. David and me were like that in prison" — here, Ben held up his hand and crossed over his first and second fingers — "so I sent another email a few minutes later saying that it was me in no uncertain terms, only this time the email I sent bounced back saying 'address unknown' — or whatever that message is you get when you get the wrong email address."

"When was this?" Richard asked.

"A couple of months back. Maybe three."

"You were in touch with Aslan three months ago?" Richard asked, to be clear.

Ben didn't know why Richard was so interested. "Yeah. Something like that."

"But we've been through Aslan's emails on his computer," Camille said. "We didn't find any emails from you."

Ben was surprised. "Maybe he deleted them. I sent them."

"Are you sure?"

"Yeah," Ben said fishing out his smartphone. "I should still have the emails on my phone. Hold on, let me do a search."

As Ben was saying this, he got up his email programme and typed into the search field. After a few moments, he handed his phone over to Richard.

Richard looked down and saw the email thread between Ben and Aslan, and it was just as Ben had said. The first message was sent from Ben's Portuguese email address at 11.05am and it said:

Hey David, is this you?
Hope life's treating you well after Brixton.

Yours
Ben Jenkins

At 11.08, Aslan had replied:

Don't contact me again under any circumstances.
I have left the past behind.

Then, at 11.10am, Ben had replied:

What?! It's Ben Jenkins here, C3397KB.
I've been speaking to Ratty. What's going on?

Richard looked up briefly from the smartphone screen. "C3397KB?"

"It's my prison number," he said, "as David knows well."

Richard looked down at the screen one more time to see that although Ben had sent the message at 11.10am, the reply had come back from the server the very same minute saying:

Mail Delivery Subsystem <*mailer-daemon@theretreat-saintmarie.com*>
This is an automatically generated Delivery Status Notification
Delivery to the following recipient failed permanently:
aslan@theretreatsaintmarie.com
Technical details of permanent failure:
PERM–FAILURE: SMTP Error (State 12): 552.5.2.2

Richard could see that Ben had re-sent his follow-up email again a few minutes later — and again a few minutes after that — and both times the message was immediately bounced back as being undeliverable.

Richard guessed what must have happened. Immediately after the first email had arrived, Aslan had added Ben's email address to his spam list and, in effect, instructed his email programme to send back a "not known at this address" email when he then got any further emails from Ben.

Richard called over to Fidel and asked him to get back in touch with Aslan's email service provider. Now they had a specific email exchange to get them to look for, there was a better chance they'd agree to do it.

"You don't believe me," Ben said.

"As it happens, I do," Richard replied. "But I'm interested in gathering evidence that will stand up in court. And if your email provider has the exact same message on its servers, then that will prove this is a real email trail."

Richard had difficulty keeping the excitement out of his voice as he said this, because there was another reason why Richard wanted Ben's email trail categorically proven and that's because he'd noticed that the whole email exchange had happened at least three weeks before Saskia, Paul and Ann had received their invites to take part in a free holiday at The Retreat. Finally — for the first time — here was definitive proof that at least one person inside the Meditation Space when Aslan was killed not only knew Aslan's real identity, but had also been in touch with

Aslan *before* he'd invited the Ponzi victims to the Caribbean.

Logically, then, Richard found himself thinking, Ben was still their prime suspect. Not that Ben needed to know this. To Ben, Richard tried to sound disinterested as he asked, "So your old mate David was shunning you now that he was going around the place saying he was Aslan. How did that make you feel?"

"It's not how you treat an old cellmate," Ben said. "I was angry. But I tried to put it to one side. If David wanted to be like that, then it was none of my business. For the next month or so, it would maybe pop into my head from time to time that he'd turned his back on me, but I tried to forget about it. Then, one day I was planning a holiday for myself, but you know what it's like. When you already live in a holiday destination, it's kind of hard to know where to go. But a mate had suggested I go to a health farm and that's when it occurred to me. I could come to The Retreat. Because Aslan might be able to fob me off with an email, but it would be harder to do it if we were face to face.

"And to be honest, I also wanted to see him because I just couldn't believe he was on the con. Honestly, this was the guy who'd turned my life around; I couldn't square that man with the one who'd sent me the email. So I booked a two-week holiday at The Retreat."

"Did you have any further communication with Aslan — or David — following that first round of emails?" Richard asked.

"No way. I have my pride. I just wanted to see his face when he saw me."

282

"And how was it when that happened?"

Ben paused a moment and finished his glass of water. He then looked at the police, briefly composing his thoughts.

"Okay, so I checked in. Didn't see him. Went to my room. Still didn't see him. And then when I went down to the beach, that's when it happened. He was coming up the path — dressed in this long white Indian-style top and what looked like pyjamas. And when he saw me, you should have seen his face. Total shock. It was kind of obvious he wouldn't be able to dodge me now. But to his credit, he came up to me, didn't say a word, just gave me a big hug. I reckoned it was his way of saying sorry.

"Anyway, within a few minutes, he'd told me everything. How he'd turned his life around. How he'd come out to the Caribbean and finally found the peace we'd both talked about when we were in prison together. But I had to know if what I'd heard was true and I told him outright that there wasn't any point lying to me, I'd heard the whole place was a con. He tried to deny it at first, but the thing is, I knew some of the details of the bank accounts in the Caribbean. How even our old mate Ratty knew what he was up to. And the more I told him what I knew, the more I wanted him to tell me I was talking rubbish. That it was all lies. But when I'd finished speaking, he looked at me and I could tell he was weighing up if he could lie to me like he'd lied to everyone else. He decided to tell me the truth."

"And what did he say?" Camille asked.

"That what I'd said was true," Ben said. "That he was back on the con."

Richard and Camille shared a sharp glance.

"When did he tell you this?"

"That first day I came out here."

"And four days later he was dead," Camille said.

"Nothing to do with me," Ben said, holding up his hands.

"Where did you have this conversation?" Richard asked.

"I'm sorry?" Ben didn't understand.

"Is there any chance your conversation with Aslan where he admitted he was on the con again was overheard by anyone else?"

"I don't know. We were just in the garden. You know, walking."

"Then please, think very carefully. Do you remember seeing any of Paul or Ann Sellars — or Saskia Filbee — in the vicinity — or walking past — while you were having this conversation with Aslan?"

Ben thought long and hard before answering. "I'm sorry. I've no idea. I didn't really know what any of those people looked like yet. Not until a few days later when we all went to the Sunrise Healing."

"But tell me — now you've told us this — was it you who was in Aslan's office arguing with him the night before he was killed? Telling him you wouldn't let him get away with it?" Richard asked.

Ben shook his head. "No way. I don't know who that was, but it wasn't me."

"And you expect us to believe that?"

284

Ben sat forward in his chair, clearly fed up with the whole process.

"To be honest, I don't care any more what you believe, all I know is I've now told you everything. The whole truth and nothing but the truth."

Fidel called over from his desk, indicating Aslan's laptop as it sat open on the desk in front of him. "Sir, you should know, I've been onto Aslan Kennedy's email provider. They've agreed to look for this one email exchange, but I've also been looking through Aslan's preferences for his email programme and Mr Jenkins's email address is indeed on his spam list. Any emails that Mr Jenkins sends to Aslan Kennedy are automatically bounced back, just like Mr Jenkins is saying."

"You see," Ben said, turning back to Camille and Richard. "David Kennedy might have changed his name to Aslan, but he's still the same crook he's always been. He admitted as much to me himself."

Richard and Camille looked at each other.

If Aslan had started conning people again, this changed everything, didn't it? But what was the con this time?

The office phone rang, and Dwayne ambled over to answer it. After a few moments, he turned back to his boss and said, "Chief, it's Dominic De Vere up at The Retreat. He says he's found the missing notebook."

CHAPTER
THIRTEEN

"I was just walking past," Dominic said to Richard as he stood in the main hallway of The Retreat, "and then I realised. It was back."

Dominic pointed at the noticeboard and Richard could see that what he was saying was true. There was indeed an old spiral-bound reporter's notebook hanging off the old nail. What's more, the notebook was turned over to the Sunrise Healing session that had been arranged for the day that Aslan was killed. But what was it doing there? Who'd put it back? Why had it suddenly reappeared?

"And I don't understand," Dominic said. "Because this is the list for the Sunrise Healing the day that Aslan died. But the five names chosen here aren't any of the people who went into the Meditation Space with him."

Richard could see that Dominic was right. None of Julia, Saskia, Paul, Ann or Ben's names were on the list. These were five completely different names.

Richard had a good idea how this might have happened, but he wasn't saying for the moment. Instead, he put on a pair of evidence gloves to bag the notebook, and, as he did this, he tried to work out how best to proceed. First Ben had been missing. Then they found him. Then Ben had told them that Aslan had admitted that he was back on the con again. And now a crucial piece of evidence had suddenly turned up — but with a different list of names to those that had attended when Aslan was killed.

On the way back to the police station with the notebook, Richard got Camille to stop off at a local general stores where he bought a children's silvered helium balloon with the words "4 TODAY" on its outside.

Richard knew how odd it must have looked, a middle-aged man in a suit buying a helium balloon, but he wasn't saying. And he knew how intriguing this must have been for Camille — but seeing as she already knew that Richard was trying to tantalise her, she refused to mention the balloon.

Which suited Richard just fine.

So, Detective Inspector and Detective Sergeant drove all the way back to the police station in silence with a silver helium balloon bobbing on its string in between them both.

Camille lasted right up to the moment that they started walking up the steps to the station.

"Alright!" she finally said, utterly exasperated. "I have to know. Why have you got a kid's balloon?"

Richard looked at the balloon, as though he was just as surprised as Camille to find that he was holding it. "What? This?"

"Yes. The helium balloon."

"Well, that's obvious, Camille. We're going to use it to reveal the identity of our killer," Richard said, and continued on and into the station.

Once inside, Richard found Fidel with all of Aslan's financial papers spread out.

"Honestly, sir," Fidel said before he'd realised that his boss was holding a balloon. "I'm going through Aslan's bank accounts for the hundredth time and he only gets that $1,000 a month from the business — most of which goes to an orphanage at the end of each month. And as for the hotel, I've never been able to identify any kind of financial wrongdoing there, either. It does well, but every cent seems to be accounted for if you ask me."

"Then what about Ben Jenkins's service provider?" Richard asked. "Have they been able to confirm if the email correspondence Ben showed us between him and Aslan was real?"

"Sure have, Chief," Dwayne said from his desk. "And they confirmed that Ben sent five emails to Aslan Kennedy's account three months ago. Just like he said."

"Which is interesting," Richard said as he went over to his desk and tied the balloon to the back of his chair. "Because that suggests that Ben's telling us the truth. In which case, maybe Aslan's back on the con again. But if he is, then how come we can't find any evidence?"

Richard looked at his team, knowing how desperate they were to ask about the silver balloon that was now bobbing on its string just behind his right shoulder.

"Um, Chief —" Dwayne eventually asked.

"He's going to use it to reveal the killer," Camille said, trying to spare them Richard's grandstanding.

"And that's where you're wrong, Camille," Richard said, delighted to have a chance for some grandstanding. "Because the children's balloon will reveal our killer's identity, but we're also going to need the toner cartridge from our photocopier and the office's stun gun."

Richard was delighted with the looks of surprise on his team's face.

"So go on, Dwayne. If you would, could you get the stun gun from the office safe? Camille, could you get the toner cartridge from the photocopier?"

Still no one moved. But that was because they were still trying to process the picture they now had of their uptight boss in a woollen suit asking for a stun gun while he stood next to a jolly helium balloon that said "4 TODAY" on it.

"Sorry? Am I invisible?" Richard said, having more fun than he'd had in months. "Or perhaps you've all suddenly gone deaf? Camille: toner cartridge, please. Dwayne: the stun gun. Thank you!"

Putting on his evidence gloves again, Richard got out the reporter's notebook from the cellophane evidence bag. It was still turned to the list of names that had been written out for the Sunrise Healing session on the day Aslan was killed. And, as Dominic had pointed out, there was no getting away from it: none of the names that were there had been in the Meditation Space when Aslan was killed. So what had happened that meant that this group of people hadn't attended and an entirely different group had instead?

As Richard got the notebook nice and straight on his desk, he took a moment to marvel at how decisive he'd become since he'd finally managed to get rid of his lizard. There was no doubt about it in Richard's mind. His lizard had been the albatross around his neck.

Camille managed to clunk the toner cartridge out of the photocopier and bring it over, and Richard decided it was time to explain what he was up to.

"Right, then, Camille. It's clear from the notebook here that Aslan wrote out a list for the Sunrise Healing the day before he died, all as normal. This list here is definitely his handwriting; all of the other pages in the notebook confirm that. But I think the killer was waiting nearby, and the moment that Aslan hung the notebook back up on its nail, the killer stepped in, turned the list over to a fresh page and wrote out a new list of names — the list of people who ended up going to the Sunrise Healing the next day."

"A list that's now missing," Camille said.

"Agreed," Richard said. "Which suggests that after the murder, the killer came back to the notebook and tore off the incriminating page with their handwriting on, and then turned the page back to reveal Aslan's original list."

Fidel interrupted, excited, "Then how about they went down to the cellar and burnt the incriminating page of names — in the killer's handwriting — in the hotel furnace?"

"My thinking exactly!" Richard said. "Which is why you found a few remnants of burnt paper in the furnace."

290

"But sir," Fidel continued, "if the killer tore off the one incriminating page with their handwriting on, why did they then have to remove the rest of the notebook?"

"Well, I'd say that was obvious, Fidel. The page that Aslan wrote on, as we can see here" — Richard indicated the notebook on his desk — "quite clearly shows him choosing a completely different set of guests for that day. But I bet the next page still carries the indentations from the killer's list of names that was on the page after it. And I want to reveal those indentations."

"Using a helium balloon," Dwayne said, unable to keep a sceptical tone out of his voice as he entered the room holding a small silver flight-case, "some photocopier toner and a stun gun."

Richard smiled. "Indeed."

He then looked at his team and knew it was time to explain.

"So my theory is that the killer flipped over to a fresh page to write the incriminating list of names out — and, in doing so, the pen he or she was writing with would have made indentations on the page underneath Aslan's original list."

"That makes sense," Dwayne said, "but it was more the balloon I wanted to know about."

"All things come to those who wait," Richard said. "First, can you get out the stun gun?"

Dwayne opened the latches on the flight-case and lifted the lid, revealing a grey foam interior that housed a stun gun. The weapon itself was like something out of a sci-fi movie: a grey plastic box about the size of a chunky mobile phone with two metal prongs sticking out of it. It looked both humdrum and entirely scary. Especially when Dwayne turned it on and electricity arced between the two prongs with a nasty crackling sound.

"This thing is evil," Dwayne said, summing up the feelings of them all.

"Have you ever had recourse to use it?" Richard asked.

"No way. This is not how we roll on Saint-Marie."

Richard looked at Dwayne and knew it was true. There was no way any of his team would ever use such an instrument on another human being.

"Right," Richard said. "So let's find out who wrote out the missing list."

Richard pulled his penknife from his pocket, carefully opened it, turned, and stabbed the balloon with it. There was a wet pop as the blade went in, and then Richard held the silvered balloon in his hand as it deflated.

"Have any of you ever wondered what they make these helium balloons out of?"

Richard looked at his team, but they had the good sense to stay quiet.

"Because they're not rubber like a normal balloon. And although it looks like silver foil, it isn't metal, either, is it?" Again a dramatic pause that his team were canny enough not to prolong by asking any questions. "Well, silver balloons like this are made out of a substance called Mylar, which is a metallised polythene. And as such it's perfect — when used alongside a stun gun and some photocopier toner — for creating an electrostatic detection device, or EDD for short."

Fishing out a pair of scissors from his desk tidy, Richard started to cut a square from the balloon that was quite a bit larger than the reporter's notebook.

"And, as I'm sure you all know, electrostatic detection devices are perfect for picking up even the faintest of indentations in paper. So, if the killer flipped over to a fresh page to write out a different list of names — as I'm sure must have happened — then whatever pen he or she used will have left indentations on the page underneath."

Richard indicated the blank page following the list of names that Aslan had written out and briefly paused for his team to ask any follow-up questions. A little disappointed that there weren't any, he continued, "So what you do is you place a square of Mylar polythene over the paper that you think has got indentations on it . . . just so." Richard placed the square of silver over the blank page. "You then turn the stun gun on." Richard picked up the stun gun and pressed the trigger mechanism, electricity starting to arc between the two metal nodes. "You then waft the stun gun over the Mylar, making sure the charge goes down into it."

Richard put the nodes up close to the silvered square, at which point the electricity stopped arcing in between the nodes and started to stab down into the plastic.

As Richard moved the miniature lightning back and forth across the silver square of child's balloon, he carried on explaining. "The objective is to produce an evenly distributed electrostatic charge across the surface of the Mylar. Because once the Mylar's been suitably charged, the most incredible thing happens . . . yes, that should be enough."

Richard turned the stun gun off and carefully placed it to one side.

There was no visible difference to the silvered square of Mylar.

"Sir," Fidel asked, "what happens?"

"Everything, Fidel, because the surface of the Mylar is now differentially charged depending upon whether or not an indentation was underneath it or not," Richard said, really selling the magic of the process.

His team were nonplussed, as he knew they'd be.

"Which is why we need the photocopier toner."

Richard got the ancient black toner caddy and shook it. As was usual, a fine dusting of black toner powder fell out of it. Richard had been trying to get the caddy replaced for months, but now he was glad that it was so decrepit.

"Watch this," he said as he held the toner cartridge a foot or so above the clear silver square. "Because every grain of toner powder is negatively charged. And the principle of how a photocopier gets its ink to stick to paper is the same that we're now going to use on the Mylar because — remember — it's now positively charged where there aren't any indentations underneath and negatively charged where there are."

Richard started to shake the toner cartridge from side to side and toner powder began to waft down onto the silver square of Mylar. And, to his team's amazement, the black powder seemed to form into

294

certain curls and swirls on the silver — and within ten seconds it was possible to see that the inky powder had in fact now "stuck" to the silver in such a way that words could be seen. The team had to squint a bit to make out what was written, but there was no doubt about it, the toner had revealed the indentations from the missing page that had been removed and destroyed.

The ink on the silver square read:

You are invited to the Sunrise Healing!

Julia Higgins
Saskia Filbee
Paul Sellars
Ann Sellars
Ben Jenkins

7am, Morning swim and stretching on the beach.
8am, Sunrise Healing in the Meditation Space

Attendance is free and highly recommended!
Aslan

This was a facsimile of the incriminating page, and it was obviously not Aslan's handwriting, so that begged the question: whose handwriting was it?

Richard realised first.

"Wait!" he said to his team as he went over to Camille's desk and started looking for the witness statements among the mess of files.

"What are you looking for?" she asked.

"Hold on," he said, having difficulty keeping his irritation in check. But now was not the time to lecture Camille on her "clear desk" policy, and instead he grabbed up the witness statement he was looking for.

He returned to his desk with the page of handwriting and put it down next to the silver square so they could compare the two samples.

And now it was time for Richard's team to be stunned.

They were looking at Julia Higgins's witness statement — and the incriminating list of names was the exact same handwriting.

It had been Julia who'd replaced Aslan's list with a new set of names.

"I don't believe it," Richard said, amazed.

Had Julia been playing him from the start? After all, even Paul Sellars had worked out that Julia was their most likely killer. She'd been at The Retreat the longest time: six months. Who else of the suspects had a better opportunity to discover Aslan's real identity and then to get him to invite the other Ponzi victims out to The Retreat at the same time?

But how did she work it out?

With a sudden flash of understanding, Richard remembered that Julia's job at The Retreat was to help for a few hours a day in the office. What if she'd been at Aslan's computer when Ben Jenkins's email came in? It clearly called Aslan "David" and referred to Brixton Prison. It would have been entirely natural for Julia to ask Aslan what on earth the email meant, and either Aslan told her the truth there and then or she was able to work out the truth on her own later on.

Richard continued to try and step through the logic of what Julia would have done next, because — now she knew that Aslan was in fact the David Kennedy who'd caused her father's death — she must have wondered how on earth she ended up being offered a free holiday in the Caribbean by the man responsible.

She'd have asked Aslan, wouldn't she? And he'd have had to explain that the "You Have Won a Prize" competitions were his way of giving something back to those he'd stolen from in the past. God knows how Julia took this news, but she obviously didn't let her real feelings show, because Aslan continued to employ her at The Retreat.

Richard banged the palm of his hand down on his desk at his own stupidity. He'd never really considered what it must have been like growing up without a dad because he'd committed suicide. The shame Julia and her mum must have felt. And, as Julia had been forced to admit — and the Met Police files confirmed — Julia's dad had lost everything including his house before he took his own life. So not only had Aslan taken Julia's dad from her, he'd also taken all of his money and the house they lived in.

And now she'd discovered she was working for the man who'd destroyed her family?

It was clear that Julia had made a simple decision.

Aslan had to die.

And with that realisation, Richard finally understood why the murder had to be carried out in front of a load of potential witnesses.

After all, if Aslan had been still living in the UK, Julia would have been able to make it look as though she was miles away at the time of the murder. But on a small island like Saint-Marie, even if she made it look as though she'd been on the other side of the island when Aslan was killed, the fact that she had a motive at all would be suspicion enough. And, seeing as she *was* the killer, the police would no doubt be able to break her alibi.

So, if you're the only person on a tropical island with a motive to kill someone, what's the best way of using this fact to your advantage? Richard realised a daring and — though he had to admit it to himself — quite brilliant plan was born.

Julia decided that she would try and hide herself in plain view.

Because there's no way a rational killer would lock herself inside a room with the victim, that's precisely what she'd do. And because no killer would ever let herself be found standing over the corpse holding the murder weapon, that's also what she'd do. But she'd stage the scene so everything would make it look like she was being just as manipulated by a shadowy killer in the background as everyone else.

Thinking with hot shame back to his night-time walk with Julia, Richard now realised that she'd orchestrated the whole tantalising encounter so she could ask him if she could go back to the UK. And knowing how seductive Julia had been, Richard knew that if she had decided to work her charms on Aslan, she'd have been able to convince him that it was okay to start inviting other Ponzi victims out to the Caribbean again, and — not only that — maybe he should invite a few at a time, rather than the usual one?

So, that's how Paul, Ann and Saskia all ended up at The Retreat at the same time. Julia got Aslan to invite them out.

Then what about Ben Jenkins, Richard found himself thinking. How did he get there? Well, what was it Ben had told them? He'd booked his holiday at The Retreat entirely normally. Well, Julia already knew all about Ben from the email she'd intercepted and which had started her off on her journey of discovery. What's more, she knew from the email that Ben had known Aslan when he'd been in Brixton Prison. If what Julia wanted to do was fill a room full of people all of whom had nefarious connections with Aslan's past, what better way than to use Ben's holiday at The Retreat as the anchor that she'd tie the rest of her plans to?

So, with Ben's dates at The Retreat fixed, Julia got Aslan to invite Paul and Ann Sellars and Saskia all out for the same time.

Finally, Richard realised that Dominic's apparent burglary was almost certainly true. Julia had been going out with Dominic for nearly six months, she could easily have found out from him what would be the best sedative to make people woozy. She could even have learnt how to make the gamma-hydroxybutyric acid herself. Or Dominic had some anyway. But either way, it was clearly how Julia got hold of a source of GHB. She stole it from her boyfriend.

Then all Julia had to do was wait until Aslan wrote up his list of names on the board and then intervene by going to the board, turning the page over, and writing out a new list of the people she wanted to be with her as her camouflage the following day.

Richard went over to the whiteboard, almost quivering with anger as he realised how the rest of the murder must have played out.

Julia must have seen Ann doing the drying the night before in the kitchen and decided that the largest carving knife she'd touched would be the perfect murder weapon. Then — either later that night, or early the next morning — she got the knife with Ann's fingerprints on, went to the Meditation Space and used drawing pins to fix it in the shadows of the eleventh pillar along.

She was ready.

Ever since his days at school, Richard had vowed he'd never allow himself to get pushed around again, but that's exactly what he'd allowed Julia to do to him. She'd pushed Aslan around; Dominic around; Ben around; the Ponzi victims around; and, finally — impossibly — she'd pushed Richard around with her string of double bluffs.

After all, murderers don't make sure they're locked in the room with the victim. Murderers don't make sure they're found standing over the body of the victim. Murderers don't premeditate a murder and then apparently botch it by screaming. Murderers don't reveal the real identity of the victim under hypnosis, especially when it reveals that they've got a motive to want the victim dead.

And — finally — left-handed murderers don't commit murder with a knife right-handed.

Except for in this case. Julia must have positioned herself to commit murder with her weaker right hand. It wouldn't have been easy, but then Richard realised — wanting to kick himself for his stupidity — in most knifings, the victim is trying to fight back. In those circumstances, it's almost impossible to strike properly with your weaker hand, but that wasn't the case here: Aslan had been sitting quite still, his eyes closed, headphones over his ears. Julia would have been able to take her time as she lined up that first right-handed blow to his neck.

And, because she was a master of manipulation, Julia no doubt only then went over to the drugged tea. She then drank a decent dose, returned to the body, transferred the knife to her left hand, and only then started screaming.

"Camille, get the jeep," Richard said darkly.

He'd allowed himself to be taken for a fool. But that was about to end. Richard was going to make the arrest himself. He was going to close the case.

But Richard was wrong. He wasn't about to make an arrest or close the case, because when they got to Julia's room, they discovered that Julia wouldn't be standing trial any time soon.

Julia Higgins was lying on her bed, stone-cold dead.

CHAPTER
FOURTEEN

When Richard and the team had got to the hotel, they'd first bumped into Dominic. He knew the room Julia was staying in and was happy to take the police there. On the way, he'd prattled on about how he'd realised how bad it had looked when the police had found his homebrew lab, so he'd decided that it was time to pack in the search for the perfect legal high. In fact, maybe it was time to move on from The Retreat altogether. After all, he couldn't be expected to be a handyman his whole life. Richard only half-listened to Dominic — although he couldn't help but note that Dominic was now the second person who'd told him he was considering returning to the UK.

As they reached Julia's room and started knocking, Richard had found himself musing that Julia was at least about to get her wish. She was going to return to the UK; but under police escort.

Then, when Julia didn't answer, it was Dominic's idea that they go in anyway. As the hotel's handyman, he had a pass key that could get him into any room, and he was happy to open the door.

And that's when they'd found Julia sprawled on her bed, her arm outstretched, a drinking glass on the floor, a clear liquid still glistening inside.

The moment that Richard realised that the woman who'd agreed to go out for a drink with him was dead, he'd shut down his emotions at the same time as his heart had swelled in panic. But — trying to remain entirely professional — he'd kept his focus on the smaller parts of the picture: no fabric or skin had got caught under the victim's fingernails. There was no sign of a forced entry to the room. The window was locked from the inside.

Richard got down on his hands and knees and tried to see what he could make of the liquid in the glass. It was entirely clear, and didn't seem to smell of anything. He dipped his little finger into the liquid and tasted it. It was tasteless as well. But it couldn't be just water. Not if it was the last thing that Julia drank before dying.

Camille came in from the bathroom.

"You should see this," she said.

Richard joined Camille in the white-tiled bathroom next door. She lifted the lid on the metal bathroom bin. There was a little brown glass bottle inside. Reaching in, Richard pulled it out and saw that it was an empty medicine bottle. He then fished out the white plastic screw-top lid that had been lying next to it in the otherwise empty bin.

He smelled both. There was no odour. And whatever liquid it had contained had been clear.

Camille had already got two see-through evidence bags ready and Richard slipped the bottle into one, and the lid into the other.

Was this what had killed Julia? Almost certainly.

Richard returned to the main room and Fidel said, "So what do you think, sir? Julia realised we were closing in on her — were about to arrest her for the murder of Aslan Kennedy — and so took her own life?"

Richard scanned the room before answering. "Could be. But if so, where's the suicide note?"

"There isn't one, sir," Fidel said. "Not that I can see."

This gave Richard pause. Suicides usually left a note behind to explain their actions. When the suicide was because of guilt — for example, because they'd killed someone else and were now wanting to end the shame of their life — there was *always* a note.

And as much as Richard was trying to keep a lid on his emotions, there was a feeling that was bubbling up inside him. Irrespective of the facts. Irrespective of the clues. He'd gone for a nocturnal walk with Julia, and although he was prepared to admit that maybe she'd been trying to manipulate him — whatever her motives — she hadn't acted like someone who was about to take her own life. In fact, as Richard ran his mind back over the short time he'd spent with her, and how uncluttered her mind had so obviously been, he realised that she wasn't someone who'd even remotely been contemplating suicide.

So: no suicide note. And no indication of a disturbed mind, either.

And there was something else. How come the notebook had reappeared just before her death? After all, Richard and his team had only arrived at Julia's room because they'd worked out that the list of names for Aslan's murder had been written out by her. And they only found the notebook because someone had put it back on its nail on the noticeboard. Was it Julia who'd put the notebook back herself before she took her own life? It was a possibility, Richard supposed, but it didn't seem very likely. There were surely more direct ways of confessing to your guilt. For example, like writing a suicide note, which Julia had so patently failed to do.

Richard went over to the window and looked out over the sparkling Caribbean sea, deep in thought — and what he kept coming back to was the fact that he only really considered that Julia was the killer because the notebook had reappeared on its nail on the noticeboard. Didn't he? And, in the excitement of working out that it was Julia who'd written out the incriminating list of names, he'd jumped to all sorts of conclusions. That Julia had the wit to plan such an involved murder as Aslan's; that she'd knife someone to death five times over, using her weaker hand.

And, as Richard's thoughts ranged over Julia's death, he allowed an ice-cold rage to clutch at his heart, because there was one thing he began to realise above all others: he was still being manipulated, wasn't he?

Manipulated by the real killer.

Julia didn't kill Aslan any more than she'd just killed herself. She was never a likely murderer. But so clever was the real mastermind behind Aslan's murder that he or she knew that all they'd have to do was return the missing notebook to its nail and the police would soon come to the conclusion that Julia was maybe Aslan's killer — and, when her body was found dead from an overdose, they'd then no doubt believe that she'd just committed suicide because of the guilt she'd felt since killing Aslan.

The more Richard considered his theory, the more he realised that he was almost certainly correct. Julia hadn't killed Aslan. One of Paul, Ann, Saskia or Ben had killed Aslan. And now they'd also killed Julia Higgins.

But of the four remaining witnesses, who was their killer?

Richard turned to his team and said, "This is a murder scene. And I don't care how you do it, but I want you to work out how Julia was killed."

Ten minutes later, Ben Jenkins, Saskia Filbee and Paul and Ann Sellars were waiting for Richard on the hotel's verandah. As Richard approached with Camille at his side, he tried to gauge the suspects' mood.

Ben was looking tanned, relaxed and wearing a Hawaiian shirt, shorts and cheap flip-flops. Saskia was looking entirely demure in a plain cream top and simple olive-green skirt, but she looked worried. Nervous, even. As for Paul, he wasn't sitting near his wife, and was instead on his own with his smartphone in his lap, his typically impeccable comb-over, polo shirt, slacks, and deck shoes all correctly in place. And that left only Ann, who had come to the interview dressed in a typically flamboyant kaftan, but Richard once again noticed how she was looking a lot more sombre than she used to. More watchful, even.

Mind you, considering the circumstances, it was perhaps understandable.

"Is it true?" Saskia asked as Richard approached.

"Is what true?" Richard dead-batted back.

"That that poor girl . . . Julia. Dominic's saying she committed suicide . . . ?"

Richard now understood why Saskia was looking so nervous. "At the moment, we're trying to establish the cause of death, but we're not ruling anything out."

Ann stood up, her hand going to her heaving breast. "You mean, it might have been murder!?"

"I think it was."

Richard was watching as carefully as he could, but all of the witnesses seemed equally shocked by this news.

Paul recovered first. "But it has to be suicide."

"And why do you say that?"

"Because it's obvious. Julia killed Aslan. Well, that's no surprise. We all saw her with the knife standing over his body. And, come on, man, she even confessed to the murder. And now, wracked with guilt —"

"She's taken an overdose of drugs," Richard finished the sentence for Paul and was pleased to see the colour drain from his face.

"You know what sort of drugs?" Paul asked after a moment.

"Not yet," Richard said. "But you're a pharmacist, Paul. What do you think it could be if the liquid that killed her was odourless, colourless and tasteless?"

Paul looked at the police like a landed fish. "You're not suggesting I had anything to do with this, are you?"

"I'm not suggesting anything, Paul. But when Aslan was killed, we know the witnesses were all drugged with gamma-hydroxybutyric acid — the very same drug you've been stealing from your pharmacy in the form of Xyrax. And now here's another drug turning up in the context of another death."

"It's a coincidence. It must be," Ben said.

"And that's where I'm pretty sure you're wrong," Richard said. "Because, in my experience, when it comes to murder, there's no such thing as coincidence."

"But it has to be a suicide," Ben said again, even more insistently.

"And what makes you say that?" Camille asked.

"Because if Julia's been murdered, then that kind of suggests that she wasn't the person who killed Aslan."

"Ah," Richard said, "I see that you now understand."

"And that means that one of us four must have killed Aslan. And has now killed Julia."

"My thoughts exactly," Richard said.

"But that's not possible," Ben said. "Because I can imagine one of us four wanting to kill Aslan. Don't get me wrong. I don't think any of us did it. But maybe I'm wrong and one of us did. But Julia? What did any of us have against her? We didn't even know her."

Richard looked at Ben — and noticed how he seemed to have taken over as spokesperson for the group. Paul was looking like a little lost boy, Saskia was looking introverted and worried, and Ann was trying to look bland, but Richard knew better. She was watching like a hawk, but staying silent.

The police had already discovered that Julia was last seen at breakfast that morning at 8am, after which time she apparently went back to her room upstairs and hadn't been seen since. Not until her body had been found. So Richard asked the four witnesses if they'd seen Julia at any time that morning. Perhaps unsurprisingly, they all said that they hadn't.

Under further probing, though, Richard was able to establish that none of the four witnesses had a watertight alibi from eight that morning until the time Julia's body had been found. Ann had been on the beach on her own during that time, or so she said. Paul had been on the balcony of his room reading a book. Or so he said. Saskia said she'd been by the spa pool, and Ben had gone for a long walk along the coast.

None of the four could categorically prove that they hadn't slipped up to Julia's room at some time after breakfast and offered her a drink laced with poison.

As for the missing notebook that had suddenly reappeared on the noticeboard, the witnesses denied all knowledge. They said they hadn't noticed it, and they had no idea who might have put it back up on the board.

Richard tried to put his frustration at their answers to one side, but without any properly incriminating evidence against any of the witnesses — and no proof yet that Julia had categorically been murdered — he had no choice but to release them and let them get on with their day.

He and Camille stood in the shade as they watched the witnesses leave. Saskia, Ben and Paul all went off together, talking — united by their recent experiences — whereas Ann made her excuses and went into the main body of the hotel on her own. Was she shunning the other three? Or were they perhaps shunning her?

Once the police were back at the station, Camille picked up on Richard's mood.

"You alright, there, sir?"

Richard had been sitting at his desk not doing anything for the last few minutes.

"Sorry?" he said, returning his attention to the room.

"You seem quiet."

The last time in his life that Richard had talked about his true feelings was when he had been seven years old. It was just after his mum had explained to him what a boarding school was and that he was about to be sent to one. So Richard wasn't going to start talking about his feelings now.

"The murderer's struck again, Camille. What are you expecting from me? A song and dance routine?"

Camille put her hand on her hip, irritated. She knew Richard had feelings for Julia, why couldn't he admit it? It would have been wrong if they didn't get upset when someone they'd come to know got murdered.

Richard barked from his desk, "Come on, team, I want the evidence processed — fingerprints taken off the glass Julia was drinking from — and off the bottle we found in her bin. I want to know, if this was murder, just how was it done?"

310

Richard was standing at the whiteboard mopping his neck with his hankie when Fidel announced he'd finished dusting the medicine bottle from the bin and the glass Julia had been holding.

"And the only prints I've been able to raise so far from the glass Julia was holding belong to Julia."

"I see," Richard said.

"But as for the medicine bottle from the bin, I've been able to raise four clear prints from it and none of them belong to Julia."

"They don't?" Richard asked.

"No, sir — and none of them match any of the witnesses, either."

This gave everyone pause.

"I'm sorry?"

"None of the prints on the medicine bottle match the prints of any of the people who were in the Meditation Space when Aslan was killed."

"Then who put the bottle in the bin?" Dwayne asked.

Richard looked back at the whiteboard a long moment before he realised.

"Fidel. We've never taken Dominic's exclusion prints, have we?"

"No, sir."

"Then give Dominic a ring, would you? I want him in here and I want his fingerprints checked against the prints you're finding on the medicine bottle."

"Yes, sir."

An hour later, and wearing an old vest, torn shorts and ancient leather sandals, Dominic flapped into the station, hot and bothered. He was uncooperative — like a teenager — as Dwayne took his exclusion prints, but then, Richard supposed, Dominic had discovered his ex-girlfriend's dead body only that morning; it would take the wind out of anyone's sails.

"Is that all?" Dominic asked once Fidel had his prints on the regulation card.

"Maybe," Richard said. "But can you tell me where you were this morning from about 8am until the time we found Julia's body?"

"What is this?" Dominic asked in a grump.

"Just answer the question."

"I was on the beach. Okay?"

"With anyone?"

"Sure. There were hotel guests around the whole time."

Richard remembered what the witnesses had said earlier. "Did you by any chance see Ann Sellars when you were down there?"

"What?"

"Seeing as you were on the beach. Did you see Ann Sellars at all?"

Dominic thought for a moment before answering. "I don't think so."

Richard considered this. After all, Ann had said she'd been down at the beach on her own the whole morning. Was it likely that Dominic wouldn't have seen her?

Richard continued, "Then can you tell me what you were doing on the beach this morning?"

"There'd been a storm out at sea a few days ago. Debris has been washing up. So I spent a couple of

312

hours this morning clearing seaweed and driftwood from the shoreline."

"And you didn't slip away — even for a few minutes — at any time?"

"No. You just ask the guests. I was there the whole time and it was only when I was coming back from the beach that I bumped into you lot and took you to Julia's room."

"How convenient," Richard said.

"What is this? I don't need an alibi. I'm nothing to do with this."

"I'm not so sure about that," Fidel said, turning to Richard. "Because, sir, I've already found a match."

Richard went over to Fidel's desk where he'd been matching the exclusion prints Dominic had just given against the prints Fidel had been able to lift from the medicine bottle they'd found in the bin in Julia's bathroom.

"Wait, what's that doing there?" a horrified Dominic said, looking at the little brown medicine bottle in its evidence bag on Fidel's desk.

"Why don't you tell us?" Richard asked politely.

Dominic started to bluster. "But that's what I'm saying. That looks like one of my medicine bottles. You know, from my lab at home. If you're saying my prints are on that . . .?" Dominic trailed off as he realised the implications of what he was saying. "Where did you find that bottle?" he eventually said.

"In the bathroom of Julia's room."

"But that's not possible. I've not been in her room in ages. You know, we're not going out with each other any more."

"Now it's funny you'd bring that up," Richard said. "Remind me. How did you feel when Julia told you it was over between you both?"

Dominic looked at Richard and was briefly speechless.

"It's a fair question," Camille said. "Seeing as your prints are on the bottle that contained the poison that almost certainly killed your ex-girlfriend."

"I told you at the time," Dominic said, but Richard noticed how nervous Dominic was looking. "I was fine. It happens."

"Really?" Richard asked.

"Alright. Then if you must know, I was pretty upset. Okay? But it's not the end of the world, there are other fish in the sea. And do you really think that if I killed my ex-girlfriend, I'd leave a bottle covered in my fingerprints at the murder scene?" As Dominic said this, he got increasingly agitated. "In fact, if you ask me, it's obvious what's happened. That bottle's what was stolen in the burglary I told you about. And now it's being used to set me up as Julia's killer. Do I have to do all your work for you? You know, you're pathetic."

Dominic turned and started to leave, although he had to pause as Dwayne took half a step away from his desk to block his exit.

"You want to stop me from leaving," he said to Dwayne, "then you'll have to arrest me."

Richard knew that there was a lot of sense to what Dominic was saying. No one killing their ex-girlfriend would leave a bottle of poison covered in their fingerprints at the scene of the crime. But here it was again, a piece of incriminating evidence that pointed

314

very specifically at one person — just as Julia had confessed to the murder, even though Richard was now sure that she hadn't done it.

Richard sighed to himself. Once again, he felt as though he was looking at jigsaw puzzle pieces that came from completely different jigsaw puzzles.

Richard nodded once for Dwayne — he stepped aside — and Dominic left, shaking his head at the police's incompetence.

No one spoke for a few moments, but then Richard went over to the board, saying as he went, "Come on! Julia was murdered, I'm sure of it! Murdered by the same person who killed Aslan. We must have found some evidence — either in Julia's room — or on her body — that suggested it was murder!"

"I'm sorry, sir," Fidel said. "Not yet. Maybe the autopsy will pick something up."

Richard gritted his teeth in frustration, picked up a board marker and crossed out the details they'd so far collected on Julia Higgins.

When he'd done that, he took a moment to steady himself, and then he turned back to his team. "Julia didn't kill Aslan Kennedy. Nor did she commit suicide. And Dominic's right. If he killed Julia, he wouldn't leave a medicine bottle with his fingerprints on it at the scene."

"Unless it was a double bluff, sir," Fidel offered.

"Agreed, Fidel," Richard said, "but that's some double bluff and I don't think Dominic's capable of such bravery. No, this case has always been about the people who were in the Meditation Space with Aslan when he was killed. And with Julia now dead, that leaves us with only four possible killers: Saskia Filbee, Ben Jenkins, Paul Sellars or Ann Sellars. So which one of that lot's our double murderer?"

The Murder of Aslan
Five guests go for a swim
Paul hands out robes
Aslan prepares the tea
5 guests + Aslan go into Meditation Space
Aslan locks it down from inside
Someone laces tea with GHB or Xyrax — a sedative
Drink tea — all cups turned over
10–15 minute window for murder, (8.00–8.10/8.15).
Right-handed killer!

Investigation / Leads
WHY KILLED IN PAPER HOUSE?
3 x drawing pins in the Meditation Space. Used to pin the murder weapon to a pillar. No prints on any of them
Another drawing pin in the cellar
Who was in Aslan's office the night before @6pm shouting "You're not going to get away with it"?
The notebook reappeared before Julia's body was found. Why?
What's the burnt paper in the furnace?

The Murder of Julia Higgins
She wrote out the names for the Sunrise Healing in the notebook
Took overdose / murdered
BUT no suicide note

Outside the Meditation Space

Rianka Kennedy
Wife
Knew Aslan when he was David — but left Aslan when he was convicted
Took Aslan back 15 yrs ago when he came to the island

Dominic De Vere
Ex-hypnotherapist. Now handyman
Sacked by Aslan
Argued with Aslan
Caught returning to Scene of Crime
Has drugs lab in his house — could have munufactured GHB
His bottle / fingerprints found at murder scene of Julia

Inside the Meditation Space

Aslan Kennedy
Victim. Everyone says he's nice
Real name is David Kennedy

Ex-conman — ran art-lease Ponzi scheme, stole
£2m
Went to prison 20 years ago, served 5 yrs
STILL A CROOK? Admitted to Ben he was still
on the con . . . but is that true?

~~Julia Higgins~~
~~Worked at The Retreat last 6 months~~
~~Confessed to murder — but drugs in blood — and~~
~~lack of real motive — and LEFT-HANDED~~

Ann Sellars
Housewife
Married to Paul
Arrived on island 7 days before murder
Lost £20k in Ponzi scheme
Her fingerprints are on the murder weapon — but
she dried knife the night before
Had her dreams as a singer ruined when she lost
£20k
Clearly hates her husband, Paul
Says she didn't recognise Aslan / David

Paul Sellars
Arrived on island 7 days before murder
Handed out the white robes
Pharmacist — who stole Xyrax from work
KNEW ASLAN'S REAL IDENTITY
Wife Ann lost money in Ponzi scheme
Hates his wife, Ann

Wife NO LONGER alibis him for argument at 6pm

Saskia Filbee
Single, 45 yrs old
Here on her own. Arrived night before
Heard argument in office night before — at about 6pm — a man, but couldn't identify him
Lied that she'd lost £50k in Ponzi scheme — she lost £500,000
Says she didn't recognise Aslan / David, but she was his lover . . . ! Maybe she did

Ben Jenkins
Arrived on island 4 days before murder
Property Developer. Portugal
Served 3 yrs for Wounding With Intent and was Aslan / David's cellmate in 1997 for 1 year
Lied that he didn't know him — had been in email contact — 3 months before murder
No alibi for time of argument at 6pm

"You know," Camille said, "if Julia was murdered, it was to make it look like she'd committed suicide because of the guilt she was feeling since killing Aslan Kennedy."

"That's right," Richard said.

"But we still don't know why Aslan was killed, do we? I mean, not really."

Dwayne said, "It's got to be connected to his past. From when he was running his Ponzi scheme. Seeing as everyone in the room with him when he was killed was connected to his past."

Richard could see the logic of this. After all, Aslan had stolen millions of pounds twenty years ago. But how did a crime that long ago connect with Ben's statement that Aslan had admitted that he was back on the con again just before he was killed? Had Aslan been conning one of the Ponzi victims? Or maybe, the con involved Aslan being in cahoots with one of the Ponzi victims — who then turned the tables on him by killing him?

"Fidel," Richard said, "how are you getting on with Aslan's bank statements?"

Fidel indicated the mess of paperwork on his table. "Still looking, sir. But honestly, I can't find anything incriminating at all. Aslan didn't ever seem to spend money."

"Maybe that's because he had a different source of income elsewhere," Dwayne offered.

Richard turned back to the board and kept on thinking. Was Aslan on the con — even though they could find no evidence that proved this? And if he were, how did it tie up with Paul, Ann, Saskia or Ben? Or was Ben lying to them? In which case, why?

Was Ben perhaps the killer trying to throw them off the scent? But why would Ben want Aslan dead? And why would he then need to kill Julia?

As the afternoon wore on, Richard found his mind wandering towards the evening he was about to spend on his own. Somehow, now he had to face his first night without Harry for company, he wondered if maybe he'd acted rashly. Of course he still resented how Harry would walk around the shack as though he owned the place — but there was no denying that he was at least someone else in the shack that Richard could interact with, even if that interaction was furious frustration.

In a post-Harry world, Richard knew he'd now be entirely alone.

"Sir," Fidel said from his desk, breaking Richard's reverie.

Richard looked over at his subordinate's desk and saw Fidel staring in puzzlement at his screen.

"What is it?" Richard asked.

"Well, it's the labs in Guadeloupe. They've finished analysing the paper we sent them."

It took Richard a moment to remember that they'd sent the scraps of burnt paper Fidel had found in the hotel's furnace to the labs for analysis.

"Better late than never, I suppose," he said.

Fidel was still looking at his monitor; and still frowning.

"What's wrong?" Camille asked, noticing Fidel's indecision.

Fidel looked up from his monitor. "The report here says they used all of the techniques available to them, but they were unable to reveal any handwriting under the burns."

"They weren't?" Richard asked.

"In fact, according to the report here, there was no writing of any sort — or printed ink — or anything at all on the scraps of paper before they were burnt. They were just clear white paper."

"Are you sure?" Camille asked.

"Wait!" Richard said, suddenly holding up his finger for silence.

Dwayne, Fidel and Camille shared a sharp glance. They knew full well that when Richard suddenly froze like this it could mean he was beginning to piece the case together.

Richard went over to the whiteboard, his mind a whirr.

"What gsm do the labs say the paper was?"

"Sorry, sir?" Fidel replied.

"Gsm. Grams per square metre. It's how you measure paper thickness. What's the gsm of the scraps of paper they tested? Come on, it's important!"

"Hold on, sir," Fidel said in a panic, turning back to his monitor and scrolling through the document on his screen with his mouse.

Dwayne looked at Camille, baffled, but they both knew to keep their mouths shut.

Fidel found the entry among all of the technical data that had been gathered at the bottom of the report.

"It says here, sir, it's 225 gsm."

"Ha!" Richard clapped his hands together and spun back to the board, calling back to his team as he studied everything that was written there. "And normal writing paper is only 80 gsm. And our reporter's notebook was probably less, it's so lightweight. Possibly as low as 70 gsm."

"Is this important?" Dwayne asked.

"Sure is," Richard replied, "because it means that the paper that was burnt in the furnace under the house didn't come from the notebook Julia wrote in. And that means . . .?"

As Richard trailed off, Camille, Fidel and Dwayne all looked at each other, no more enlightened. What did it matter that the paper they sent off for analysis didn't come from the reporter's notebook? In what way was that important?

"Good grief," Richard said almost to himself before turning around and looking at his team as though he'd finally solved a crossword clue that had been set weeks ago.

And then something happened that almost never happened on the island of Saint-Marie.

Richard Poole smiled. He actually smiled.

Fidel said, "Sir, you can't have worked it out?"

"On the contrary," Richard said, "because I think that's exactly what I've done."

"You know who killed Aslan Kennedy?" Fidel asked.

"I do. And Julia Higgins."

"But is it the same person, Chief?" Dwayne asked.

"Oh yes," Richard replied.

"It wasn't Dominic, was it?" Fidel blurted, hopefully.

"Good heavens no, Fidel. He wasn't inside the Meditation Space when Aslan was killed, he can't be our killer."

"So you're saying that Aslan was killed by one of the people who was locked inside the room with him?" Fidel asked.

Richard looked at his team as though they were all a bit slow.

"Of course," Richard said. "Only one of the people who was inside the Meditation Space with Aslan Kennedy when he locked it down could ever have been his killer."

"Then who was it?" Camille asked, unable to resist asking any longer.

Richard looked at his partner and couldn't help himself.

He waggled his eyebrows.

"I'll tell you in a minute," he said. "But first we've got a con to prove."

CHAPTER
FIFTEEN

Richard had asked everyone to join him in the Meditation Space, but as he stood sweating in his suit and tie, he wished he hadn't. It really was very hot. But he had a theory to prove, and that meant that he had no choice over where he did this.

It didn't help that the room was made all the more sweltering with the presence of eight other people. There was Camille and Dwayne, of course — Fidel was currently elsewhere running an errand for Richard — but there were also all the other interested parties: Saskia Filbee, Paul and Ann Sellars, Ben Jenkins, Rianka Kennedy, and — last of all — Dominic De Vere.

One of these six people killed Aslan Kennedy and then killed Julia Higgins, and Richard was about to reveal their identity.

"Do you really know who the killer is?" Dominic asked, unable to hide his amazement.

"Oh yes, Dominic," Richard said, and smiled for Dominic's benefit. "But let's first remind ourselves of what we're dealing with here.

"Because we've got Rianka and Aslan running a spa hotel in the Caribbean. It's popular. They do well. And we know that Aslan in particular has found a degree of

325

peace embracing the more spiritual side of life. Or is that true? After all, as we all now know, Aslan Kennedy was once David Kennedy, a dangerous conman who was given a seven year sentence for stealing two million pounds in an art-lease Ponzi scheme. And we know his past as a conman is an important part of this case because, when he was killed, four people who he'd previously stolen from just happened to be in the same room as him, and the fifth person had once been his ex-cellmate.

"But why did he have to die? That's the question. Or to put it another way: can a leopard change its spots? Seeing as Aslan was such a crook in the past, could we really believe that he was now on the straight and narrow? When Ben Jenkins told us that Aslan confessed to him that he was still on the con, it chimed with what I suppose we'd always expected to hear. Aslan was a crook in the past. He was still a crook. But here's the interesting thing. I've had one of my best officers examine Aslan's bank statements and records. Aslan took a small salary from the business, he barely spent even that — and what was left over at the end of every month he gave away to charity. And we already know he lived at The Retreat, didn't go on expensive holidays or buy expensive cars. Or even artwork or fine wine. If he was on the con again, it was hard to see how he was in any way benefiting from it.

"So I started thinking. We only had Ben's word that Aslan was on the con again. As far as everyone else could tell us — from Aslan's wife to the Commissioner of Police — no one had a bad word to say about Aslan.

Apart from you, Dominic," Richard said this to Dominic with a smile. "And I look forward to coming to you in a minute."

Dominic looked back at Richard, and it was clear that he was worried.

Richard turned back to the room. "But putting Dominic to one side for a moment, everyone else adored Aslan. For his pure soul. His kindness. So let's see where the balance of evidence lies. If dozens of people are saying that Aslan was an innocent who no longer cared for money, why should we believe the one person, Ben, who's saying that Aslan confessed to being on the con — in a conversation, I hasten to add, that quite conveniently no one else overheard. And Ben's a one-time violent criminal. Why should we believe what he told us?"

"Are you saying I lied to you?" Ben said with a barely concealed hint of menace. "Because I'm telling you, Aslan told me he was still on the con."

Richard looked at Ben a moment. "You're really not prepared to change your story?"

"No way," Ben said. "It's what happened."

"Very well. But everyone should bear in mind that there was only ever one person who said Aslan was back to being a crook. So now let's look at the day of the murder.

"Aslan Kennedy locks himself inside a wood and paper structure with five other people. The door's not opened at any time, but when it's unlocked twenty minutes later, Aslan is dead. So who killed him?

"Well, let's see what we know. The tea was drugged with a mild sedative to make everyone docile and less responsive. So that when everyone started to drift off, they really drifted off. As you all know. You were all a touch woozy when you woke up, weren't you?"

Richard could see that Paul, Ann, Saskia and Ben all agreed with his assessment of the situation.

"Except for the fact," Richard clarified, "the killer no doubt took their dose of sedative-laden tea *after* they'd committed murder. After all, you wouldn't want to knife someone to death while drugged up, would you?" Richard held the four suspects' attention for a moment, before continuing. "And as for the knife that was used to kill Aslan? Well, it was obvious from the drawing pins we found at the scene of the crime that the killer had previously set the knife behind a pillar and was able to get to it while the rest of you were lying down wearing eye masks and headphones.

"And yet, none of what I've just said is in any way true. The killer didn't take their dose of sedative-laden tea after they'd committed murder. And that's not how the knife was hidden in the room before the murder."

This got everyone's attention.

"Come on," Dominic interrupted, "just tell us who did it."

"Very well," Richard said. "Because now we come to the only four people who could ever have killed Aslan. The people who were inside the room with him when it was locked down." Here Richard looked at Saskia, Ben, Paul and Ann. "And because Aslan had stolen from three of you in the past — and the fourth of you was in prison with him — it's easy to imagine you all having motives.

"Starting with you, Saskia, you lost the most to Aslan in the Ponzi scam twenty years ago. By some distance. Half a million, up front, and that alone would be enough to commit murder. But that's not what interested me. Because I was always much more impressed with the half a million you then spent trying to get that first half a million back. Which shows how you don't forgive. Or forget. What's more, it made it quite clear — to me at least — that you were prepared to risk everything to get back what you felt was yours. Even though you've always made sure you came across to us as demure. Timid, even. But that can't be the whole story. A timid person wouldn't have pursued their lost money for so long — and to such a ruinous extent."

Everyone could see that Saskia was looking anxious at Richard's words.

"You don't understand," she tried to say.

"I understand too well," Richard cut back. "So don't even think about denying it. Underneath your quiet exterior — your prim secretarial exterior — you're prepared to go to the ends of the earth to get revenge. Aren't you?"

Saskia didn't dare say anything.

"But did you do it?" Richard continued. "That's the question. After all, you only arrived on the island the night before Aslan was killed. So even if you'd already worked out that Aslan was David Kennedy, I don't see

329

how you could have staged such a complex murder by 8am the following morning."

"You don't think I did it?" Saskia asked, hope desperately flashing into her eyes.

Richard looked at Saskia. "That's right. I don't."

Saskia gulped. And then frowned. And then bobbed her head in appreciation to Richard. For his part, Richard next turned to Ben Jenkins.

"So let's look at you, Ben Jenkins," Richard said. "Because Aslan's murder was so violent, surely we needed look no further than the only person here who already had a history of violent crime to unmask our murderer?"

"I served my time," Ben said with the sort of edge that suggested he hadn't quite put his violent past as far behind him as he'd have liked people to believe.

"But you're still consorting with other criminals. As your friendship with the ex-con Ratty proves."

"I told you all about him voluntarily."

"Hardly," Richard said. "You were trying to make sure you didn't get arrested for murder at the time. I think you were throwing us a bone to distract us. Just as I think you were trying to distract us when you told us that Aslan confessed to you that he was on the con again."

"But that's what he told me!" Ben said, no longer able to keep the anger out of his voice.

Richard tilted his head to one side as though he were an art expert deciding if a painting was fake or not. "Again. Interesting."

330

Richard turned back to address the room. "It was also true that you were the person in the murder room who'd known Aslan's true identity the longest. In fact, you'd worked out that Aslan was David a whole three months before he died, as you were forced to admit when you showed us your email correspondence with him. Which, I can't help noticing, was weeks and weeks before Aslan decided to invite all the Ponzi victims out to the Caribbean — a stark change in his policy. Was it you who told him to invite Paul, Ann and Saskia out here all at the same time?"

"But you saw my emails to him!" Ben said. "I tried to make contact, but his emails kept bouncing back to me."

Richard replied darkly, "There are ways of communicating other than via email, Ben. And seeing as you knew you'd eventually have to explain to us how you ended up on Saint-Marie, perhaps you created the email trail to Aslan to give yourself a plausible cover story."

"This doesn't even remotely stack up," Ben said.

"A man with a violent past who's known Aslan's real identity for long enough to dupe the victim into inviting the others out here — and who's the only person on the whole island who's been saying that the victim was still up to no good? It sure looks to me like you're our most likely suspect."

"But why did I want him dead?" Ben asked through gritted teeth.

Richard held Ben's gaze a long moment.

"And there you have me," Richard conceded. "Maybe it's something to do with your time you spent in prison with Aslan? Or the confidence trick he's now apparently trying to pull off?"

Richard was looking hard at Ben to see if a moment of fear would slip into his eyes like had happened before.

It didn't.

"And that's the thing. Because you're right. Although you'd have been the most likely person to carry out a violent crime like this, I've never been able to uncover a single reason why you'd want Aslan dead. So, I don't see how you could be the killer."

"You don't?" Ben asked, somewhat stunned by Richard's sudden change of direction.

"That's right. I don't think you killed Aslan Kennedy."

This took a moment to register with Ben, and then he briefly threw his hands up in the air with a sudden exhalation of contempt, for the police in general — and Richard in particular.

"Which leaves only two remaining suspects," Richard said as he turned to face Paul and Ann Sellars. "And this is where it gets interesting."

All the colour had already drained from Paul's face, but Richard could see that Ann was trying to look composed.

She was failing. Very well. So be it.

"Because here we have a couple," Richard said, "who quite clearly don't get on. And one of them, Paul, stole a bottle of gamma-hydroxybutyric acid — trade name,

332

Xyrax — that we now know was used to sedate the witnesses just before the murder was carried out. What's more, Paul had even secretly been phoning Aslan from his office phone — apparently behind his wife's back. And, as Paul was eventually forced to admit, he'd recognised that Aslan was David the moment he saw his face in the hotel's leaflet."

"Now look here," Paul started.

"No, you look here, Paul," Richard said, "because you should know that I don't think you killed Aslan Kennedy."

"You don't?" Paul said, almost deathly pale by now.

"As it happens, no," Richard said. "Even though it was undoubtedly your Xyrax that the real killer used to lace the tea you all drank that morning."

At different speeds, everyone in the room realised what this must mean. They all turned and looked at Ann, who was standing stock still. Like a suspect about to receive their sentence, Richard found himself thinking.

"Why are you all looking at me like that?" Ann asked.

"Because," Richard said, "only someone locked in the Meditation Space with Aslan could have killed him, and it wasn't Julia, Saskia, Ben or your husband. So, by a simple process of elimination, that leaves only you. Good-time Ann. Who wears wild clothes — obviously has a good laugh wherever she goes — if only as an antidote to living with her turgid husband. And yet, let's stop and think what these last twenty years must have been like for you. Because, as you eventually had to admit to us, you once had a dream. A dream you were realising when you were studying to be a singer. And that's what shattered when Aslan stole the twenty thousand pounds you'd set aside to pay for your fees."

"I didn't kill him!" Ann said, horrified.

"You didn't?"

"No!"

Richard looked at Ann a long moment, and then his face softened.

"I know," he said.

This got a reaction from the witnesses.

"You mean," Ann asked, "you don't think I killed Aslan Kennedy?"

"That's right," Richard said, quite unperturbed, as he turned back to look at Ben, Saskia, Paul and Ann. "But I want you to know the process of elimination that led me to understand how Aslan was really killed. Because it had to be one of you who killed him and yet I never could quite make it fit. It was as though I had lots of different jigsaw pieces, but they all belonged to different puzzles. And I was right. That's how the murder was made to look.

"We had Ben, who was the most violent of you, but it was only Julia and Ann whose fingerprints were found on the murder weapon. And as for Julia, she confessed to the murder, but was left-handed and therefore couldn't have carried it out. Whereas you, Saskia, always had the best motive, but you only arrived on the island the night before. And Paul seemed to have no motive at all. But then, it was Paul's drugs that were used in the tea — I know that now. And it was Ben who'd been in touch with Aslan the longest. Each one of you had something incriminating about you, but you also seemed to have something else that suggested you couldn't have done it. It was almost as if you'd taken all of the necessary elements of a single murder and shared them out among yourselves. And it was only when I realised this that I managed to make a connection that I maybe should have made much, much sooner.

"You see, other than Aslan, there were five people in the murder room when he was killed. And there were five knife strikes in his neck and back. And that's when it occurred to me.

"What if you were all in this together? After all, I'd been trying to work out how and when the killer had managed to drink down the drugged tea without being seen. And how the killer managed to lace the tea with gamma-hydroxybutyric acid without being seen. And how the killer smuggled the knife into the Meditation Space without being seen. And — finally! — how the killer managed to kill Aslan without any of the rest of you noticing. One explanation for how all this was achieved would be that the murder wasn't carried out secretly at all. Remember: five people. Five knife strikes. It couldn't be a coincidence, could it?"

Richard took a moment to see that Ben, Saskia, Paul and Ann were all looking increasingly worried — exchanging panicked glances — and Richard watched Ben wipe some sweat from his brow.

"And it wasn't a coincidence. Because when I started to think of the five of you working together, the murder

335

finally started to make sense. This was it! How Aslan was killed! It was the only way!

"Or so I thought until I remembered the drawing pins. Because if you were all in on this together, there'd have been no need to pin the murder weapon behind this pillar here."

As Richard had been speaking, he'd moved over to the far corner of the Meditation Space and now he indicated the pillar that he and Camille had found the drawing pin stuck into.

"So why did we find a drawing pin stuck into this wooden pillar here?" Richard next indicated where they'd found the second and third drawing pins on the floor. "In fact, why did we find a second drawing pin on the floor just here? And another one over there? And, above all else, why did we find a fourth drawing pin in the cellar under the main hotel? And to answer that, we have to address the one aspect of this case that has irritated me more than any other. Just why was Aslan killed inside a Japanese tea house? And that's when I finally understood: although it wasn't a coincidence that there were five knife strikes, this wasn't the five of you working together. This was indeed a solo murderer. Someone who'd been manipulating us from the start. A shadowy figure we'd never properly considered."

As Richard finished talking, everyone realised that he was now looking squarely at Dominic De Vere.

After a long moment, Richard said, "And this is where I owe you an apology, Dominic, because you unwittingly revealed the killer to me a long time ago. And I didn't believe you."

Richard turned back to Rianka. "Because it was you, Rianka, wasn't it? It was you who killed Aslan Kennedy and then killed Julia Higgins."

"What?" Rianka said, stunned.

Behind her, Dwayne and Camille took half a step forward so that they were now flanking Rianka on either side.

Ben was the first to find his voice.

"But how can that be? She was outside the Meditation Space when I opened the door."

"I know," Richard said entirely unfussed.

"And none of us let her in while we were inside," Ann said, just as amazed.

"I know," Richard said. Again, entirely untroubled. "But that's how clever she was."

"But you don't understand," Paul said, wanting to make his point clear. "There's no way Rianka could have been hiding inside this room before we locked it down. I mean, look about you, man!" Here, Paul indicated the completely empty paper box they were all standing in. "There's nowhere to hide."

"And that's where you're wrong, Ben, because she was hiding in this room before you got in here."

"But that's impossible," Ann said. "This is a completely empty room."

"Precisely!" Richard almost bounced on his feet as he said this. "And seeing as all along I've been trying to work out why you'd kill someone inside a Japanese tea house, it is entirely gratifying to discover that I was on the right track. After all, as I kept on asking myself, why not kill Aslan in his bedroom? Or in his office? Why on earth would you choose to commit a murder in a building that was no more than a wooden frame covered in paper? There had to be a reason. And there was.

"It wasn't that it was possible to break in from the outside. The rusting staples around the outside of the Meditation Space make it clear that the paper walls have been in place for months. And anyway, any attempt to break in through the paper would have involved cutting a hole large enough to climb through. And seeing as we found no cuts in the paper, that rules that option out. To all intents and purposes, although the tea house is only made of wood and paper, it might just as well have been constructed from brick or stone. It's impregnable." Richard pointed at the latch lock on the door, "and the moment Aslan locked the only door into the room, that ruled out anyone getting in from outside. So how was it done? Fidel?" Richard called out. "Are you ready?"

"Yes, sir," Fidel said from outside the building.

The door opened, Fidel entered, and under his arm he had one of the rolls of paper that Camille had found in the cellar underneath the hotel. Although it looked cumbersome, Fidel was able to get the long roll of white paper into the room by bending it around the door — and he brought it over to where Richard was standing by the far wall.

"You see," Richard said, "my mistake was to keep looking at the outside walls. Because there's something about paper that makes it very different from any other kind of building material. And that's that you can put up an internal paper wall in minutes, and remove it just as quickly. Particularly when you've already got a ready-made frame to pin the paper to."

As Richard said this, he indicated the wooden pillar towards the end of the room that he'd found the drawing pin stuck into.

"You'll notice that this pillar is only a couple of feet in from the end wall, and it runs vertically up to the ceiling" — Richard pointed up the pillar as he said this — "where it meets the horizontal beam that goes across the room" — here Richard walked along the width of the room indicating the ceiling beam above his head — "where it meets another vertical pillar which, like the first, is set only a couple of feet into the room."

Richard turned and looked at Rianka. "In effect, these two verticals and cross beam — set, as they are, just in from the end of the room — are perfect for hanging a false wall from. All you'd need is a roll of paper and a load of drawing pins so you could pin the paper to the far side of the wood."

Everyone in the Meditation Space finally understood the truth of what Richard was saying. If a paper wall had been hung towards the end of the room — attached to the pillar and cross beam — would anyone have noticed that the room was a couple of feet shorter than it should have been? Or that there were now only eleven vertical pillars visible along each side of the paper box when there should have been twelve? And while the cavity that Rianka would have created would have been only a couple of feet deep, it would have been just enough for her to hide inside.

"And now everything begins to make sense," Richard said, turning to Ben. "It was indeed your initial email to Aslan that started the clock ticking. But it wasn't Julia who intercepted it as we'd originally thought. It was Rianka. After all, it's her office as much as it's her husband's, it's no surprise she picked up the email through The Retreat's website.

"It was Rianka who then sent back the email to you, telling you not to contact Aslan again — and who then set up the spam filter that meant that none of your emails would get through to Aslan's computer ever again. And, having done that, Rianka must have hoped she'd dealt with the danger. She'd got rid of you. She was safe again.

"But then, a few weeks later, Rianka discovered that you'd booked a holiday at The Retreat, and this was when she realised how much trouble she was in. As to why she was in trouble, I'll come to that in a moment, but, suffice to say, Rianka knew that if you got to speak to Aslan, the game would be up for her. She had to start preparing for the worst. And that's when I think she realised. She was so desperate to keep her secret, she was even prepared to kill.

"And here I have to apologise. Because the apparent narrative of the murder was so compelling that when I was trying to work out who among the suspects might have known Aslan's true identity, I never properly considered that there was one other person on the island who'd known his real identity the longest — for the last fifteen years, in fact — and that was his wife, Rianka. And who'd always been best placed to convince

340

Aslan to start inviting multiple Ponzi victims out to the Caribbean? Again, that was Rianka. And I didn't consider her because she had an alibi for the time of the murder: she'd apparently been outside the room at the time.

"And all along I've been trying to work out why the killer had been happy to commit murder inside a locked room in front of a load of potential witnesses. Why hadn't the killer sorted themselves out with an alibi? Well, they did: Rianka made sure that her husband was killed inside a locked room that contained a load of people all of whom would swear on oath that she wasn't inside the room with them at the time of the murder. And let's be honest, you don't get many better alibis than that."

Here, Richard paused to revel in the moment. His dark suit was broiling him, his face was streaming in sweat — the food on the island was too spicy — he hated living in a tin-roofed hovel — he'd recently had to catch a lizard in a biscuit tin, for heaven's sakes! — but this was what made it all worthwhile. Why he was a policeman. Not because he got to deliver justice — although it was, of course, partly because of that. It was more that Richard was offended by the mess and barbarism of a murder. The way it left lives broken and destroyed. The way it upset the acceptable order of things. When he solved a murder, then, most of Richard's satisfaction came from the fact that he was reimposing order on a world that, without him, would otherwise be full of chaos.

"So now," Richard said, "we come to the night before Aslan was killed, and the argument that Saskia overheard in his office." Richard looked at Saskia. "And here, I think you made a mistake, Saskia."

"I didn't," she said. "I heard a man shouting 'you're not going to get away with it'."

"Oh no, I know that's what you heard, but tell me, how did you know it was two men in the office having the argument?"

"Well," Saskia said, puzzled. "It was Aslan's office. I heard a man shouting, and then, a few seconds later, Aslan came out — and he was looking upset."

"And that's where you made your mistake," Richard said. "You presumed that Aslan was fleeing from the man who'd been shouting at him. In truth, it was Aslan who had been doing the shouting — and the person who he'd been shouting at was Rianka. Again, I'll tell you why in due course, but — for the moment — all you need to know is that it was Aslan who was telling his wife that she wouldn't get away with it. But with those words, Aslan was inadvertently signing his own death warrant."

Richard turned to address Rianka.

"Not that your husband knew at that point, of course. And I bet you made all sorts of promises to him later on that night to buy yourself time. Knowing you as I do now, I bet you even promised to make a full confession in the morning."

As Richard said this, he was pleased to see the tiniest flicker of guilt flash into Rianka's eyes.

Got you, he thought to himself.

"Thought so," he said to her, knowing that Rianka now knew that she'd shown the first chink in her armour. "But all that mattered to you that night was that you bought yourself time until the following morning. Which you self-evidently did. And that allowed you to put your plan into action. Because you'd already lined up your chess pieces, hadn't you? That's what you were doing when you convinced Aslan that it would be fine to invite out a few more Ponzi victims — and all at the same time. You were making sure you had an insurance policy. And once you knew that the game was up for you, you decided it was time to put it into action.

"So, following your argument with Aslan, you got hold of Julia and asked her to write out a new list of names for the Sunrise Healing session. A list of names that you'd chosen. And I'm sure Julia was only too glad to help. Partly because she was a trusting soul — partly because I bet she was thrilled when you told her she could add her name to the list — but mostly, if I'm honest, because it was her job to offer you secretarial support. That was the condition of her staying at the hotel for free. Wasn't it? And what could be more secretarial than writing out a list of names for one of your bosses?

"As for how Rianka got hold of the murder weapon, I don't think that was hard, either. Ann?" Here Richard turned to Ann. "Was Rianka one of the people doing the washing up with you the night before Aslan was killed?"

Ann looked at Rianka, her memory slowly coalescing as she thought back to the night in question.

"You know what?" Ann eventually said. "She was! In fact, it was Rianka who suggested I come and help with the washing up in the first place. I remember now!"

"Which we should have realised sooner," Richard agreed. "Because, after you told us you'd done the washing up, we rang Rianka to find out if it was true — and it was Rianka who confirmed that you had indeed been doing the washing up the night before her husband's death. And, when you think about it, how could she have confirmed that piece of information unless she herself had also been doing the washing up at the same time?

"So," Richard said, "Rianka was standing at a sink that night, wearing Marigold gloves and washing carving knives that she then handed to you to dry and get your fingerprints all over. Am I right?"

Ann didn't need to say anything, it was obvious that what Richard had said was true.

"As I've been saying all along," Richard continued, "our killer was an arch-manipulator. She managed to get Julia implicated when she wrote out the replacement list of names. And she managed to implicate you, Ann, when she got you to dry the kitchen's carving knives.

"As for implicating Paul, that was even easier. Because when you stay at any kind of spa or health farm, you have to fill in a form saying what sort of medicine you're on. It wouldn't have been hard for Rianka to discover that the Xyrax that Paul listed was a brand name for gamma-hydroxybutyric acid and a sedative. And nor would it have been hard for her to use the hotel's pass key to liberate some of the Xyrax from Paul's bottle of pills. And it would have been easy for her to then leave out the teapot and cups on a tray all ready for her husband to pour water into the following morning. An act of kindness, or so it appeared on her part. But Aslan wasn't to know that his wife had crushed up a load of Paul's Xyrax pills and mixed them in with the tea leaves at the bottom of the teapot. All ready for him to activate when he poured in the boiling water the following day.

"So that was Paul also implicated in advance. As for Saskia and Ben, you weren't able to pin anything directly to them, but you weren't too worried about that. Saskia was already the person who'd lost the most money to Aslan's con twenty years ago, surely that was implication enough? And Ben was an ex-convict who'd shared a prison cell with her husband. No one could appear more like the murderer than someone who'd already done time for actual bodily harm."

Here Richard took out his hankie and mopped his brow. He could see that Ben and Paul were looking impressed with him — as though they were both finally acknowledging that maybe Richard wasn't such a waste of space after all. As for Ann and Saskia, Ann was watching events unfold with slack-jawed wonder — and Saskia was clearly just as astonished, but she didn't need to bob her head around to follow proceedings, as Ann did.

As for Rianka, Richard noted that she'd taken to staring straight ahead in silent horror. She was guilty as hell and she knew that Richard knew it.

"So now we come to the day of the murder," Richard said, "and now I'm going to tell you how Rianka killed her husband."

CHAPTER
SIXTEEN

"Aslan got up with the sun," Richard said. "We know he didn't like alarm clocks. He then went down to the kitchen where he found a teapot and cups had already been set out for him on a tray. He maybe thought it was a peace offering from his wife following their argument the night before — or maybe he thought it had been laid out for him by the ever-thoughtful Julia — but it hardly matters. He put the necessary boiling water in, never knowing that he was inadvertently making a drink that was laced with a sedative.

"Now, I imagine that Rianka had already got the spare roll of paper wall into the Meditation Space before that morning. But whether she'd already started to hang it the night before — or did it all that morning while Aslan was making the tea and the unsuspecting guests were on the beach stretching and swimming — Rianka slipped into the Meditation Space and finished pinning up the paper wall so no one would know she was hiding behind it. Fidel, if you would?"

As Richard went over to the end wall, Fidel stood the roll of paper up by the vertical wooden pillar that Camille had found the second drawing pin pushed into. As he did this, Fidel made sure that the trailing flap of paper was running flush up against the vertical post. The roll fitted the height of the building perfectly. Of course it did. It had been designed for the building. Fidel then got out a little box of drawing pins from his pocket and started to push a few drawing pins through the edge of the paper and into the vertical beam. As he did this, Richard continued speaking.

"And here I have to admit to a failing, because I should have realised that a roll of paper had been used in the murder of Aslan Kennedy much sooner. When Camille found the spare rolls of paper in the hotel's cellar, it was Rianka who told us that they were all present and correct, but she said this even though there were only four rolls. Because — think about it — the Meditation Space doesn't just have four walls, it actually has four walls *and one roof*. There should have been five rolls in the cellar that day, but Rianka's quick thinking distracted us from the truth that it was her who'd used the fifth roll of paper in the murder of her husband. Thank you, Fidel. If you'd now brick me up."

Having secured the roll of paper to the pillar, Fidel was able to unroll it across the room — just inches in front of Richard's nose — rather like someone unrolling a twelve-foot tall tube of cling film — until he reached the opposite pillar, which is where the paper naturally ran out. Of course it did. It was designed to fit the width of the room just as it was designed to fit the room's height.

From everyone else's viewpoint, Richard and Fidel were now hidden behind the fake wall at the end of the room. And, because Fidel had pinned the paper on the "far" side of the wooden posts, it wasn't even possible for anyone inside the Meditation Space to see any of the drawing pins. In fact, from everyone else's point of view, the end of the room looked entirely normal. It was just the usual wooden frame with a paper wall attached to the further side of it.

But there was now a narrow cavity at the end of the room that Richard and Fidel were hiding inside, although their bodies could still be seen as dim shadows through the translucent paper.

Richard called out from behind the paper, "And while you can no doubt see our shadows on the fake paper wall, that's because this is the westernmost wall of the room and the sun is beginning to set behind us. But think about it. When the murder was carried out, the sun was still only just rising in the east. Whatever shadow Rianka cast that morning would have gone behind her and wouldn't have shown up on the internal wall at all. In fact, all Rianka had to do was wait silently in here until the room was locked down and everyone was lying down and drifting off. Then she removed the drawing pins that were holding the paper up."

As Richard said this, Fidel magically reappeared as he started to roll the paper back across the end of the room, turning the flat sheet of paper back into a tall roll. Half way across, Richard was revealed.

"And with the others in the room already sedated, lying down and listening to the sounds of the deep on headphones whilst their eyes were shut behind eye masks, Rianka was able to roll the wall back up and get it ready to remove from the scene of the crime.

"And this is the other advantage a house constructed from paper has over a house constructed from brick or stone. Because not only can you hang a fake internal wall in two seconds flat, you can also fold it up when you're done with it and carry it out of the room with you."

As Richard said this, Fidel finished rolling the paper up and detached the drawing pins from where they'd been holding it to the pillar. He then folded the roll of paper over so that the tube became flat and half the length it had previously been. He then folded it over one more time so that although it was now thick — maybe about the thickness of a shoe box — it was only three feet long. And throughout the whole process, Fidel had managed to be almost entirely silent. As long as the others kept their eye masks and headphones on, they'd have failed to realise there was someone else in the room with them.

"After the murder," Richard said, "when Aslan's body was found and the Meditation Space was opened up, Rianka was sitting on the verandah with her sewing basket, entirely innocently. Or so it looked. But I think she had her sewing basket with her that morning because it's what she'd used to smuggle the murder weapon and a pair of gloves into the Meditation Space. In my imagination, the gloves she wore that morning were the same Marigolds she'd used to do the washing up the night before. But the sewing basket also allowed her to smuggle the fake wall out of the room once the murder was done. And it was also the perfect receptacle for the drawing pins as she removed them from the wooden pillars. Although we now know that one of the drawing pins had got stuck so far into the pillar that Rianka was unable to remove it. And another two drawing pins rolled away and got lost entirely. But then, they were only drawing pins. I'm sure Rianka presumed the police wouldn't be able to make much of them." Richard smiled at this.

"But what if one of us had woken up?" Ben asked.

"That would have been unfortunate," Richard said, "but remember: while she was removing the paper wall, she'd not committed any crime yet. And I'm sure Rianka would have just laughed off her hiding behind a fake wall as a silly prank she was about to play on her husband.

"But the key point is this: no one did wake up. Or hear her. Or see her. Not in their sedated states. So, still wearing her gloves, Rianka got the knife from her sewing basket. Right-handed. Of course she did. She's right-handed. She then approached her husband as he sat directly in front of her in a lotus position on the floor, his back already turned to her — his headphones on, his eyes hidden behind a mask.

"And only now that she's sure that no one's even realised she's in the room, does she commit her crime. She stabs her husband five times in the neck and back — another piece of circumstantial evidence she knew might later point the finger of suspicion at the five other people who'd been in the room when he was killed.

"She then puts the knife down, and this was Rianka's final stroke of genius. Because although the room was locked down from the inside, it was only a latch lock —

a common-or-garden Yale lock such as you'd find on any front door anywhere in the world — and she knew that although no one could get in from outside while it was locked down, there was nothing stopping her from unlocking it from the inside. And, once she'd slipped out of the Meditation Space and closed the door behind herself, the lock would lock itself behind her again.

"And here, Rianka displayed nerves of steel: she had to leave the Meditation Space as though she were entirely innocent. But then, if anyone saw her, what in fact would they have seen? The owner of the hotel calmly leaving one of the treatment rooms with her sewing basket under her arm. Would they really recognise the significance of the wodge of white paper in the basket? Or know if this was before or after Aslan had gone inside? Or before or after Aslan was slain? Because I think Rianka presumed that the sedative she'd put in the tea would knock everyone out inside the Meditation Space for long enough that it would later on prove almost impossible to pin down the exact time when Aslan had been killed.

"As it happened, no one saw Rianka leave, and this allowed her to take the folded-up paper to the cellar under the house and burn it in the hotel's furnace. In the process, she dropped one of the drawing pins she'd used. A small clue perhaps, but it was enough to make me realise that the killer had possibly been in the cellar under the house. And that's what made me ask Fidel here to sift through the ash of the furnace — a furnace, I now remember," Richard said, turning to Rianka, "that you didn't want us to shut down. Of course you didn't, you guessed we might find charred bits of paper from the spare roll of paper you'd burnt on the morning of the murder. Not that we knew the importance of what we were doing from your manner. I almost take my hat off to you. You've had us turning this way and that from the start."

Richard turned back to address the room.

"But having killed her husband — and burnt the roll of paper in the furnace — Rianka then went out onto the verandah and started darning a sock so that later on — when we asked — she'd be able to give false testimony that the whole time Aslan had been inside the Meditation Space, she saw no one enter or leave; another way of making it look as though the killer had to be one of the people who'd been locked inside the room with her husband.

"And this is where Rianka had a stroke of good fortune, because Julia was the first to come round from the drugged tea, and, in her confusion, she went to the body and picked up the knife while she was still groggy. And being the somewhat impressionable and credulous young woman that we all know she was, she erroneously came to the conclusion that she must have killed him.

"Although I'm not sure you necessarily saw it as good fortune. After all, Julia had written out the list of names on your say-so. And you didn't want us finding that information out until you'd decided it was time to commit murder again."

This got everyone's attention.

"That's right. I think Rianka was always prepared to commit a second murder if she had to. Whether it would be Julia she killed — or one of the others who'd been locked up with Aslan — I don't think she yet knew, but she was always prepared for the possibility. And I know this because it was Rianka who broke into Dominic's house long before Aslan had even been killed, wasn't it?"

"But why would I do that?" Rianka asked, finally finding her voice.

"Because you wanted a bottle with Dominic's fingerprints on. Remember, we know your *modus operandi* now. You sew confusion by implicating others — indiscriminately — and you don't care who goes down for your crimes as long as it isn't you. So yes, it was you who stole Dominic's bottle — the autopsy report will show whether you also stole some of his poisons as well — and it was you who killed Julia with a drink she no doubt received from you without even the first hint of suspicion that it was laced with poison. But tell me, Rianka, did you return the notebook to its nail for us to find before you'd killed Julia? Or after?"

Rianka was looking at Richard, but she wasn't saying.

Richard wasn't that bothered as he continued, "Either way, you knew that when we analysed the notebook we'd find the indentations of Julia's handwritten list on it. And, seeing as Julia had already been found standing over the dead body with the murder weapon in her hand, you knew we'd jump to the only logical conclusion: Julia was the killer. And when we found her body, you hoped we'd think she'd killed herself out of guilt."

"These are all lies!" Rianka said, a desperate edge to her voice. "It was Julia who killed my husband. She killed my husband, and then she killed herself!"

"Hey!" Dwayne said to Rianka's side. "Save it for the jury."

"Indeed," Richard agreed. "But you should know, I already have enough evidence to convict you for the murder of your husband, but I'm not going to rest until you're also convicted for the murder of Julia Higgins as well. Do you understand?"

Richard looked at Rianka with an intensity that was frightening. But she had to know. She was going down for both murders; not just for one.

"But I don't understand!" Ann interjected, unable to keep silent any longer. "Why did she do it? Why did she kill her husband?"

Richard turned to look at the witnesses, and sighed.

"Ben, you heard in Portugal from your old mate Ratty that Aslan was on the con again. But how could this be? Everyone said how Aslan wasn't interested in money any more. And his bank account confirmed as much. But tell me: when you confronted Aslan, he was shocked at first, wasn't he?"

"Sure," Ben said.

"In fact, he denied being on the con, didn't he?"

"Yeah."

"He denied it a lot."

"That's right," Ben still agreed.

"And then there came a moment when he changed his mind and seemed to accept what you were saying?"

"That's it exactly. It was like he didn't want to disagree with me any more."

"And here's what I take from that. Ratty was right when he said that David Kennedy's off-shore accounts were up and running again, but he was wrong about who was using them. It wasn't David. It was Rianka." Richard was looking at Rianka as he said this, and he could see that the blow had landed.

Richard turned back to Ben. "So, to you, Ben, Aslan denied being on the con right up until the moment he realised that maybe it was Rianka who'd been accessing his old off-shore accounts. At which point, Aslan changed his story and agreed with you. Partly from a tragically misplaced sense of loyalty to his wife, but also because it closed the conversation down with you. He had to go and see his wife at once and find out if she'd been up to anything."

"And what had she been up to?" Ann asked, all agog.

Here, Richard held everyone's attention a moment before answering.

"Money laundering," he then said.

There was a gasp — a sudden intake of breath — and Richard was pleased to see that it had come from Rianka.

Richard turned to Dominic. "And this is the apology I mentioned earlier that I owe you, Dominic. Because it was you who told us that Aslan and Rianka didn't get on as well as everyone suggested. In fact, they argued. That's what you told me. And I should have listened."

356

Here, Richard turned to look at Rianka. "But what did they argue about? That's the question.

"I think the answer's in the very fabric of this place. Because you, Rianka, live in luxury inside a beautiful mansion. Admittedly, it's also your place of work, but there's no getting away from it. You surround yourself with the finest imported furniture — the best quality food — the best health and spa treatments — and the most immaculate grounds. But then, your insatiable taste for luxury was surely what first attracted you to the conman, David Kennedy. The fast cars. The hotel suites. Just as you told us.

"When Aslan came and found you out here after he'd served his time in prison, it had all gone well. At first. Yes, he was more spiritual than he'd been before, but that seemed only to benefit the business, and I think you were genuinely happy together. But the thing is, Aslan really had changed. And he didn't stop changing. In fact, as the years passed and you became more and more obsessed with leading a life of luxury, he became all the more ascetic. He started wearing simple robes; growing a beard and long hair; living by ever-more simple values. He didn't even want money any more — and what he didn't spend he gave away.

"And now I find myself remembering that Dominic also said that Aslan was stubborn. I bet he didn't hold back from telling you that you were living your life by the wrong values. I think that that's why the pair of you had been arguing.

"Maybe a different person would have reacted differently, but what I don't think Aslan quite

357

appreciated was the fact that you'd never forgotten that there was a time — twenty years ago — when your husband had been so obsessed with luxury and fast living that he'd stolen money from hundreds of innocent people. And here he was hypocritically lecturing you on morals? How that must have grated. Week after week. Month after month. Year after year. Living with someone who disapproved of you even though, to your eyes, you were less guilty of greed than he'd ever been.

"I don't exactly know how you got the details of the offshore bank account your husband had hidden his millions of pounds of ill-gotten gains in all those years ago — and with Aslan now dead, I don't suppose we'll ever quite know. Maybe you got him to give you the details of where he was hiding his money. Or maybe you came across the details by accident. Or maybe he told you years ago and you've been sitting on the information ever since. Anyway, you finally decided that your husband could disapprove of you all he wanted, but he wasn't going to get away with such rank hypocrisy. If he was so happy to go without money, you'd take his money from him. The money that was sitting in an off-shore account just waiting to be spent. By you. But how to do it without Aslan realising what you were up to? That was the question.

"And this was when the 'You Have Won a Prize' competition was born, wasn't it? But it wasn't Aslan who came up with the idea — like you told us — it was you. And poor, trusting Aslan was happy to agree."

"How the hell do you know all this?" Paul asked, amazed.

Richard turned to Fidel. "Perhaps you'd like to explain?"

"Yes, sir!" Fidel said, proud to bursting that he was being asked to contribute. "Well, it was almost impossible to spot at first, but when we really drilled down through The Retreat's accounts, we finally realised that they claimed that the hotel was running at one hundred per cent occupancy. And what hotel runs at one hundred per cent occupancy? Especially when, for most weeks of the year, there was always a Ponzi victim staying at the hotel for free. Which should have been hitting the hotel's income massively. But according to the accounts, it wasn't.

"So we started looking at how the accounts recorded the free holidays for the Ponzi victims, and we were amazed by what we found. Because, the bills that these people were running up weren't just written off — as you'd expect — they were all being paid in full by an off-shore company based in Turks and Caicos. A company, we guessed, that was where Aslan's money was hidden."

"But why would she use Aslan's money to pay for the free holidays?" Paul asked.

"It's a classic way to launder dirty money and make it clean," Richard said. "Each free holiday generated thousands of dollars of bills and receipts — for treatments, food and alcohol — but rather than writing these bills off, as Aslan thought was happening, Rianka was using the account in Turks and Caicos to settle the bills."

"By our reckoning," Fidel said, "there have been over sixty Ponzi guests stay at The Retreat for free over the last three years — but by getting the company in Turks and Caicos to settle all of their bills, Rianka's been able to wash over $450,000 from Aslan's off-shore account into the hotel's bank accounts. And how would the tax office ever know? Year after year, the hotel's income perfectly matched the bills that the business was apparently generating."

"It was such a clever con," Richard said, again to Rianka. "And like all good cons, you were hiding your lust for money behind apparent altruism: the free holidays you were offering here at The Retreat. But once Aslan realised what you'd been up to, you knew he'd go to the police. You'd be looking at a good ten year stretch in prison. And, from your point of view, your husband had already ruined your life once — when he was arrested twenty years ago. You weren't prepared to let him ruin your life again. That's the way you saw it. So you decided he had to be stopped from going to the police — and stopped permanently. As for whether or not you'd have to kill anyone else to cover up the first murder, you didn't much care, did you? That was just collateral damage. All that mattered to you was that you didn't lose your life of luxury here."

Richard was looking at Rianka as he said this, and he was pleased to see that she was finally looking worried. There was a streak of pride in her that he knew he could exploit.

360

"But the thing is, Rianka, that's exactly what you're about to lose. Because it's going to be twelve feet by twelve for you for the next twenty-five years at least — fetching outfits in orange — and prison food." Richard could see a quiver in Rianka's lip, but he didn't feel even the tiniest spark of compassion. He was talking to a double murderer.

Richard turned to Dwayne. "You know what? You can take her away now."

Dwayne pulled out a pair of handcuffs, clicked them tight onto Rianka's wrists and read her her rights. As Dwayne then led Rianka off to the police jeep across the immaculate lawn, Richard and the others drifted out of the Meditation Space to watch.

"That bitch," Ann said.

This pretty much summed it up for them all and they stood in silence for a while.

"You know," Saskia continued, "I never thought I'd ever say this, but that woman's almost made me feel sorry for David Kennedy."

Everyone turned and looked in surprise at Saskia, so she clarified. "Almost."

"You know," Dominic said, "I was convinced back there for a moment that you were about to reveal that I'd killed Aslan."

Richard turned and looked at Dominic. "But how could I do that? I always said the killer had to be one of the people inside the Meditation Space, and you were never inside."

Dominic took a moment to work out what Richard had said, but once he'd got his head around that, he thought for a moment longer and then suddenly froze in wonder.

"Hey, I don't believe it," Dominic said. "You're glowing."

Richard was thrown. "I'm sorry?"

"I didn't notice before, but you do have an aura after all. And it's golden, man. A golden halo of light like an avenging angel. *That's* your aura."

Richard couldn't help himself, and he found himself smiling for the second time in a day.

"You just tell people what they want to hear, don't you?" he said.

Dominic shrugged. "There are worse crimes," he said.

Together, they turned and looked at Dwayne as he put Rianka into the back of the jeep, closing the door on her with a metallic clang.

"You're right, I suppose," Richard said. "There are worse crimes."

It turned out that the moment Rianka was banged up inside one of the police station's cells — with an iron bed, iron bars, a strip of window and peeling paint on the walls — she'd been consumed by a deep depression. Not that she'd confessed to either murder yet, but Richard guessed it was only a matter of time. After all, the only way she'd be able to minimise her time in prison now was if she pleaded guilty.

Two days after Rianka's arrest, Richard was standing alone on his beach when he got a call on his mobile.

It was Camille.

She told him how the labs had analysed all of the material they'd found in Rianka's sewing basket and found spots of Aslan's blood. There had also been a number of drawing pins. They were the same brand of drawing pin as Richard and Camille had found at the Meditation Space — and one of the drawing pins had a spot of blood on it that also belonged to Aslan.

As Camille explained all this to Richard, he took a moment to consider Aslan's character. A one-time crook who'd changed his ways so much that he'd not touched any of his stolen money since coming out of prison.

Maybe people were capable of change after all?

Camille was then able to say that the autopsy report had also come in on Julia Higgins and the pathologist had found a lethal cocktail of drugs in her bloodstream, including ketamine and cyanide — which suggested that Rianka had indeed stolen the poisons from Dominic's lab as well as the bottle she had put them in. However, the report said that Julia had actually died of asphyxiation. And the cotton fibres that the pathologist had been able to pull out of her mouth and throat matched one of the pillows that had been by her head after her body was found.

Whoever had given her the poison to drink had then smothered her to death with a pillow over her face to make sure.

Camille said, "So I just confronted Rianka with all this new evidence."

"You did?" Richard asked, his interest finally coming into focus.

"And she broke down and confessed to everything. To killing Julia. To killing her husband. She's currently making a full statement to Fidel."

Richard didn't say anything.

"This is where you say well done, Camille."

"No. Of course," Richard said. "Very well done. It's just . . . Camille, I'm busy this second, but I'll be back at the station in half an hour. Okay?"

There was a pause from Camille on the other end of the phone before she said, "You're busy?"

"Yes."

"Doing what?"

"Oh," Richard said, immediately guarded. "Nothing."

"You're busy doing nothing?"

"That's right. But thank you for all your work on this case. It's been excellent. As ever."

After a moment, Camille said, "Thank you, sir," accepting the tiny olive branch she was being offered. "And you should know. Dwayne's organising a big party down at *Maman*'s bar tonight. You know, now that Rianka's confessed to both murders. And the Commissioner's going to be there, too. Everyone's coming."

"They are?" Richard said with a rising sense of panic.

"And I'm telling you in advance so you can come up with a decent excuse this time when you try and get out of coming. Okay?"

Richard couldn't help himself and smiled.

"Thank you, Camille."

"Unless you want to come to the party, of course. It's a pretty major success we've all had."

"I'm sorry, Camille," Richard said. "I'd love to — really I would — but I've already set aside tonight to rewire my bedside lamp."

There was a long pause from Camille.

"I said, a good excuse."

"But it's not an excuse," Richard said, a little hurt. "I really am doing that tonight."

Richard heard Camille sigh at the other end of the phone.

"You'll be back at the station in half an hour," she said.

"Yes, Camille. That's the plan."

"Then I'll see you then, sir," Camille said.

Camille hung up, and Richard put his mobile away.

So that was it. They'd caught their murderer.

Richard remembered back to the moment when he'd stood over Aslan's body and made his solemn promise. He'd sworn he'd catch his killer; and he'd done just that.

So he was trying to feel satisfied that he'd delivered justice — and restored order to the world — but, in truth, Richard just felt empty. And this was because what he couldn't get out of his mind was the memory of his brief encounter with Julia on the beach.

Because he now knew that Julia had been entirely innocent all along. She'd never been manipulating anyone. And that meant that when she'd come to his beach — and gone for a walk — and tried to go swimming with him — that had all been entirely genuine.

As, indeed, had been the moment when she'd kissed him.

And when she'd agreed to go for a drink with him.

Richard bent down to the sand and picked up another round pebble. This one was about the size of a side plate he decided — but much heavier, of course — and he carried it over to the little tower of washed-up pebbles that he was building on the beach. It was hard work getting about the sandy beach in a suit and brogues, but only ten minutes later he was able to stand up and look at his handiwork.

He'd constructed a little wishing tower on his beach. It was, in truth, a touch lop-sided, and it was nowhere near as tall as the one he'd seen here with Julia, but it was nonetheless a tower entirely built with his own hands.

And although he knew that what he was doing was ludicrous, Richard made himself close his eyes while he made a silent wish.

Once he'd finished making his wish, he opened his eyes in time to see a stone slip from the top and the whole thing collapsed in a heap of rubble.

This was just typical, Richard thought to himself. The one time in his life he tried to open himself up to a new experience, of course it went wrong. And, now he was thinking about it, what on earth was he doing in the middle of a beach wearing a woollen suit and brogues? He needed to get back into the shade and get the sand out of his shoes and socks.

He returned to his shack across the sand and, by the time he'd reached the verandah, he was berating himself for having even tried to build a stupid tower of stones in the first place. You couldn't wish for a companion for life and have them turn up just like that. Life wasn't a fairytale where wishes came true.

Richard caught a flash of movement out of the corner of his eye.

No, he thought to himself, dread clutching at his heart. It couldn't be.

Ever so slowly, he turned his head and found himself looking into a pair of beady eyes sitting atop a devil-may-care grin.

A little green lizard was sitting on the balustrade.

And in that awful moment, Richard realised that somehow — impossibly — Harry wasn't just an ordinary lizard.

He was a homing lizard.

Acknowledgements

First of all, I'd like to thank Tony and the team at Red Planet who bought my original *Untitled Copper in the Caribbean* pitch and then, through equal parts inspiration and sound judgement, helped me shepherd it to the screen. So, to Tony Jordan, Belinda Campbell, Simon Winstone and Alex Jones I owe the show's very existence and success on TV. I'm also grateful to the BBC, who gave a prime-time series to a writer with no previous broadcast credits — and for that I have to thank the commissioning genius of Polly Hill and Ben Stephenson.

As for *Death in Paradise*, the novel, I've had direct help from a few key friends. To start with, just as each script for the TV show is developed under the masterly guidance of James Hall, James was also kind enough to read early drafts of the treatment for this book and stop the more excessive mistakes I was otherwise about to make.

Then, once I had a half-way decent treatment, I have to thank both my literary agent, Ben Mason, and TV agent, Charlotte Knight, for putting the deal together with Harlequin UK, who have been an inspiration to me: from Donna Hillyer's help at the start of the process through to Sally Williamson's life-saving interventions towards the end — and all overseen by the ever-sparkling Alison Lindsay. An author couldn't have wished for a more supportive team.

There are those closer to home I also need to thank: Richard Westcott read an early draft of the book and gave life-saving notes, all of which I then incorporated into the second draft; Nicholas Dunham put up with my idiot questions about the UK legal system and always found time to answer; Molly Ker Hawn made critical interventions before, during and after the process of writing; Georgie Bevan read the nearly finished manuscript and her words of encouragement helped massively; and I should also like to thank my mother, Penny Thomas, who not only read the manuscript and cheered me on (as she's always done), but also gave me a lifelong love of reading in the first place and crime thrillers in particular. I must also thank my children, Charlie and James, for their tolerance of the fact that Daddy seems to spend most of his life in a shed tapping away at a computer.

And finally, I must thank Charlie and James's mother, my wonderful wife, Katie Breathwick. She's read and responded to every draft of everything I've ever written over the last decade-and-a-half and she's always given her unwavering support, even to the duff stuff. It's been a long journey getting here, it's not always been an easy ride, and whatever professional and personal success I've subsequently had I owe entirely to her. Thank you, Katie.

Other titles published by Ulverscroft:

THE CURIOUS AFFAIR OF THE SOMNAMBULIST AND THE PSYCHIC THIEF

Lisa Tuttle

For several years, Miss Lane was companion, collaborator and friend to the lady known to the Psychical Society only as Miss X; but then she discovered that Miss X was actually a fraud. Now Miss Lane works with Mr Jasper Jesperson as a consulting detective, though the cases are not as plentiful as they might be, and money is getting tight — until a wife's concern for her husband's nocturnal ramblings piques their interest. But there's more to it than an oblivious somnambulist, for mediums are disappearing all over London, and the Psychical Society suspects the supernatural. There is only one team with the imagination and intelligence to uncover the nefarious purpose behind the vanished psychics and the somnambulist's wanderings. Jesperson and Lane: at your service.

BLOTTO, TWINKS AND THE STARS OF THE SILVER SCREEN

Simon Brett

The Dowager Duchess of Tawcester knows America is full of wealthy young men, all of whom will fall in love with her daughter, the supremely gifted Twinks — and marriage to a Texan millionaire would solve the Tawcester financial problems once and for all. So, along with trusty chauffeur Corky Froggett, the intrepid Twinks accompanies her brother Blotto on his Californian cricket tour. On arrival in Hollywood, they are invited to a glitzy party where they are introduced to a firmament of Hollywood stars, directors and gossip columnists; but the mood of the party suddenly curdles with the breaking news that beautiful starlet Mimsy La Pim — the (former) love of Blotto's life — has been kidnapped. And Blotto is determined to make it his personal mission to rescue her . . .